END OF DAYS
AN APOCALYPTIC ANTHOLOGY
VOLUME 3

EDITED BY
ANTHONY GIANGREGORIO

OTHER LIVING DEAD PRESS BOOKS

DEAD THINGS (W/AN EXCLUSIVE DEADWATER STORY)
JUST BEFORE NIGHT: A ZOMBIE ANTHOLOGY
NIGHT OF THE WOLF: A WEREWOLF ANTHOLOGY
THE WAR AGAINST THEM: A ZOMBIE NOVEL
CHILDREN OF THE VOID (FOR ALL AGES)
BLOOD RAGE & DEAD RAGE (BOOK 1& 2 OF THE RAGE VIRUS SERIES)
DEAD MOURNING: A ZOMBIE HORROR STORY
BOOK OF THE DEAD: A ZOMBIE ANTHOLOGY
LOVE IS DEAD: A ZOMBIE ANTHOLOGY
BOOK OF THE DEAD 2: NOT DEAD YET
ETERNAL NIGHT: A VAMPIRE ANTHOLOGY
BOOK OF THE DEAD 4: DEAD RISING
END OF DAYS: AN APOCALYPTIC ANTHOLOGY VOLUME 1 & 2
DEAD HOUSE: A ZOMBIE GHOST STORY
THE ZOMBIE IN THE BASEMENT (FOR ALL AGES)
THE LAZARUS CULTURE: A ZOMBIE NOVEL
DEAD WORLDS: UNDEAD STORIES VOLUMES 1-6
FAMILY OF THE DEAD, REVOLUTION OF THE DEAD
RANDY AND WALTER: PORTRAIT OF TWO KILLERS
KINGDOM OF THE DEAD, DEAD HISTORY
THE MONSTER UNDER THE BED
DEAD TALES: SHORT STORIES TO DIE FOR
ROAD KILL: A ZOMBIE TALE
DEADFREEZE, DEADFALL, DARK PLACES
SOUL EATER, THE DARK, RISE OF THE DEAD
DEAD END: A ZOMBIE NOVEL, VISIONS OF THE DEAD
THE CHRONICLES OF JACK PRIMUS
INSIDE THE PERIMETER: SCAVENGERS OF THE DEAD

THE DEADWATER SERIES

DEADWATER, DEADWATER: Expanded Edition
DEADRAIN, DEADCITY, DEADWAVE, DEAD HARVEST
DEAD UNION, DEAD VALLEY, DEAD TOWN, DEAD SALVATION
DEAD ARMY (coming soon)

COMING SOON

BOOK OF THE DEAD 5: BACK TO THE GRAVE
CHILDREN OF THE DEAD: A ZOMBIE ANTHOLOGY
END OF DAYS: AN APOCALYPTIC ANTHOLOGY VOLUME 4
DEAD WORLDS: UNDEAD STORIES VOLUME 7

END OF DAYS VOLUME 3

Copyright © 2010 by Living Dead Press
ISBN   Softcover ISBN 13: 978-1-935458-58-6   ISBN 10: 1-935458-58-2
All stories contained in this book have been published with permission from the authors.

This is a work of fiction. Names, characters, places and incidents either are the product of the author's imagination or are used fictitiously, and any resemblance to any actual persons, living or dead, events, or locales is entirely coincidental. This book was printed in the United States of America. For more info on obtaining additional copies of this book, contact:

www.livingdeadpress.com

Table of Contents

PLANT PLAGUE

JESSY MARIE ROBERTS

1
Meteor Seed

Kennedy checked herself in the mirror one last time before she sprinted down the stairs. Her mother, Grace, was standing in the entryway, her well-plucked eyebrows drawn together in a dainty frown.

"I'm not sure I like this idea, Kennedy. Your father has been gone for three months. I'm sure he would like to see his only daughter when he gets home."

The teenager rolled her eyes and gave an exasperated sigh. "Dad leaves all the time, Mom. Why should I sit around at home and wait for him to grace us with his presence? He missed my high school graduation and I'm sure he'll miss my college graduation, too, just like he missed every other important milestone in my life. He's too busy being a hero to be a father. This is the last time I'm going to see all of my girlfriends before we all leave for college. So I'm going to this party, Mom."

Grace forced a smile on her quivering lips. "Of course you're going to go to the party, honey. I'm sure your father would want you to have a nice time with your friends." A single tear escaped the corner of her eye and she hastily wiped it away with her left hand, the shine of her wedding band sparkling for a brief moment in the chandelier's crystal light.

Kennedy leaned over and kissed her mom on her damp cheek. "I love you, Mom," she said, and put her hand on the doorknob. The typical heat of mid-August was scorching this year; the summer had been unseasonably hot. TV scientists blamed the temperature shift on the meteor and considering the alternative result if the meteor had impacted the planet—namely the total annihilation of the Earth—most people were happy to suffer the blistering heat wave sweeping across the Northern Hemisphere. "Don't wait up."

Her mother gave a short laugh and pulled Kennedy close. "I'll always wait up for you. It's a mother's prerogative." She watched as her daughter pulled open the front door and stepped onto the well-lit porch. "Wait a second, honey," Grace called, halting her daughter's progress.

Kennedy turned around, an expectant, impatient look flashing across her face. "What, Mom? I've gotta go. I'm already late and I still need to pick up the pizza."

"He loves you, you know. He's sacrificed a lot for this family. I know you're angry about…"

"Stop, Mom, please!" Kennedy interrupted in a frustrated shout. "He chose to go on this last mission. He *volunteered* to go. There were plenty of other soldiers who would have been happy to shoot down the meteor."

"It was his duty, Kennedy," Grace said softly. "Now, go and have fun with your friends, but please think about what I said. He saved the world, honey. You should be proud of him."

Kennedy laughed harshly. "Proud of him? I barely know him. I hope you enjoy yourself tonight with my sperm donor." With a glare, Kennedy slammed the door and jogged to her hand-me-down compact car.

She was in tears by the time she backed out of the driveway.

* * *

The sleek black car pulled up to the curb in front of the well-appointed, suburban home. Grace held her breath until she saw her husband step out of the passenger's side of the government vehicle, still in his U.S. Air Force uniform. With his hat covering his thinning hair, and the shadows of dusk concealing the lines etched into his ruggedly handsome features, he looked exactly as he had at twenty, the first time she had waited at home for him to return from a combat mission.

His back erect, his shoulders pulled taut in perfect military posture, he stood in the front yard and watched the car until it rounded a corner and was out of sight. Then his head dropped to his chest and his rigid muscles slackened as he leaned over and picked up a heavy camouflaged duffle bag.

Grace's breath caught in her throat—he looked weary.

She knew the potentially catastrophic events of the last few months had been hard on her husband. He had volunteered to be part of the 'Rescue Earth' mission, had been the leader of the UN-sanctioned international contingent of fighter pilots to bombard the planet-wrecking meteor with the greatest firepower human technology had invented. The military operation had been successful, shattering the alien rock into thousands of shards. But though the rock shower had altered the Earth's climate, raising its temperatures, the planet had been spared.

She was married to the man who had saved the world.

Her constant worry about her husband's safety, her argument with Kennedy, and the stress of keeping her family together fell away the second he dropped his gear on the ground and wrapped her in his strong arms. She rubbed her face against the starched fabric of his formal uniform, sniffling back tears of joy.

"You're home," she whispered. "You look tired, Brigadier General Scott Buchanan."

"Oh, yeah, I got a promotion," he said after a stilted laugh, the amusement not quite reaching his tired blue eyes.

Grace smiled. "I know. I saw you on the TV. You could have let me know you were meeting the President."

Scott shrugged. "I didn't want to brag."

They stood at the front door, an awkward silence encompassing them. The first hour or so after his long absences were always strained. She was suddenly grateful Kennedy had gone to the party. Things would be back to normal in the morning.

"Well, leave your bag and come into the kitchen. I have a casserole in the oven and you look like you've lost a couple of pounds," she said, breaking the quiet with forced enthusiasm. "It's your favorite."

"Okay," Scott agreed, "Let me change out of this uniform." Grace waited at the foot of the stairs until he returned, dressed in an Air Force Academy t-shirt and old jeans. He took her hand and led his wife into the kitchen. "Where's Kennedy? Did she already eat?"

Grace shook her head, her smile dropping away. "She's at a party. We didn't know when you'd be in, so we decided she should spend some time with her friends. We'll have a nice breakfast together in the morning."

"She's pissed off?" Scott guessed, heaping a spoonful of hamburger and rice with mushroom gravy onto a plate. "I wanted to be there, Grace. But the meteor…" his voice trailed away. He sat down at the small dinette tucked into the corner of the kitchen, set his plate in front of him, and picked up a fork.

"I know, Scott. You're a soldier. She'll understand when she gets older," she consoled, taking a seat across from her husband and placing her hand over his. "I'm sure in a couple of days this will…" she stopped in mid-sentence as the doorbell rang, interrupting her thoughts.

Scott pushed back his seat, ready to stand, but Grace stopped him with a firm hand on his shoulder. "No, I'll get the door," she said. "You stay here and eat before you turn into a walking skeleton." Without another word, she walked to the front entrance, peeked out the peep hole, and let the door swing inward.

Katherine Harris, their next door neighbor, fell to the tiled entryway with a thud, her pudgy frame in the throes of a seizure.

"Scott!" Grace screamed, dropping to her knees next to her friend. Katherine's head was smashing into the cold, hard tile with each vicious spasm wracking her body, the wet crunch of bone reverberating through the air. A dark red pool of blood formed, splattering the crimson fluid onto Grace with each jarring impact.

"Protect her head!" Scott shouted, racing to the front door. He snapped a limb off of the coat rack by the front door and fitted the slat of wood between Katherine's teeth. "To make sure she doesn't bite off her tongue," he said, gesturing at the makeshift mouthpiece. "Hold her head tight, don't let her do anymore damage to it. I'll call for an ambulance."

Grace nodded and placed her hands on either side of Katherine's shaking face and lifted her friend's gushing head into her lap. Hot, sticky blood soaked through the fabric of her printed dress. "Hurry, Scott. I'm not strong enough to hold her still for long!" Grace cried.

Scott returned to the entryway holding the portable phone out in front of him. "There's no charge, Grace. The battery's dead. And I can't find the other handset. Where's your cell?"

"I loaned it to Kennedy for the evening. Where's yours?"

"I think I left it in the drop-off car. Damn it!"

"What're we going to do, Scott?"

"Hold tight while I run next door and use their phone," Scott said, hopping over the crumpled heap of his neighbor. He was just about out of the house when Katherine stopped shaking and went limp.

"Oh my God, Scott. I think she's dead."

Scott dropped down to one knee and pressed two fingers against the base of Katherine's throat, checking for a pulse. "She's still alive, Grace. Let's get her some help."

"Don't leave me here. I don't want to be alone with her if she dies."

Scott stood to his full height of six-feet and stared down at his wife. After a minute, he nodded, relenting. "Fine. I'll carry her; you follow us." He scooped up Katherine, grunting at her chubby weight, then balanced her in his arms. "Let's go, quickly. She's not getting any lighter."

Grace jumped up and her feet splashed through the pool of blood on the tile on her way out the door.

* * *

Balancing two large pizzas, Kennedy leaned against the doorbell at her best friend, Simone's, house. Loud music poured through the cracked window and she recognized the chorus of Dusty Springfield's *Son of a Preacher Man.*

"Come on, you guys, you'll all starve if you don't let me inside!" she yelled. Simone's parents were out of town and they had the house all to themselves.

She waited a couple more minutes, alternating between ringing the doorbell, pounding on the door and screaming, before she gave up.

"They're never going to hear me over the music," she muttered, setting the pizza's down on the front porch's welcome mat. "I'll grab the food when I get inside."

Swinging her purse over her shoulder, she made her way around the side of the two-story A-framed house and jumped over the chain-link fence into the backyard. She saw a couple of blonde heads bobbing in the pool.

"You guys are assholes!" she shouted while laughing. "Couldn't you have waited for me to get the party started?" She waited for her friends to turn and greet her, but there was no movement inside the pool.

Frowning, she walked past the boom box perched on the glass patio table in-between two half-full ashtrays and a handful of Bud Light bottles. Finding the volume dial, she turned it all the way down until an eerie silence descended over the backyard.

"Simone? Nicole? Marie? What's wrong with you guys?" Kennedy asked. She walked closer to the pool, saw her friends' arms and legs kicking softly, treading water, with their backs to her. "Is this some sort of game? Couldn't you have waited until we had some pizza before swimming?"

She crossed the yard and stopped at the edge of the pool to see Simone spinning slowly in the water. Kennedy screamed and jumped backward when she saw her friend's face.

"Help us," Simone croaked in a hoarse whisper. "So thirsty."

Simone's face was as wrinkled as a woman facing her hundredth birthday, scrunched up and dehydrated like a prune. Her body was in the same condition as her face, nothing but a sun-dried mess of nooks and crannies that contorted her flesh.

"Get out of the water!" Kennedy screamed. "There's something wrong in there!" She leaned over and gripped her friend under the armpits, and with a grunt and a heave, pulled her out of the water and onto the patio. "All of you, get out!"

Kennedy realized with frightening certainty that Nicole and Marie were in the same sorry debilitating state as Simone. "Oh my God, get out of the water! Swim to the side of the pool and I'll help you!" Her two friends, their heads barely above the surface, leaned forward in the water, trying to swim toward the pool's edge. "Hurry up!" Kennedy shrieked.

Simone shook and then went still. With a gasp, Kennedy dropped beside her friend and put her hand over her mouth. She didn't feel any air. Desperate, she upended her purse, letting the meager contents fall to the concrete. She sifted through a pack of Marlboro Lights, a lighter, her wallet, checkbook, and lipstick until she found her mother's cell phone. Flipping it open, she dialed for help.

"9-1-1 Emergency," came a calm, professional voice through the phone's speaker. "Please state your emergency."

"My friend, she isn't breathing. I think she drowned or something."

"Okay, what's your location, miss?"

Kennedy gave the address to Simone's house. "What do I do?"

"Have you attempted CPR?"

"No," Kennedy said, chewing her bottom lip. "But I'll try"

She linked her fingers together and placed the base of her palm over her friend's heart, as she had seen on television. "I hope I'm doing this right," she whispered, then pressed down hard against Simone's breastbone.

There was a sickening crunch as she broke the sternum. "One, two, three," she counted, applying pressure against the heart with each beat. "Four, five, six," she continued, praying her friend would open her eyes and inhale air. "Seven, eight, ni—*ouch!*" she screeched, pulling her hand away from Simone. Blood dripped from the palm of her hand and splashed against Simone's prone form. Some of the dark red droplets mixed with the chlorinated water in the hollow of her stomach and filled the deep crevices decorating the unconscious girl's skin.

A sharp brown length protruded from the concave indention in Simone's chest. "What the hell?" Kennedy whispered, leaning over her friend to get a closer look. About two inches long, it looked like a small, jagged tree branch growing out of the shallow hollow between Simone's bikini-covered breasts.

Greenish tendrils were spiraling out from the protrusion, looking like putrescent veins, just under the surface of the puckered skin. The spidery webs turned a darker shade of murky brownish-green, and then the protuberance shot out of the desiccated skin by a couple more inches, doubling in length within less than a minute. Its base grew thicker and small nubs formed around it. A minute later, spindly branches that looked like pine needles grew out from the nubs.

Kennedy looked up from Simone when she noticed Nicole and Marie at the edge of the pool. Nicole struggled to lift her hand out of the water and stretched it for help. Kennedy gasped to see that growing out of the center of Nicole's hand, pushing out of her palm like a newborn seedling, was a small plant unlike anything she had ever seen before with the exception of in her worst nightmares.

2

Seedlings

"Grace, run back to the house, grab my duffle bag, and start the car. I'll be there in a minute," Scott said calmly as he laid Katherine down on the brown suede couch in her living room. His neighbor's three children were lying huddled together in the middle of the floor, hunched in the fetal position, an occasional grunt or moan escaping their dried, chapped lips.

Grace hesitated, torn between getting out of the house and her maternal instinct to help the children. "Are we taking them to the hospital?" she asked, her voice cracking with fear.

Scott shook his head slowly. "We'll send help their way. I'll call for the paramedics when you leave. Start the car and wait for me."

"Okay," Grace agreed with a whisper.

"And Grace?" Scott continued. "Windows up and lock the doors till I get there."

She nodded and rushed out of the house. Scott walked to the window of his neighbor's house and watched as his wife made her way across the lawn and into their home. When she was out of his line of view, he turned his attention back to the woman on the couch and her three children.

There was a telephone on the end table on the opposite side of the living room and he hurried toward it, his progress halted by a high-pitched wail of pain. Garrett, the oldest child, about twelve years old, let out another shout and clenched his hand over his abdomen.

Scott knelt beside the boy and removed his hands, disturbed to see a patch of blood soaking through his t-shirt. "Hold on, son," Scott crooned. "Let me see what's going on."

"Thirsty," Garrett stuttered, the words broken and hoarse as they forced their way up through his parched throat and dry, cracked lips.

"I'll get you something to drink in a minute," Scott answered. "First, I want to look you over. Just relax."

Garrett closed his crinkled eyelids, hiding his bloodshot eyes. "Hurry," he croaked.

Gingerly, Scott slid the t-shirt up the boy's abdomen until it bunched up around his chest. His stomach was as crumpled as the rest of his skin, as if every bit of moisture in his entire body had been sucked out of him, leaving him looking like a pasty raisin. There was a growing lesion in the center of his stomach, right above his belly-button. Greenish brown lines squiggled across the crevassed skin, streaking in every direction. The lines wriggled beneath the flesh, like worms working their way through mud.

A parasite? Scott wondered. *Had the family been exposed to some sort of new, aggressive tapeworm*? Scott's skin itched from head-to-toe as he looked down at the boy, fearful that whatever had invaded Garrett's body was contagious and had now infected him as well.

Garrett let loose another cry, this one deeper, more guttural, reminding Scott of the way Grace had sounded when she had delivered his daughter eighteen years ago. The boy's stomach began to undulate, moving with the rhythm of something living under his flesh. A small, brown length worked its way out of the boy's stomach through the open lesion. Scott watched the growth's progress with morbid fascination as it jutted out of the body one inch, then two, then popped out four more inches in an incredible spurt.

Tiny nodules grew around the head of the thickening projectile, and then slender, sharp-tipped needles shot out of the nodes. "It's a goddamned plant," Scott muttered, rising to his feet. "But how?" He sprinted to the kitchen, grabbed a dish towel off the counter, and hurried back to Garrett's side. The base of the plant had doubled in size, its roots stretching along the contours of the youth's lanky frame, pressing against the skin until Scott was terrified they would burst through.

Dropping the towel over the head of the plant, Scott gripped it with both hands and pulled. He heard the clatter of high heels clinking on the hardwood floor and looked up to see Grace in the living room. "What are you doing?" she cried as she rushed toward them.

"Get out of here, Grace!" Scott shouted.

She ignored him and drew closer. "What are you doing to Garrett? Are the paramedics on their way?"

Sweat beaded on Scott's forehead as he tried to pull the plant free of Garrett's midriff. Needing leverage, he placed his foot right over the teen's bellybutton, relieved the pressure on the plant, and then, with a cry of exertion, jerked the invasive protrusion with a mighty tug.

A wet, thick sound reverberated through the room as the plant came loose. Momentum forced Scott onto his back, the towel-covered vegetation still clenched tight within his grip. A high-pitched scream warbled out of Grace's mouth as she brought one hand up to her chest, over her thundering heart, and pointed at the end of the plant with a manicured fingertip.

Scott retched when he saw the boy's stomach organ glistening on the far end of the plant, with green, fibrous roots wrapped around its rubbery shell. A long, viscous rope of large intestine connected the organ to the gruesome crater above the boy's abdomen, swaying from side to side like a cable attached to a suspension bridge on a windy day. Garrett's eyes were wide open and dull with death. He threw the plant and its grotesque attachment to the side and staggered to his feet.

Scanning the room, he saw small, shrub-like infections growing on the other two children who were still writhing on the floor. One was protruding out of one of the children's shoulder blade, the other through the child's armpit. Their mother made a gurgling noise and Scott shuddered as he watched a tree-trunk like protuberance sprout out of Katherine's mouth. Her tongue flopped out, dangling between her ruined lips, and it was covered in a mess of wriggling roots.

"Stay there," Scott ordered his wife. He dashed across the room, picked up the telephone, and dialed 9-1-1. The line was busy.

"Are they coming?" Grace asked tremulously.

"Busy signal. Something's very wrong here, Grace."

"No kidding. What do we do about them?" she asked, gesturing to the bodies wracked with pain on the living room floor. "We can't just leave them here. They're suffering."

Scott closed his eyes and whispered a prayer. "You're right, Grace."

With quick, meticulous, military precision, Scott leaned over the bodies of the two children on the floor and snapped their necks. With a grim expression, he moved over to Katherine. "I'm sorry," he whispered, then twisted her neck until it cracked, leaving her head bent at an unnatural angle.

*   *   *

Kennedy sat on the front step of Simone's house, a couple of cold pizzas next to her, as she smoked a cigarette. She blew out a blue cloud of smoke in relief when she saw the ambulance, red lights flashing, pull into the driveway.

She tossed her half-finished Marlboro to the ground and crushed it out with the sole of her sandal, waving her arms over her head. "In back! My friends are in the pool!" she shouted, trying to gain the driver's attention.

The uniformed EMT slumped over in the driver's side seat, his head smashing into the steering column to press against the horn. A loud, constant wail deafened Kennedy and she pressed her hands over her ears as she hurried toward the emergency vehicle. When she reached the driver's side door, she pulled it open, then pushed the slouched body backward so the man's forehead was no longer engaging the horn.

She gasped when she saw, growing out through both of his nostrils, twin plants, each sprouting needle-like branches, growing longer by the second. She stumbled backwards, putting her hand over her mouth to stifle the scream growing inside of her chest.

Roots slithered beneath the man's cheeks and forehead and their searching ends peeked out from both of his ears and between his lips. Finding air instead of flesh, they maneuvered their jagged ends until they found skin and dug down deep inside.

The paramedic was as dry and withered as her friends had been. Kennedy noticed three empty water bottles on the empty passenger's seat.

A low moan, coming from the back of the ambulance, captured her attention. She sprinted around the van to the double doors at the rear of the vehicle and flung them open. Lying on a cot was a second paramedic, a saline IV plugged into the crook of his left arm, feeding a vein.

He looked better than her friends or his partner; while his skin was still slightly wrinkled, he had some color left in his cheeks and his eyes were bright and alert. "How can I help you?" she asked, jumping inside the van.

"Dehydrated. Something's wrong," he grunted, the effort of speaking almost too much for his thirsty mouth. "My foot."

She glanced down to the leg he barely lifted off the cot, indicating which one was infected. Unsure of what to do, she unlaced his black boot and pulled it off his swollen foot. She took a deep breath and peeled his sock down his ankle, around his heel, and across his arch.

Dark green lines arced around his foot. As she watched, a root wiggled on the edges of his exposed extremity and up and over the bony prominence on both sides of his ankle.

"Okay, listen to me," Kennedy began, "I know you're going to think I'm crazy, but you're going to have to trust me. There's a plant-thing growing inside of your foot and it's moving up your leg."

The EMT sat up, groaning with exertion. "A plant? What are you talking about?" he demanded, his voice weak and hoarse.

Tears streaked down her cheeks. "My friends, the driver, they all died because some sort of plant was growing inside of them. Take a look at your foot if you don't believe me!"

He bent over at the waist and cursed, seeing the evidence stretching up into his leg. "Whatever the growth is, it's already moved up past my medial and lateral malleolus. Must be why I'm so damned thirsty—the plant's using the water in my body to feed itself with." He looked up, his bright blue eyes calm and steady. He reminded Kennedy of her father for a second, and for the first time since her dad had left to shoot down the meteor, she wished he was with her.

"Sounds reasonable," she agreed, returning her gaze to his foot. "Oh my God, it's growing so fast! It's going to be all the way up to your knee in the next couple of minutes! What do we do?"

"Cut it off," he said after a moment of silence. "It'll be all the way to my stomach and intestines by the time we get to the hospital, and that's if we don't hit any traffic. We'll take off the leg at the knee, then you'll drive me to the emergency room as fast as you can. Okay?"

Kennedy stared at him, horror written all over her face.

He reached out and grabbed her arm. "Hey, I need your help here. Can you do it?"

Shaking out of her thoughts, Kennedy nodded. "I'll help you. What do I do?"

"Can you get some ice? We need to numb it. Plus, it'll slow down the bleeding. I have some pain killers in here. I'll have you administer the drugs after you get the ice."

Kennedy nodded and started running toward the back fence, sparing a final look at his leg as she ran. The ropy roots were already halfway up his shin bone. Rounding the corner, she tried to avoid looking at her friends, but found her gaze morbidly drawn to their corpses. The plant shooting out of Simone's chest had grown exponentially, already reaching two to three feet. Its roots had slid out of Simone's body and bobbed in the water, sucking in nourishment.

She yanked open the sliding glass door and found a plastic Ziploc bag, which she filled with ice from the automatic dispenser on the refrigerator, then jogged through the house, unlocked the front door, and darted back to the ambulance.

Panting, she pressed the ice bag over his foot when she reached the van. "What now?"

The paramedic had the tip of a hypodermic needle shoved into a small vial. "Give me this injection before you start sawing," he replied.

A car skidded around the corner of the cul-de-sac and Kennedy let out an elated cry when she recognized the man driving and the woman clutching the dashboard of the vehicle. Her parents had arrived.

Relief flooded through her, making her lightheaded. Her last thought before she fell out of the ambulance unconscious and to the driveway, was that her mouth was dry.

*   *   *

Scott lifted his daughter's head off the driveway and placed it in his lap. Then he broke the smelling salts the paramedic had procured from his kit. Kennedy came awake with a startled yelp.

"Dad?" she asked. She smacked her tongue against the roof of her mouth, then her tongue flicked out to lick at her lips. "I'm so thirsty."

Scott exchanged a concerned look with his wife. "We'll get you something to drink as soon as you get into the car, honey. Go with your mother."

"But the paramedic. We need to cut off his leg and…"

"I'll take care of it. Follow your mother into the car." As he helped her stand, Scott noticed the puncture wound in his daughter's palm. "What happened to your hand?"

She glanced down at the inflamed wound, red and caked with dried blood. "I was giving Simone CPR. The plant-thing stabbed me when I pressed down on her chest."

Scott cursed under his breath, certain his only child was infected with the plant plague. He turned and looked at the paramedic strapped into an IV, then down at where an oversized, ice-filled plastic bag covered his leg. If taking off his leg worked, then he could sedate Kennedy and take her hand. Bile rose in the back of his throat as he contemplated removing his daughter's hand, but if the brutal action would spare her life, he would perform the field amputation.

He waited until Grace had helped Kennedy into the car before he leaned over the EMT and took the bone saw from the first aid kit. "You sure about this?" Scott asked.

"Don't forget to give me the shot," the paramedic said with a crooked smile. "I don't really want to remember any of this."

Scott grimaced and picked up the needle. "Do you have more of this? In case I have to do it again on my daughter?"

The paramedic nodded. "Yes. Now, hurry up. Let's get this over with."

Scott removed the ice bag and set it aside for Kennedy. He looked down at the foot and squinted, sure his eyes were playing tricks on him. "I don't see anything wrong with your foot. Are you sure you were infected?"

The paramedic shot straight up and leaned over to get a better look. His foot was bright red from being exposed to the ice, but other than that, his skin was unblemished. "I'll be damned. It's gone! The ice?"

Scott grabbed the ice pack and darted to his car.

3

And the Plants Shall Inherit the Earth

Scott glanced in the rearview mirror, glad that Kennedy was asleep. She had seen enough to give her nightmares for the rest of her life. He was glad she was spared the images laid out before him. Bodies, with plants in different stages of growth, were scattered across the sidewalks. Men, women, children, animals. No species was spared.

They had driven through the long night and the dawn brought on an onslaught of visual nightmares so vivid that Scott knew their images were forever burned into his mind.

A young boy, seven or eight years old, lay in the middle of the street, his red bicycle atop him. Green vines grew around the spokes of the bike and a thick, four foot tree trunk grew out of his chest. His eyes were wide open and pleading, even in death.

Cars were haphazardly parked on lawns, plants forcing their way through cracked windshields and open windows.

"Turn off the radio," he muttered to Grace, sitting in the passenger seat, her head bowed. After the first couple of minutes of daylight, she had refused to look out the window at the carnage, her eyes on her lap. He wished he could do the same. "I don't want them up yet, they need their rest."

The paramedic, who had introduced himself as John Williamson, was passed out beside Kennedy in the back seat. Both had recovered from their infection, but they were out cold. Scott had slipped an Ambien from his wife's purse into each of their soft drinks when they had stopped at the gas station to fuel up the car. They were unconscious within minutes, their sleep spawned by exhaustion and the sleeping aid.

The gas station attendant and seven customers were all dead, and for quite a while, if the growth of the plants using their decaying bodies as fertilizer was any indication. Scott had helped himself to a couple of coolers, filled them with as much ice as he could carry, as well as some high-calorie food and drinks, and had placed them in the trunk of the car. He didn't know when they would be able to pick up more supplies.

Then he had collected all of the gas cans in the service station and filled them to the brim. He had quite a drive ahead of him, and they would need gasoline to make the journey. His plan was to drive straight north, into Canada, to the coldest section of North America he could find. They would be out of California in about four hours and would follow I-5 all the way through Oregon, then up into Washington, and eventually into Canada.

With the deft fingers of a fighter pilot, he checked the controls on the dashboard of the car, making sure, for the twentieth time, that the vents were closed and they were breathing recycled air. He wasn't taking any chances with his family. Those plant seeds weren't going to find a way into his vehicle if he could help it.

The radio stations had reported massive casualties before they went off the air, repeating emergency warnings in a pre-recorded broadcast. Scientists had attributed the plague to seeds—trapped inside the meteor—then released into the atmosphere and spread over the world when the massive space rock had been blown to smithereens.

Scott had been responsible for unleashing this pandemic upon the world and guilt ate away at his gut. Instead of saving the world, he had caused the creatures of Earth to become fertile soil for an invasive race of alien plants. The planet would have been better served by total annihilation. At least they could have collectively come to terms with their fate, said goodbye to their loved ones, passed on with dignity.

"What if everyone in Canada is dead, too?" Grace asked quietly, wrapping her arms around her midriff. "What if *everyone* is dead? What if we're the last people left in the world?"

"We're going to be fine, Grace," Scott said. "If ice killed the plants growing in Kennedy and John, it stands to reason that the seeds would have been destroyed in the colder climates liker Antarctica." He cranked up the air conditioning to full blast. "We've got plenty of ice in the coolers. If one of us gets infected, we'll freeze the plant-bastards out."

It was a miracle his family was still alive. He had escaped implantation in a vacuum-sealed government facility as he debriefed the Secretary of Defense on his mission. He thanked his lucky stars that Grace and Kennedy had volunteered at a local food shelter, spending most of their afternoon in the soup kitchen's walk-in freezer, organizing donations. Their charity had saved their lives.

Grace rubbed her slender fingers over her arms, shivering. Scott looked sidelong at his wife, and then reached behind her seat, unzipped his duffel bag, and pulled out his flight jacket. He placed it on her lap, then diverted the vents so they weren't blasting straight at her. "Why don't you get some sleep?" he suggested softly.

His eyes scanned over her body, looking for signs of plant infection. While she looked exhausted, her eyes bloodshot from crying, her skin had a healthy glow and she hadn't asked for anything to drink the entire time they had been in the car.

"Are you sure?" she asked hesitantly, chewing on her bottom lip. "What if you get tired?"

Scott smiled. "The traffic is pretty light right now, Grace. What am I gonna hit?"

Unbidden, giggles arose in Grace's throat. She bit down on her finger to squelch the laugher, but it came pouring out. Scott joined in, his deep laugh in harmony with her tinkling squeals of mirth.

"What's so funny?" Kennedy asked from the backseat, her voice gruff with sleep, her drug-induced slumber interrupted by the chorus of chortles.

Her laughter spent, Grace turned around and stroked her daughter's cheek. "It's nothing, love. We have a long trip ahead of us. Why don't you try to get some more sleep."

* * *

Kennedy awoke with her cheek pressed against John's shoulder, an embarrassing trickle of drool wetting his navy blue paramedic's uniform. She sat up in a hurry and wiped the drool off her mouth. His breath was deep and even, and she was relieved he was unaware of her deplorable sleeping manners.

Even lost in dreams, John Williamson was an attractive man. *Hot*, she would have described him to her friends. The memory of pulling Simone from the pool, of performing CPR, crept through her mind. She tried to force the images away.

Focus on something else, she instructed herself. *Like how lucky I am that at least there's a hottie with whom to perpetuate the human race should they not find any other survivors.*

"Well, hello, sleepyhead," Scott greeted her from the driver's seat as they continued down the highway. "Feeling better?"

"I'm not five years old anymore, Dad," she retorted. "I don't usually answer to 'sleepyhead' anymore."

He sighed and captured her gaze with his in the rearview mirror. "I've told you I'm sorry a thousand times, Kennedy. When are you going to accept my apology?"

She barked out a harsh laugh. "Maybe when it's sincere?"

He sighed again, long and loud. "Everything I've done, every decision I've made, has been to protect my family. I wish you could see that."

"Yeah, you're a great martyr. Too bad you're such a shitty father."

He whirled around, his blue eyes gleaming with anger. "Maybe when you finally grow up and think about someone other than yourself, you'll have the right to judge me."

"And how would you kno—Dad, *watch out!*" Kennedy screamed, pointing out the front windshield.

Her father whipped his head around, slammed on the brake, and fought with the steering wheel to keep the car on the road. Ahead of them, blocking all lanes of the interstate, was an eighteen wheeler. Two men stood on top of the truck, semi-automatic rifles clutched in their hands.

* * *

The car came to a screeching halt, the interior of the vehicle reeking of burnt rubber. Scott slid his hand into his duffle bag and pulled out an M9 pistol with a fifteen-round staggered magazine.

"Dad? What're you going to do?" Kennedy asked quickly.

Scott slid the handgun into the back waistband of his jeans. John was still passed out in the backseat, snoring, and blissfully unaware of the danger they were now in. He had keeled over from the motion of the car coming to a stop, and his head fell into Kennedy's lap.

Grace was awake now too, her eyes wide with fear. Kennedy had the same expression. The resemblance between mother and daughter was most prominent when they were frightened.

Scott's jaw clenched as he seethed with anger. Six combat tours, twelve special ops missions, leading the international coalition to demolish the meteor, only to be waylaid on his way to frozen safety by a couple of gun-toting morons wearing dirty Confederate flag t-shirts.

Those bastards would feel the bite of his semi-automatic, double-action sidearm before they would lay one filthy finger on his family.

"Grace, slide over to the driver's seat when I get out of the car. If anything happens to me, drive," Scott said. "Turn around and follow side streets until you find your way back to the interstate. Follow I-5 North into Canada. Don't stop until the external thermometer reads thirty-two degrees or below."

"Scott," Grace pleaded, putting her hand on her husband's arm. "Let's just do that now. Just put the car in reverse and get out of here."

Scott shook his head. "They'll just shoot us or the car the minute we try. You'll need a distraction. I have fifteen bullets that can provide one. Lock the doors behind me," he ordered, and then swung his door wide and stepped out onto the hot macadam.

"Put yer hands in the air, friend," the taller of the two men said with a sneer. His off-white t-shirt didn't quite cover the bulge of his beer belly hanging over a silver belt buckle with a swastika design.

Slowly, Scott did as instructed, and raised his arms over his head. "What do you want?" he called. From the corner of his eye, he saw Grace slide into the driver's seat and buckle her safety belt. *Good girl*, he thought.

"For starters," the throw-back to *Deliverance* said with a white-trash twang, "tell that lady of yers to get out of the car and join ya."

"That's not gonna happen," Scott snarled.

Beer belly's buddy, a short, pudgy, acne-ridden man, fired a warning shot at Scott's feet. The bullet ricocheted off the black tar and struck the side of the car, leaving a small hole in the metal. "Next one's goin' through yer lady's head," the shooter warned.

"You heard my partner, friend, the first man said. "We just want to take a look at her. Then we'll check out that pretty little thing in the backseat. She looks to be just my type." Beer belly laughed, a loud, sickening sound twisted with hate and repugnant thoughts. "It's just our luck, Braxton," he continued to his friend. "Three people to play with and one to kill," he snickered, pointing the barrel of his firearm at Scott. "The first one to wet our appetite," he said with a leer, moving the gun to gesture at Grace. "And then a few to keep and have some fun with," he laughed, his gaze locked on Kennedy.

Scott looked at the two men, wondering if the idiot on the semi was smart enough to count to four, but Beer Belly and Braxton were still chuckling with murderous glee. It looked like they hadn't see John slouched in the back seat, his head cradled on Kennedy's lap. Scott prayed the EMT had awakened during the conversation. The element of surprise might be the only way for them all to survive.

"If you don't have yer lady out of that car in three seconds, friend, I'm gonna tell Braxton ta shoot ya in the leg. One, two, thr…"

"Okay, okay! Don't shoot!" Scott shouted. "I'll do it!"

Scott turned and opened the driver's door, the now open door blocking the two men's view of his waist to his shins. "Grace, reach behind me and give my gun to John," Scott whispered out of the corner of his mouth, trying to conceal his speech. Then, louder, he yelled, "Do you promise you won't hurt my wife? If we do what you want, will you let us go?"

Beer Belly howled with merriment, tilting his head back and cackling toward the sky. Braxton followed suit, his weird laughs sounding like a demented coyote with a bad case of the hiccups. Scott felt the gun slide out from his back.

"Okay," Grace whispered, indicating she had passed the gun into the backseat.

"Well?" Scott hollered. He knew the two men were going to lie. He had just wanted their false promises to buy some time.

"Sure, friend. I *swear* we'll let ya'll go as soon as we're through with ya!" It was the most insincere thing Scott had ever heard.

Scott grabbed Grace by the hand and helped her out of the car, shielding her body with his. "Are you infected?" he asked. "I don't want my wife infected with the plants."

"We ain't infected. We figured out right quick what killed the plants. If you send yer pretty little wifey our way real nice-like, we'll tell you how we did it."

"Walk slowly, Grace," Scott whispered as he pulled his wife from behind him. "Sounds fair," Scott agreed. When Grace was about halfway to the semi, Scott shouted, "Well, what's the cure?"

"Ice," Beer Belly shouted, then turned to Braxton and said, "Shoot him."

"With pleasure," Braxton squealed, his finger twitching on the trigger. The loud crack of a gunshot split the silence and a blossom of red formed on the front of Braxton's t-shirt, soaking through the Confederate flag. A second shot followed and Scott smirked when he saw Beer Belly's brain explode out of the back of his skull.

Grace screamed and ran back toward Scott. "Get in the car, Grace!"

John stepped out of the car, the smoking M9 in his right hand. "You're a crack shot, son," Scott complimented the paramedic.

"A tour in Iraq before I became a paramedic," John explained, the gun still trained on the semi. "You think that was all of them?"

"I don't know. Let's find out."

* * *

Two siblings, a boy and a girl, were wedged between Kennedy and John in the backseat. An infant, their baby sister, was cradled

21

against Grace's chest in the front seat. Their rescue mission had just gained three survivors.

"We should have taken the semi," Kennedy complained, jostling for arm room in the backseat. "It's a little crowded in here."

"We're better off in the car, Kennedy," Scott explained for the third time, impatiently. "This is faster, more fuel efficient, and we can all drive it in case something happens to me."

"Whatever," Kennedy muttered, staring out the window at the desolate Washington landscape. They hadn't run into another living soul since the attempted hijack in Northern California. They had seen plenty of death, mostly at the hands of the foul plants growing out of human flesh, but they had also seen evidence of the horrors human beings are capable of during a disaster—houses and businesses burned to the ground; people run over by cars, their insides splattered to the wind; gas station attendants in a bloody heap, gunshots wounds scattered over their corpses, the cash register drawers hanging open and empty.

Scott was worried that only the worst of humanity had survived the plant plague. Survival instinct was primitive and base, devolving mankind into a beast within hours. *A hundred thousand years of evolution down the toilet*, he thought.

The children, their three newest passengers, were victims of people rather than plants. Their parents had figured out how to fight the plants, only to be murdered by the would-be hijackers. When Grace had asked why, the boy had answered, "They were going to sell us."

The slave-trade was alive and kicking in post-apocalyptic America. Scott hoped Canada had fared better.

"We're almost there," Scott said. "We'll be in Vancouver in a couple of hours."

"Will it be frozen there?" Kennedy asked.

"If not, we'll keep going north," Scott answered.

4

The Unfrozen North

One Year Later

Scott awoke with a start. He glanced out the window and saw the August sun creeping up in the sky. It was dawn.

He placed a quick kiss onto Grace's forehead and slid out of bed, pulling on a pair of jeans and a t-shirt before making his way into the kitchen to make coffee. Despite the tragedy of the past year, he felt hope for the future—his family was safe, they had welcomed three children into the fold, and he was about to gain a son-in-law in John. He was pleased Kennedy had fallen in love with the easy-going, capable paramedic. He was a strong and dependable man.

Time and patience had gone a long way toward rebuilding his relationship with his daughter. With each day, she seemed to forgive him a little more, and she gave him smiles rather than eye-rolls more often than not.

Their log cabin in the northern-most region of Canada was self-sufficient. They used a generator for power and wood for warmth in the wood stove and fireplace. Four loaded shotguns were at ready, mounted to the wall on a gun rack, next to the front door, but they hadn't been used for over six months. Isolated from the rest of mankind, they did their chores, ate their meals, and lived their lives in relative peace and harmony.

"Papa Scott!" Logan, the boy they picked up on their northern journey, shouted as he and his sister, Paula, flew inside the cabin, panting. Bundled in heavy winter coats, their red cheeks and noses gave testament to the cold weather.

"Catch your breath, son," Scott said with a laugh, tousling the boy's brown hair. "You two are sure up early. Did you feed the chickens?"

"Yes, sir," Paula said, "but…" her childish voice trailed off.

Scott frowned. "But what?"

"The snow's melting," Logan said.

"*What?*" Scott ran to the window and looked out at the ground. Sure enough, it was melting. The climate change had reached their neck of the woods. Scott cursed. "Get your mother up, kids. And wake up John and Kennedy. We've got to get moving."

"Okay," Logan said. "Can I get something to drink first? I'm really, really thirsty."

THE AIR ITSELF

ANTHONY GIANGREGORIO

"Well that's it, the filters are clogged with ash again," Dr. Frank Mathis said as he climbed down from inside the ventilation shaft leading to the surface.

"Great, so what do we do now?" Bill Johnson asked as he helped the man off the ladder.

"It's simple, really. We have to do what we've done before. Someone needs to go outside and clean them."

"But that's a death sentence," another man said.

There were a total of six men gathered around Dr. Mathis and Bill, each with concern clearly written on their faces.

"Yes, I know, but we don't really have a choice now, do we. If we don't get those filters clean, we're all dead anyway. Better one dies than all of us."

"Easy for you to say, Doc," one of the men said. "We all know it won't be you that has to die."

"What do you mean by that? I have as much chance as going as the next man," Dr. Mathis replied.

Bill shook his head. "That's not true, Frank. We can't afford to lose you, and you know it. No matter what, it can't be you who goes up there."

Dr. Mathis frowned as he made eye contact with each of the other men, but he knew Bill was correct. Though he wasn't afraid to do his part, he was the only one of them that knew how the vent and filtration system worked, and if he wasn't around to fix it when it became clogged or needed to be calibrated, then they were all dead.

"Well, that may be true, but if there was anyone else that could do my job, I'd be there like the rest of you," Dr. Mathis said sadly.

"Sure you would," one of the men said under his breath, the sarcasm obvious.

Bill turned and glared at the men, hearing the remark but not who said it. "Shut it, all of you. I want to know who said that." No one answered. "Dr. Mathis is the only reason we've survived for as long as we have. If not for him, the filters would have clogged more than a year ago, and with no way of knowing how to flush and clean the system, we all would've suffocated a long time ago."

"That's easy for you to say, Bill. You're the only one with a woman," one of the men said and Bill saw it was Brad, a twenty-two year old college drop out. Not that it mattered anymore what Brad had done before they all became trapped inside the bunker. Now they were just human beings, no one man better than another.

Bill knew what Brad was talking about instantly. There had been a total of five women in the bunker with them when they had sealed themselves inside it, but through fate or bad luck, four of the women had died. Two had died from pneumonia, one had suffered an accident while preparing a meal and had bled out after severing a major artery, and the last had killed herself, not able to handle the pressure of perhaps spending the rest of her life underground. That left his wife, Sheila, as the last woman in the bunker and for all he knew, the last woman left alive on Earth.

And Bill knew the other men coveted her badly, each one wanting to be with her. After months of being celibate, the men had needs and Sheila was the only one who could fulfill those needs. A few of them had become gay out of necessity, such as in a prison, but most saw Sheila and wanted her for themselves.

So far no one had tried to take her, though Bill saw the way the other men looked at her during meal time. There was a hunger there that no food could ever fill and it scared him, not for himself, but for the woman he loved.

"That's beside the point at the moment, gentleman," Dr. Mathis said, trying to change the subject. "Nothing else matters but getting those filters clear of ash. As of now, we only have what recycled air is inside the bunker with us and given the amount of people down here, I'd say we have about two days worth of air and by the second day it will be thin at that."

"So someone has to sacrifice themselves again, is that it?" a man asked.

Dr. Mathis nodded. "I'm afraid so. Look, we've been through this before. We don't have a choice in the matter. Either one of us sacrifices himself or we all die. It's as simple as that."

Arguing and angry voices filled the passageway and Bill raised his hands over his head and bellowed loudly, "Enough! That's enough! Christ, what the hell are you yelling about? Look, you can argue all you want but the end result is still going to be the same. One of us dies so the rest can live, end of story. Now, listen, we don't have to decide right now so everyone, please, go back to your quarters and we'll meet in the rec room tomorrow morning. Then we'll decide who is gonna do it."

More grumbling filled the passageway.

Bill lowered his right hand to the .45 pistol on his hip. He was the only one with a gun, the rest of the weapons locked up in the armory and he with the only key, and though he hated it, sometimes it was the threat of the handgun that kept the others in line.

"I said that's enough. Let's not make this any more difficult than it has to be."

A few of the closer men saw where Bill's hand was and could read the hard look in his eyes.

More than a year ago, before they had agreed that Bill would be the leader, there had been an altercation by a small group that wanted to leave the bunker, despite it being suicide. They believed it was safe outside, that the air had cleared, and they wanted to leave.

It got out of control and three hostages had been taken, one of them Dr. Mathis. When the men refused to listen to reason, Bill had shot the leader at point blank range in the face, killing him instantly.

The fight had left the others then and Bill's dominance had been established in blood, and though he had always felt guilty for killing the man, he knew it was the right thing to do.

So when he placed his hand on his .45 now, the men knew what the gesture meant and their voices faltered and they began to disperse. When only Bill and Dr. Mathis remained, the doctor leaned against the wall and rubbed his face with his hands.

"It's getting harder to keep them in line, Bill, you see that don't you?"

"Yeah, I do. Ever since Carol took her life it's been like this."

"Do you ever worry about Sheila? I mean, really worry," Dr. Mathis asked.

"All the time. I see the way they look at her and it fills me with dread, but what can I do?"

"There's nothing you can do," Dr. Mathis said as he turned to walk away. "But I'd be more on guard than ever before. Remember, one of those men is going to be committing suicide tomorrow and I doubt he'll go with a smile. That man will have nothing to lose before he goes."

"What are you saying?" Bill asked.

"I'm saying until those filters are clean, I'd keep an even closer watch on Sheila."

With a nod and a wan smile, Dr. Mathis headed off, his destination the filtration room. The system needed constant monitoring and now with the intake clogged, he needed to shut it down. Now was the perfect time to run a diagnostic check although he would have preferred not to do one. Because the system was down meant another man would have to give up his life and that was always hard to deal with.

Bill watched Dr. Mathis walk away and he sighed heavily as he waited for the man to round the bend in the corridor. He looked up at the hatch leading to the surface and the intake vents, wondering what it was like up there.

He decided it probably wasn't very good, not if the intake filters were choked with ash yet again.

He supposed he shouldn't complain. It had been over seven months since the last time they had been clogged, the longest so far. Seven months ago another of their little group had sacrificed himself and he and every one inside the bunker owed the man a debt that could never be repaid.

Feeling survivor's guilt, but still glad to be alive, he moved off to his quarters, the burden of command weighing heavily on his shoulders.

* * *

He knocked twice on the door to his quarters, and a second later, it was opened. Sheila stepped back so he could enter.

"How'd it go?" she asked. She was wearing a bathrobe, her long brown hair covered by a towel wrapped around her head. There were a few drops of water still on her neck and the room smelled of steam. She had taken a shower, one of the few luxuries they had in the bunker thanks to the recycled water.

"Not good," he said as he kissed her cheek. She smelled of soap, clean and natural. The shampoo had run out months ago but there was still a good supply of bar soap. "The filters are clogged again."

She raised her right hand to her mouth and stifled a gasp. "Oh, no, does that mean…"

"Yeah, it does."

"Who is it this time?"

He shook his head. "Don't know yet. We'll draw lots tomorrow morning."

"Will you be there, too?"

"Yes," he said as he took her into his arms. She placed her head on his shoulder. "I have to. I'm no better than anyone else. If they're willing to do it, I have to be, too."

"I know that, of course, it's just…"

He pushed her back a bit so he could look into her eyes. "I know, Sheila, believe me I know. But we don't have a choice. Either one of us goes up there or we all suffocate."

Tears had formed in her eyes and she was doing her best not to cry. Though he was a hard man, he had to admit deep down, he wished he could join her. A good cry would help to relieve the tension he felt. But he had to stay strong; for her and everyone else.

"Look, tomorrow isn't here yet. And we still have the rest of the night."

She wiped her eyes with the back of her hand. "The rest of the night? What do you have planned?"

He smiled mischievously as he slowly opened her robe. It fell to her ankles and she stood before him, her naked body soft and supple.

"For this," he said as he took her into his arms again, their lips meeting, tongues exploring one another's mouths.

Sheila sighed as he kissed her, a slight sniffle all that remained of her tears. Though the next morning would arrive before they knew it, for now they were timeless, lost in the other's embrace, their love making them one soul.

* * *

Bill walked into the rec room early the next morning to find he was the last to arrive instead of the first. Apparently, with the fate of one of them on the hook once more, no one could sleep.

All of them were there, sitting around the three tables as they talked and watched news footage taped just before they had gone underground and sealed themselves inside the bunker.

On the television screen, a frazzled news anchor was talking about the global catastrophe that had befallen Earth while behind him, the scenes of devastation were being shown.

Bill leaned against the wall and watched the screen for a few minutes as he remembered what had happened.

No one could have imagined that the Earth would shift slightly on its axis and because of it, volcanoes across the planet erupted, spewing ash into the air to choke the skies.

The ash became so thick that airplanes and motor vehicles wouldn't run, their engines choked by the ash, and to breathe for more than a minute without an oxygen mask was death. Rebreathers were useless as the filters clogged in seconds, and before anyone realized how serious it was, people began suffocating on the streets and in their homes as the ash seeped into any structure that wasn't vacuum sealed to be air tight.

Many self-contained buildings were air tight but once their filters clogged, the air stopped circulating and soon the people died. What was amazing was how the ash got into absolutely everything. Even something such as a refrigerator in a home would be opened to find it was filled with ash.

In no time, the entire planet was consumed and with the ash in the atmosphere, it blocked the sunlight and soon all plant life withered and died.

As far as Bill knew, his small enclave was all that remained, but he was confident there had to be more survivors scattered across the globe, for to imagine there wasn't was to bring on hopelessness.

The bunker he was in had a self-cleaning filter system for the air, but even that wasn't enough to keep it clean forever, for the ash was too heavy and persistent. And every so many months, due to no fault of theirs, the filters had to be cleaned manually.

But there were no hazmat suits to be worn if someone needed to leave the bunker, just one of many oversights when it had been stocked quickly as the ash filled the sky.

So someone would have to go outside without one, and by the time they finished cleaning the filters, they would be gasping for air, their lungs coated with soot, a death sentence if there ever was one.

Bill walked over, turned off the television, then turned to look at everyone and said, "All right, that's enough of that. Let's get this done. No use putting it off."

"How are we going to do it this time?" a man asked.

Dr. Mathis stood up. "We'll draw lots, just like before. I've already taken the liberty of preparing straws. The short straw is the one that goes."

"Here," Bill said to Dr. Mathis. "Give them to me, I'll hold them."

Dr. Mathis handed them to Bill and he placed them in his hand, closing it. He looked at them sticking out of his hand and cringed, knowing one straw in there would doom one of them to death, but save the others.

"Okay, line up and each man pick one," Bill said.

Each man did as instructed and soon, one at a time, each man pulled a straw from Bill's tightly squeezed hand.

Bill looked each man in the eye and nodded, knowing that each one picked could be the fatal straw.

It went quickly and by the third to last man, the fatal straw was found.

Bill opened his hand to see that the remaining straws were all long. Ernie, a middle-aged, balding man, had picked the short straw.

Ernie stared at the straw, his eyes wide at the revelation it was him who was going to give his life so the others would live. The other men all walked up to him, shaking his hand and patting his back, thanking him for his sacrifice, the mood solemn.

But when Bill walked up to Ernie to give him his thanks, Ernie snapped, tripped Bill and pulled Bill's gun from its holster. Bill was dazed, his head striking the floor as he went down hard.

Cries of worry filled the room, each man not understanding what Ernie was doing.

"What the hell, Ernie, give that back!" a man yelled as he took a step towards him.

"Stay back, Mike, don't come any closer or so help me I'll shoot you," Ernie warned the man.

"What? Why?" Mike asked.

"Because I'm not going out there, I won't do it!"

Another man spoke up. "But, Ernie, you picked a straw like the rest of us and you lost."

Ernie shook his head as sweat beaded on his forehead. "I know that but I didn't think I would actually get the short one."

Bill was coming awake now and was slowly realizing what was happening.

Mike took another step towards Ernie and said, "Just give me the gun, Ernie. No one has to get hurt here."

Another man was sneaking up on Ernie from behind, his mouth open slightly as he concentrated on remaining silent.

"I'm warning you, stay back. I'll shoot, I swear," Ernie warned Mike once more.

Ernie realized there was someone behind him and he spun, saw the man reaching for him and in his panic, he fired. The bullet went right into the open mouth of the man, blowing out the back of his head. Brains and skull fragments painted the wall red as bits of brain slid down the surface like dead snails. As the man toppled to the floor, dead, the rec room erupted into chaos.

Some of the men jumped at Ernie after seeing what he'd done while a few others tried to run away.

Bill, seeing what was happening and knowing Ernie had lost it, turned and ran for the armory, knowing the only way to stop the unstable man was to put him down with a bullet.

Three men came at Ernie but none of them reached him. One at a time, Ernie shot each one in the face or torso. Blood now covered the floor, making standing or running treacherous, and the moans of the dying filled the air.

Ernie was now in full killing mode, his eyes so wide they looked about ready to pop out of his head. He was yelling manically as he shot anyone still standing.

A man had almost reached the doorway to the outer hallway when a round struck him between the shoulder blades. A large hole appeared in his chest as if a fist had been punched through him. With his mouth opening and closing like a landed fish, he slumped to the floor, not understanding why he was dying.

Ernie laughed devilishly and searched for another target. All around him were dead bodies.

Mike moaned loudly on the floor, his right shoulder a mass of blood and bone. Seeing Mike, Ernie walked over to him, placed the muzzle of the gun on Mike's forehead, and squeezed the trigger, blowing out the back of his head.

"Who's next, huh? Who wants to die next?" Ernie screamed as he waved the gun in the air. He caught movement to his right and spotted Dr. Mathis standing stock still, shocked by the violence before him. With a roar, Ernie raised the gun and fired but missed when Dr. Mathis dodged to the right, making a run for the door. A fist-sized piece of plaster was missing thanks to where the bullet hit the wall.

Ernie gave chase, the two men dashing through the curving hallways until Dr. Mathis reached his sanctuary, which was the air filtration room, complete with computer displays, monitors and printouts. This room was where the system was kept functioning, the heart, soul, and brains of the system.

Dr. Mathis dashed into the room and tried to close the door behind him, but a bullet ricocheting off the doorframe caused him to jump back. Ernie kicked the partially open door in and charged into the room.

Dr. Mathis tried to run but he tripped on his own feet. He fell against one of the computers that controlled airflow, his head striking a display of blinking lights.

Ernie laughed at his trapped prey, and with a guttural yell of glee, shot Dr. Mathis in the throat.

The bullet sliced through Dr. Mathis' carotid artery, severing his spine, then continued onward into the computer behind him. In a spray of sparks, the lights blinked faster and went out as blood shot into the bullet hole, saturating the wiring and making sure the machine would be ruined and beyond fixing. Not that there would be anyone with the knowledge to fix it. Dr. Mathis was the only technician and he was now sputtering his last bloody breath on the floor. His eyes glazed over as his right hand reached for Ernie, as if his killer could now somehow save him.

Ernie laughed and leveled the gun, prepared to finish the job.

A loud report filled the room and Ernie's chest disintegrated into a bloody spray of gore. His ribcage erupted outward, the bones fragmenting into razor sharp shards. Heart, lungs and kidneys were blasted into bloody pieces, the visceral mess spraying Dr. Mathis and the nearby computers.

Ernie's face took on one of confusion, and before he could get so much as a scream out in pain, his destroyed lungs robbed him of this and he fell face forward onto the floor, the gun clattering away to end up under a steel table covered in printouts.

Bill stepped into the room, the barrel of the shotgun in his hands still smoking.

Barely acknowledging the twitching body of Ernie, he went to Dr. Mathis to see if he could help him.

It was as he looked into the doctor's eyes that he saw he was too late. The eyes were glazed in death, the blood not pumping out of the gaping neck wound.

His friend was dead, gone, and worse, with him dead, there would be no one to fix the filtration system. Even if Bill went topside to clean the filters, the system wouldn't work.

As he thought this, he looked up at the vent grating on the wall and the small blue ribbon hanging from it. The ribbon hung slack, impotent, thanks to no air flowing through the air shafts.

With his left hand, Bill placed his fingers on Dr. Mathis' eyelids and closed them gently. Then he turned and walked out of the room, stepping over Ernie as he exited.

Upon returning to the rec room, all he found was more death. No man had survived Ernie's wrath—his madness—each one gunned down and murdered.

With nothing else to do, Bill turned and left, closing the door behind him.

Sheila would be worried, probably petrified from hearing all the gunshots.

He needed to tell her he was fine, but also to break the bad news to her. With everyone but him and her left alive and the filtration system destroyed, there could be only one outcome for them.

He didn't know how much time they had left, how much oxygen remained within the bunker, but however much time they had would be spent together, until the last breath was made.

And that's what they did. Bill and Sheila spent the next three days together, never leaving each other's side. They talked and made love and ate whatever they wanted, for food reserves were the least of the troubles. They dined till their stomachs were about to burst and then slept in each other's arms.

Bill woke on the fourth day to find the air was staler than ever. He had to breathe harder as his lungs struggled to pull in what meager oxygen remained in the bunker, and he had a headache to end all headaches.

As he sat up, he felt lightheaded and he knew this would be their last day together. When they went to sleep that night, he had a feeling he and Sheila would never wake up again, deprived of the oxygen they needed to survive.

It was as he looked down on her sleeping form that he decided that wasn't how he wanted to go out. He didn't want to think about him and her lying dead in their bed, the bodies forever sealed in the bunker, a giant tombstone no one would ever know about.

"Sheila, wake up," he said softly, shaking her shoulder. She stirred slightly and it took him four more times before she finally woke up.

"Huh, what? What do you want? Let me sleep, God I'm so tired," she said groggily.

"That's just the lack of oxygen," he said. "It makes you want to sleep."

"Then let me. Bill, there's nothing we can do, you know that. All we can do is accept our fate. The ones who were shot by Ernie were the lucky ones. At least they went quickly."

"No, don't say that. I wouldn't trade this last week with you for anything. At least we got to say goodbye and make our peace."

"Huh, some peace."

"Listen, I've been thinking about something and I want you to join me."

"Go on," she said, her voice slightly stronger in curiosity.

"I want to go topside." He held his hand up to stop her protest. "Wait, hear me out. There's no more oxygen left, it's almost gone. I can barely breathe as it is and I'm lightheaded. This is it, our last day, and I don't want to die down here. Let's go up there one last time. If we're gonna die, then let's do it together on the surface, not down here in this giant coffin."

"But the ash, we'll choke to death when it fills our lungs, it's suicide," she said while sitting up, her adrenalin now flowing.

"It's suicide to stay down here, Sheila and if we're gonna die, if we have no say in it, then let's go for a walk one last time together, like we used to do in the old days."

"I..." she began, but when she looked into his eyes, seeing his resolve, she stopped, nodded, and closed her eyes and said, "Okay, fine, like you said, we don't have a choice." She smiled. "I would like to go for one more walk with you, Bill...outside."

He took her hand. "Well then, there's no time like the present. Let's get dressed."

He helped her stand, and after the dizziness passed, she dressed as did he. They wore their best clothing, as if they were preparing to go to a funeral, and though they didn't discuss it, they both knew they actually were...theirs.

When they had dressed, combed their hair and brushed their teeth, both looking wonderful with the exception of their pale skin from lack of sunlight and their sunken eyes, they headed for the ladder leading to the surface.

"I'll go first," he said to her when they reached the ladder. She nodded and he slowly began to climb. He had to stop more than once and gather his strength from the exertion, the oxygen in the bunker fading fast.

When he reached the underside of the hatch, it took all his might to spin the wheel to release the locking mechanism, and he wasn't able to push it open with his shoulder, plus white spots filled his vision and he thought he was going to faint.

"Are you all right?" Sheila asked from below, holding onto the ladder with her arms wrapped around the iron rungs."

"Yeah, just give me a second to catch my breath for the hundredth time." He looked down at her. "You ready? Once I open the hatch, it won't take long for the ash to clog our lungs."

"Just do it. We've already said our goodbyes."

He nodded and winked at her, she grinning back.

"I love you," he said.

"I love you, too," she replied.

When he felt he was as strong as he possibly could get under the circumstances, he pushed one final time as more white spots filled his vision and he knew in a second he was definitely going to pass out. The hatch cracked and ash flowed inside, the vacuum of the bunker pulling it down like a depressurized airplane in reverse.

He spit the ash from his lips as he pushed the hatch open some more, then began to climb out.

Blinking black soot from his eyes, he wiped his face clean with the back of his hand, and as his eyes cleared, he gasped in shock.

With tears in his eyes he said, "Sheila, come up here, oh my God, you have to see this!" he cried in amazement.

"What is it? What's wrong?" she called, too terrified to climb up and step out of the hatch and be suffocated by the black and gray ash.

"Just come up here, hurry, oh my God! I don't believe it, it can't be true but it is!"

Sheila paused and considered his words. He didn't sound like he was choking, in fact, his voice sounded stronger. With shaking arms and her heart pounding in her chest, she climbed higher, and when her head poked out of the hatch, her mouth fell open and her lightheadedness faded as oxygen flooded her system.

"What? How, it's impossible," she gasped as clean air filled her lungs.

"It's over, Sheila, it's finally over," Bill said and spun in a circle, the ash at his feet stirring slightly but then falling back to the ground. All around him was a sea of ash, but in that ash were small seedlings, the fertile ash now giving forth lush greenery. Overhead, the clear azure sky bathed them in sunshine.

Bill took her hand and smiled as she joined him. There had been ash covering the hatch and that was what had fallen onto his face and hair when he opened it. "Since the last time we had to clean the filters, the volcanoes must have finally ceased spewing ash into the atmosphere. It all finally settled and the sun's back."

"You mean..." she began.

He nodded. "Yes, if we had stayed inside we would have died and all for nothing. Ernie, Dr. Mathis, Mike, and everyone else died for nothing. We could have left the bunker at anytime."

Sheila had tears in her eyes as she looked up at the shining sun, feeling its warmth on her face. "I still can't believe it. So, what do we do now?"

He hugged her tightly and kissed her gently on the lips. "That's simple, we start over."

THE TORRENT

KETIH LUETHKE

Dwayne awoke to raindrops splashing into the growing pool of water inside the living room. Last night, a tree had fallen on the roof, making an even better excuse for the rain to come in, not only through the windows, but now the ceiling. He watched his daughter, Ashley, as she slept, and made sure the wood ax was where he'd left it the night before.

Water splashed downstairs.

They weren't alone.

He snatched the ax immediately and stood in the doorway, waiting and listening. He stayed that way for a few minutes but the splashes never came back again.

Ashley stirred in her sleep. She rubbed her brown eyes and brushed away the dark hair clinging to her face.

"What is it, Dad? Are the bad men here?"

"Maybe, be quiet," he shushed her.

He flipped the ax in his hands, testing its weight. He could hold the weapon like this for hours at a time, and he had on occasion when the men came by in boats, but tonight it was useless. If there was someone hiding in the water, they would've made a move by now. He dropped his guard and went back to sitting on the bed.

"No bad men?"

"No," he said, shaking his head. "Get some sleep, honey. We're leaving in the morning."

"I don't want to go. I like our house," Ashley pouted.

"It's not safe here anymore, and we're out of food. We need to get to higher ground; away from the water."

"What about Snoopy? Can he come with us?"

"He's not real," he said.

She shook her head. "Yes he is Daddy. He swims in the water and he talks to me when you go out to get food. So, can he come too, please?"

Dwayne rolled his eyes, knowing his daughter's imaginary friend was a coping mechanism.

"Yes, I guess he can come," he sighed and patted her head. "Now go back to sleep."

Ashley yawned and closed her eyes.

A shadow danced along the wall and disappeared so fast he wasn't certain he'd seen it at all. He grabbed the ax and watched the water steadily climb up the stairs and down the hallway.

The world was no longer a safe place.

* * *

Cold and wet, always so cold and wet...
The man called Snoopy watched the man on the bed slowly close his eyes and fall into an uneasy sleep. He didn't like the man. He wasn't bad like the others. He didn't throw things or shoot at him. He just guarded his daughter and Snoopy's best friend, Ashley.

Little Ashley...kind and sweet smelling.
He watched her as she slept. She looked so peaceful and he could almost hear her small lungs sucking in air and blowing it out as she struggled to gain beautiful dreams, instead of nightmares. Snoopy treaded the cold water and recalled when he first met her. She was singing near the water, that was then flooding the streets and not yet in her house. He swam up to her while her father was gathering the last of his supplies. He told her he was a mermaid, which was a lie, but she believed him in child-like wonder, and the two soon became friends.

Ashley...sleep well, sleep well.

* * *

Dwayne awoke to gunshots. He found himself sitting on the bed with the ax in his hands. His daughter was still there and was also jerked awake from the sound.

Outside, a man was speaking through a loud speaker, broadcasting his horrid voice across the flooded landscape, seeking out the last vestiges of humanity.

"...And I urge you to come out of hiding. My men and I can give you food, we can give you shelter, and most of all, we can offer you a place in this new world."

Dwayne took off his shoes and shirt, and then started down the hallway, still carrying the ax.

"Dad, don't leave me," Ashley begged.

"I'm just going to have a peek. We could use one of their boats."

The little girl curled up into a ball and cried softly into her pillow.

"Be strong," he whispered to her, and slipped into the water which had overtaken the hallway and began to claim the bedroom.

When he reached the staircase, he eased into the water and let the coldness slip over his flesh. He was naked except for a cut-off pair of jeans, and the ax. He floated on the water's surface until he reached a window. From there, he spotted two motor boats trudging along the waterway. Each boat held men armed with lengths of pipe, and in the nearest one was a tall, skinny man wearing a rubber Halloween mask, and talking through a loud speaker. The man at his side had a rifle, and kept a constant visual for survivors.

"We come in peace," the masked man said. "You no longer have to hide from us. We offer you security."

"Over here!" a man called out from across the street.

Dwayne knew who it was immediately. It was his neighbor, Zack. He was a middle-aged accountant with a young wife who liked to spend his money on fancy clothing, back when money meant something.

The men in the boats directed their attention to Zack.

"We're over here, help us," Zack pleaded.

"You fool," Dwayne muttered to himself. Had he known the sniveling paper worker was next door all this time, he would've offered him spare food and protection. Now, it was much too late.

Isabella, a pretty young blond came out of Zack's attic by popping open the window at the side. Zack was still wearing his business slacks and white button down shirt, both which were discolored and slightly torn. His wife wore a pink blouse and a black dress. Her hair was stringy and uncombed. Both waved and grinned.

"Save us," Isabella called. "We're starving."

The man with the rifle pointed at Zack, a second later there was a loud report and a gaping hole appeared in his chest.

Isabella screamed and clutched her husband.

The men on the boats quickly reached her and tore at her clothes. They kicked her husband into the icy water, the current quickly carrying him away. The woman cried and begged for mercy but the men beat her into submission. Soon, she was barely conscious and the men took turns having their way with her warm flesh.

The other boat turned around and went the other way, leaving the rapists to their business.

Dwayne sucked in his lips and turned away from the horrible scene. Isabella had ceased to cry or struggle. She let the men have her.

Dwayne swam back through the house and went upstairs. There, he found his daughter sitting on the bed, clutching a small kitchen knife and her teddy bear, Mr. Ruffles.

"Where did you get that?"

"Snoopy gave it to me for protection," she said, and dropped the knife on the bed. She hurried to her father and gave him a hug, never wanting to let go.

* * *

When night arrived, he bade his daughter to cover her ears and try to sleep as he descended into the water once more. She fought and argued, pleading him not to go, but he was firm, and won in the end. He stripped down to his cut-off jeans and took the ax with him just like earlier, only this time, he ventured out the window instead of watching from behind the broken glass.

The night cast everything in a thick blanket of darkness. He could barely make out Zack's house across the street.

Cautiously, he swam with the ax. The current was strong, but he was stronger, and smarter. Instead of fighting the current, he allowed the murky water to carry him a little further down the street. Once he could see the outline of the side of Zach's house against the star-lit sky, he swam forward, cutting through the water until he could grab the roof for support. Out of breath, he wheezed and set the ax on the roof. He waited for the men to come, but they never did.

As he scanned the roof, he saw three bodies lying side by side. The slow rise and fall of their chests indicated sleep or rest; in the dark it was hard to tell for sure.

He slipped out of the water and onto the roof. He readied the ax and approached the prone bodies. The two men didn't stir and Isabella was in-between them, looking up at him. She didn't say a word, only stared, her face swollen and bruised.

He motioned for her to come to him but she wouldn't budge. One of the men groaned and scratched his naked chest.

Dwayne heaved the ax and let it fall on the man's jugular. The blade dug through skin, cartilage, and bone, but the head didn't completely come off; it hung by a bloody strip of flesh.

The other man stirred and Dwayne lifted the bloody ax high above his head. He brought it crashing down into the man's sternum with a bone crushing *thunk*. The man's body twitched and his hands fluttered to free the cold steel, but his efforts were useless, and after a while he laid still.

"Isabella, you're free," he told the woman. "Get up."

She jerked her head from side to side, looking at the dead men beside her.

He grabbed her arms and pulled until she was sitting up.

"Where's their boat?" he asked her.

Isabella slowly stood up. Her legs wobbled momentarily and she covered her nakedness with her hands. He avoided looking at her nudity and walked to the edge of the roof, searching the dark water for the motor boat.

"They...hurt me," Isabella cried.

He turned around to face her. In the dark, her pale skin was light enough to make her almost glow. She could've been a ghost.

"I'll take you with me. We'll be safe together. My daughter's upstairs back at my house. Let me get her and all three of us will head for the mountains."

Isabella stopped crying. She stared at him, not comprehending.

"Come with us. We'll go to higher ground and start fresh again, away from the gangs and thieves. We'll start a new life and look after each other."

Isabella walked to the edge of the roof and spread her arms wide. "I'm sorry. I can't go with you. Not after...the things they did to me; Zach's gone. I'll never be able to forget." Before he could stop her, she fell into the water and the current dragged her into the darkness.

He tried to grab her, but in less than a second, the strong current had swept her away. One minute she was there, the next— gone. He sighed and stepped across the roof to check the opposite side. There, tied to the top of a telephone pole, was a small motor boat, swaying back and forth in the black waters. He quickly went back to the men he'd killed. The ax buried in the heavier man's chest was stuck. He had to place his foot on the man's head and use both hands in order to wrench the ax free of his sternum. It came out with a wet sound, and a chunk of red tissue was stuck to the blade.

Ax in hand, he went to the boat, having to jump into the water in order to reach it. He tossed the ax inside and lifted himself over the side and fell into it.

Inside the boat, he discovered a blanket only slightly wet from exposure to the weather, a First Aid kit, a cooler full of beer, some *Slim Jims* and beef jerky, and a pair of women's underwear— Isabella's no doubt. He tossed the underwear into the water and started the small engine. He had to pull the rip cord twice and the motor choked, then started. He slipped the rope off the telephone pole and drove back home.

He circled around to the back of his house and tied it to the top of a lamp post sticking out of the water. But with the continual rise of the water, the boat would be sucked down or capsized if he didn't fetch his daughter soon.

Once he was sure the boat was secure, he then climbed over the roof and jumped into the water. He swam to his house and back through the open window. He rushed upstairs, but when he reached the bedroom, Ashley was missing. Only her teddy bear, Mr. Ruffles was there. He began searching the house, swimming into all the rooms now underwater. There was no sign of her anywhere.

When he was exhausted and in tears, he sat on edge of her waterlogged bed while clutching Mr. Ruffles.

* * *

A few minutes earlier.

Ashley sat on her bed, clutching her knife and waiting for her father to return. After a few minutes had passed, a dark shape slowly rose out of the water. He was hunched over, his skin extremely pale, and he smelled like dead fish. He wore a pair of scuba flippers and a diving mask.

"Snoopy!" she yelled happily and ran toward him.

"Keep your voice down," he sneered and snatched her up in his long arms. "We're leaving now."

"What about my dad? Can he come, too?"

"We're going away under the sea to live in my castle and your father can't join us," he said, squeezing her arm gently.

"Snoopy, you're hurting me."

One side of his gnarled lips curled, revealing blackened teeth. He jumped into the water, holding her tightly, and swam away from the house and into the night. He brought her to the house at the end of the street and sat her down on a weather-stained roof.

Ashley hugged herself. "I'm cold," she said, shivering.

Snoopy climbed onto the roof and slid closer to her, licking his teeth with his dark tongue. He was so hungry.

"Don't worry, you'll be safe here."

Unable to resist, he snatched her arm and took a bite.

Ashley screamed.

* * *

Dwayne heard his daughter's scream echo through the air and he snapped out of his stupor. He dove into the water and swam out of the window, wanting to get to the boat. In the distance, there came another sound and Ashley's cries suddenly came to a halt.

A motor boat was coming.

He could see the boat getting closer and saw a small beam of light–probably a flashlight–play over the roof of Zack's house and reveal the mutilated men.

The boat pulled up to the roof and two men got out and examined the corpses.

Dwayne watched and tried to ease away from the men in the dark so he could reach his daughter. He decided using the boat he'd taken wasn't an option, as the men would spot him easily; he chose to swim.

The flashlight beam darted toward him and he ducked underwater, and was forced to swim back into his house. He could hear the men cursing and the motor boat coming his way. He had to act fast if he was going to survive. He swam back to Ashley's bedroom. Once there, he tucked Mr. Ruffles into his waistband, and secured him with a belt. Then, he got his ax and swam back to the living room. He knew the men would find the other boat and take it back, and he couldn't let them. He reached the window and swam outside just as they approached. It was easy to let the current take him away from them, to drift on its black wings and avoid detection. He saw the men park the boat beside his house and tie it down to the roof gutter. One man jumped into the water and swam through the window. The other stayed with the boat. He wondered if it was the man who had worn the mask from yesterday, but it was hard to tell.

He fought against the current once he was a safe distance away, and circled around the boat, coming up behind it. The man in the boat had his back turned and was wiping the loud speaker down with a piece of cloth.

Dwayne eased onto the boat quietly, making sure he didn't alert the man. He could see the back of the rubber mask lying on the bottom of the boat.

He lifted the ax and brought it down at an angle, crashing through the skull and splitting the man's head wide open. The body toppled forward and the loudspeaker fell into the water. Dwayne tossed the rest of the man in after it, and found a rifle in the boat. He dropped his ax in favor of the rifle just as the other man appeared in the water on the side of the boat. He was thin and out of breath.

"I couldn't find him, sir. What should we do?" the man asked. In the darkness, he hadn't realized who Dwayne was, assuming he was the now dead raider.

"You can die," Dwayne said simply, and blew half of his skull apart.

The body jerked back and slid into the mirthless waters, staining it a darker color.

Dwayne started the boat with ease and drove toward where he'd heard his daughter scream. The flashlight was on the seat beside him and he used it to scan the darkness for movement. He saw something move in the water near the house at the end of the street. The house once belonged to an elderly lady and her son. They kept to themselves and he didn't recall them leaving when the flood started, despite countless warnings to do so. He steered the boat closer and saw something swimming under the water; it was as white as snow, and fast. He circled the boat around and followed the shape in the water which in turn circled around and popped up for air.

"Daddy, help me!" Ashley cried, but was then sucked back down into the water.

He panned the flashlight onto the thing holding his daughter, and a red mist flowed from her arm. Whoever had taken her was a fast swimmer, and sunk deeper into the water. After a while, the light couldn't penetrate far enough down to see them.

"Ashley!"

Dwayne circled the boat around. Minutes passed. He couldn't find them. They were gone. He circled back and stopped, cutting off the engine. He scanned the water's surface with the flashlight and by chance spotted a pale foot kicking water and then sinking deeper. He left the boat and the flashlight behind, leaving the light on in hopes to delude the man that he was still in the boat.

He then grabbed his ax and slid into the water after them. It was slow going, and every time he got close to them, the pale being would swim just a little further out of reach. Dwayne hung back, but kept pace with them, just another shadow in the dark. In time, the pale man grew tired of swimming and reached a house for a rest. He tossed Ashley onto the roof and quickly followed after, holding her down. He looked behind him and could barely see the boat with its shining light in the distance.

"Now, where were we? You soft and tasty morsel," he grinned.

Ashley struggled beneath him as he opened his mouth to take another bite of her flesh.

But before he could bite down, a sharp pain filled his backside. The man called Snoopy shuttered and looked backward. He gasped as the ax was torn away from his side and brought down again, even harder, into his lower spine. He screamed and screamed and screamed, but the man wouldn't stop chopping until there was nothing left except fragmented pieces.

Dwayne dropped the ax and went to his daughter who was shaking and staring at him with vacant eyes. He dropped the ax and held onto her.

"I'll take care of your wounds. You'll be okay. We're going to leave this place tonight. We have a boat now. I'll keep you safe, I promise."

Ashley sobbed into his chest and nodded.

He picked her up and stepped over the leftover pieces of Snoopy. He left the ax behind and slipped into the water. The boat with the flashlight had drifted away on the current but the one he'd tied up behind the house was still secure. He swam to it and put his daughter inside.

"Are we still going to the mountains?" she asked, still griping her arm where Snoopy had taken a small chunk out of it.

"You bet, but let's get that arm bandaged first."

He wrapped her wound with the gauze from the First Aid kit and gave her back Mr. Ruffles. He then put the blanket around her shoulders and tried to start the boat, but it wouldn't turn over. He cut the rope and they drifted into the darkness, letting the current take them wherever it pleased.

THE WANDERER

MARK CHRISTOPHER

The explosion of the Synergy Corporation Refinery forever changed the small town of Tin, Pennsylvania. The town had received its unusual name when a local geologist discovered a small reserve of the metal in the ground during a search for groundwater. This was puzzling as tin had never been found in the United States prior to this discovery. It wasn't long before a large smelting company decided they would buy the land and use the mined tin to plate over steel. This new company led to more jobs and the name of the town, which had been Deerfield, was formally changed to Tin in a ceremony that included champagne, dancing, and music.

As the years flew by, the smelting company was sold to a larger chemical company. Synergy Corporation had bigger ideas than just the production of a relatively useless metal. They brought vessels, cooling towers, and control rooms, and began production of a vast array of products and chemicals, including ammonia, gasoline, benzene, and hydrogen sulfide. In all, the refinery giant produced over twenty-six various chemicals and substances.

It was in the early morning of July 25, 2011 that Simon Croydon would finally accomplish something in his bleak, short life. Just an ordinary field laborer for a contract company working a turnaround in the hydrogen sulfide plant, Simon was in painful need of a cigarette. Unbeknownst to him, a small rupture had been discovered in one of the hydrogen sulfide transport lines during a routine leak check. As the operators argued in the control room about who would write the permit and whose turn it was to fix it, Simon was debating walking the five hundred yards to the plant-appointed smoke shack.

Not feeling up to the walk, he decided to take refuge in a small maintenance shed located inside the production area. As he made his way there, the unpleasant odor of foul eggs and flatulence assaulted his nostrils. The smell didn't bother him that much, as he had made worse smells in the hotel room bathroom that morning, and he entered the maintenance shed. The stench of sulfur still hung in the air and Simon didn't know that the leak, which was still being debated over, was slowly piping the colorless gas into the shed. Simon placed a cigarette in his mouth, and just before he flicked his lighter, he thought that maybe he should quit before it killed him.

I'll quit after this one, he thought as his lighter ignited.

Immediately, the air surrounding him burst into flames. Simon felt the extreme heat and the rush of fire run down his throat as he was cooked from the inside out. Within seconds, his world faded to black. Inside the control room, alarms were blaring and the control boards lit up like a Christmas tree. The operators were panicking as they frantically pushed buttons to close valves while others rushed to change into their chemical suits. But it was all in vain. In minutes, the entire sulfuric acid plant went up in a giant, toxic fireball.

The fire spread to the ammonia plant and then traveled down a natural gas line to the gasoline and benzene production areas. The fire burned so hot that it melted steel and incinerated any unlucky worker in the vicinity.

The townspeople, a few miles away, saw a large fireball erupt on the horizon. It was quickly followed by a loud bang that shattered windows and caused birds to fall from the sky. The trees ignited and burned as a wall of fire swept forward like lava flowing from a volcano. The unlucky homes and people closest to the plant were reduced to ash. Some of the people were smart enough to run to their basements where they were spared. Others, who were not as quick-witted, succumbed to the fire and poisonous breeze. To those trapped in their basements, it sounded like a raging locomotive had shot from the bowels of Hell and was sweeping over the town.

After a few hours had passed, the people of Tin began to venture out of their basements. The landscape of their town had been horrifically disfigured. The trees had burned and looked like giant scarred hands reaching out of the earth. The small creek which ran on the outskirts of the town was thick with black sludge. The air was so thick with toxic gasses and corrosives that breathing was painful. A few of the elderly townsfolk died within minutes of breathing the foul air, their frail lungs scorched. Some of the people fell to their knees and prayed. Others looked up at the sky and cursed the God that they no longer believed in. A few just sat down and laughed.

The President vowed quick action. The fire at the plant was eventually extinguished, though it was never revealed to the public that it was allowed to burn out first. Food and water was brought into the town by the Red Cross. A group of celebrities were already banding together to make a song. The nation was pulling for Tin, the little town that no one had ever heard of.

However, something had changed. In the days that followed the explosion, a Red Cross truck was attacked and overturned. The volunteers were savagely beaten and killed; their shipment of medical supplies and MRE's stolen. A young camera man caught the attacks on tape during a live feed. The last thing he recorded was a group of people smashing him to a gooey pulp with various tools. The nation was shocked and scared. The National Guard was mobilized immediately and a perimeter ten miles around the town and refinery was constructed. Only once did the deranged citizens of Tin test it and they were sent back in a hail of gunfire. The President consulted with his team of experts who told him the land was ruined and so were the people. Their advice was to quarantine it and let them die off. They could not possibly live longer than a few months. Then they could do with the land whatever they pleased. With a heavy heart, the President agreed. In a few months, he figured, he would turn the land into a memorial park. That would serve as a nice backdrop when he sought a second term.

It was one year later and Martin was still having weird dreams. The first few months, his sleep had been haunted by images of his wife, Sarah, who had gone into town that fateful day with her mother to shop at the antique store. The dreams used to be of Sarah waving to him and telling him that everything was going to be fine.

Recently, they had been of her bathed in fire, screaming for him to help her as the fire licked the flesh from her bones. Each dream would jar him awake, covered in perspiration as he breathed heavily in his sweat-soaked bed. On nights like that he would read from the Bible and try to make sense of it all. The book had once brought him great comfort but was now causing him confusion. Why had he been spared when so many had perished?

He was lucky for starters, his home was situated within the Tin city limits but as far from the refinery as one could get. He also had a fully stocked basement filled with canned goods and pallets of drinking water. His paranoia of a terrorist attack crippling the United Stated had paid off.

As the days went by, the dreams of Sarah faded all together. Though he was happy he didn't have to witness her suffering, he still missed seeing her face.

He didn't remember when the new dreams started, if they could even be considered dreams. He never could see their faces, but he heard their voices. They were the voices of men and women, of people young and old. They were voices that swirled around his head like water spiraling down a drain, always urging him to get out of the house. Every once in a while he would catch a quick glimpse of a face, an arm, even an eye; but nothing more. He had ignored these dreams as nothing more than his mind playing tricks on him. As the day passed, the voices that visited him grew more persistent and louder. The last time he dreamt of the voices, it had truly terrified him. As the voices swirled around his head, they started to shout. The shouting turned to yelling which in turn gave way to screaming. Horrible screams of people consumed in agony. Suddenly, the face of his wife appeared, her burned bald head possessing a few strands of singed, black hair, her eyes nothing but empty sockets. She raised her hands to her face, and when she pressed her cheeks, they seemed to melt and ooze around her charred fingers.

"Get out, Martin!" she screamed in a voice that shook him from the inside. "Come be with me!"

Martin's ears were still ringing as he woke in a panic.

Just another dream, he thought as he lay back down and drifted off to sleep. He had just closed his eyes when a wave of light washed over him. Martin opened his eyes and squinted and made out the outline of a person walking towards him in the honey-yellow light. The silhouette came forward out of the light and he was awestruck when he recognized the curvy shape of a woman. The woman's white face sparkled like a thousand diamonds. Her long black hair flowed from the top of her head and touched lightly on her rosy cheeks. Her body was adorned with a flawless white silken tunic. She was barefoot and appeared to float to where he was sitting up in his bed with his eyes transfixed on the manifestation before him.

"Sarah?" Martin stammered.

"Yes, honey, it's me. Why haven't you come looking for me?" she asked, a hurt look painted on her face.

"I...I thought you were only a dream."

"They were dreams, but it's through them that I can talk to you. I'm so lonely and cold out here. I need my husband, I need you."

"I'm sorry, Sarah. Please forgive me. I...I didn't know," he said as he began to weep.

"I do forgive you, Martin. But it's time you left here and joined me. I've been waiting for you this entire time. I need you to continue my journey."

"Is your mother with you?" he asked as tears continued to roll down his cheeks.

"No. I haven't seen her since it happened. It was so fast and people were running and clawing at one another to get out of the streets. I held her hand but felt it jerked away from me. When I looked back, she was gone."

Martin rose to his feet.

"Well, what do you want me to do? Where should I go to find you?"

"Go to the scene of where the world ended. You'll find me there waiting for you, but be careful. What's out there waiting for you is sinister and evil. The town of Tin isn't what it used to be."

"I'll be careful," he said as he started to choke on his words, the tears falling freely. "I miss you so much, so damn much. I never stopped missing you."

"I know, and I miss you, too. Soon we will be together again. Just come find me."

"I love you, baby," he whispered.

"I love you, too," she said with a smile as she faded away.

Martin woke up; his heart feeling like it would explode in his chest as it thumped with anxious anticipation. The sweat dripped down from his hot cheeks but he paid it no mind as he leapt out of bed. He walked over to where he had witnessed her standing. He bent down and touched the floorboard where she had been and noticed they were unusually hot in the cool room. He walked over to the small table near his bed and removed the Colt .45 from the drawer. He went to his bedroom window and stared out into the dark wasteland. He could hear the light patter of acidic rain hit the bedroom window and he hoped the rain would pass by before he began his journey. He had only attempted to leave the house once since the explosion occurred and when he had, the burning rain poured down on him. He remembered how horrible it felt as he rushed back into the house and doused himself with a case of bottled water. Still, he remembered the tears that ran down his face, burning more when he realized Sarah was never coming home. But now he was filled with hope. He would see her again, and soon.

He decided to leave at daybreak.

Martin was too excited to sleep as the thoughts of what was to come rushed through his head. He decided to wait the morning out by thumbing through his Bible, most likely for the last time. As he read it, he didn't feel as confused and torn as before. He glanced out the window again and noticed the black sky already starting to lighten to a pitch gray. Yes, when morning came, he would start wandering.

The hours went by fast and soon, the inky black night had turned into morning as the sun stretched its fiery head over the hills in the distance. Martin debated the choice of clothing he would wear for his search and find mission. At first he selected the suit he wore for Sunday services, but then dashed the idea as the thought of walking in the hot suit was already beginning to make him miserable. He decided on a pair of clean jeans and a button-down red cotton shirt. He roped a black leather belt around his waist and slipped into a pair of brown leather, steel-toed boots. He picked up his gun and made sure it was loaded. Six bullets were in the chamber. He removed them and drew a small cross on the rim of each one with a black marker. He had six shots; he hoped he wouldn't need more. When he felt he was prepared, he opened his front door and stepped out into the bright world. He had a smile on his face as he left with his gun and the thought that Sarah was waiting for him.

The first thing he noticed about this new world was the sky. It had once been crystal blue with little fluffy clouds rolling around it like tiny sheep. Now it had been reduced to a dark red that reminded Martin of condensed tomato soup. The sun itself glowed not as a ball of yellow, but a pale orange. As he walked under the atomic sky, he was shocked at the drastic change in the topography. The lush greenery he remembered was now replaced with bare ground. Not even a speck of grass or troublesome weed could be detected. There were no clues left behind that at one point the area had been alive.

I'm in Hell, Martin thought and strangely enough the thought excited him. He whistled 'Onward Christian Soldiers' as loudly as he could as he made the long walk into the town of Tin.

The walk into town was uneventful and a wave of relief washed over him. The road leading to Tin was quite remarkable and strangely beautiful as the orange sun reflected off the metals and corrosives that were imbedded in the asphalt road. It gave the road a color of gold. Littered across the road were various bones that had been bleached white and stripped of any flesh or muscle. He saw the outline of the town and he knew he would be there soon. His legs were growing tired and he was breathing heavily. It had been a year since he had walked a distance further than the layout of his home.

"Halt!" a high-pitched voice broke out.

Martin stopped immediately.

People, he thought as he felt his heart rate quickened. He was surprised when a boy who appeared no more than eight years old walked out from behind a large rock and stepped onto the golden road, blocking Martin's path. The boy's long, black hair hung like a greasy mop around his pale, thin face. His eyes were wild, like those of a feral wolf, and black as a pool of ink. He was shirtless and his chest moved up and down quickly, exposing a gaunt body where Martin could count all the boy's ribs. Various scabbed over scars and sores were visible on the boy's body and he wore a pair of jeans with holes throughout and no shoes covered his dirty feet.

"What can I do for you, young man?" Martin asked.

"No one enters Tin unless I say so!" the boy shouted, exposing a mouth filled with jagged and broken teeth.

"And why is that, child?"

"Because I said so! And don't call me child!"

"What if I said I have to go into Tin to meet someone very important to me?" Martin asked with a slight smile.

"The hell with your meeting! The hell with you!" He turned and called to someone over his shoulder. "Hey, Dad, get out here now!" the boy cried as he turned to the rock he had just come from.

Martin saw a figure rise up and slowly make its way to the road. Martin was saddened to see the desperate man lurch forward and come to a stop next to his son. He was short and very thin. His bald head had been burned badly by the hot sun and a thick brown beard covered his mouth and chin. A broken pair of glasses sat on his large nose. A tattered and stained white shirt hung loosely over him and a pair of olive-green shorts was held on his waist by a duct tape belt. His feet were bare as well. Martin could see the look of submission and shame in his eyes.

"Dad, this man refuses to listen to me. Kill him!" the boy commanded.

"Son, how about we let this one pass," the man said weakly.

Suddenly, the boy lashed out and struck his father in the chest. The man bent over and the boy kicked his legs hard and shoved him to the ground. The boy continued to kick his defenseless father wildly.

"Let one pass!" the boy shrieked. "I'm starving!"

"Hey, kid, you stop that right now!" Martin shouted. "How dare you treat your father that way!"

The boy stopped, and as Martin finished yelling, a smile broke across his young face and he laughed like a maniac as he shook his wild hair. In his laugh, Martin could hear the cackle of demons.

"My father? This stupid coward had no problem letting my mom and sister die! I saved him when he was too stupid to move! I tell him what to do!" the boy screamed as he began to pull his father up off the ground. "Get up, you old bastard. You've let him live long enough."

His father stumbled to his feet and glumly removed a dull hunting knife from its sheath. He came at Martin slowly with the knife raised high. Martin took aim, fired, and the Colt boomed across the empty road.

The man looked down at his chest and noticed a large hole over his heart. *It doesn't even hurt*, he thought as he died before his body hit the ground.

"Dad!" the boy cried as he ran to his dead father.

He looked up at Martin with the hate in his eyes burning like the fires of Hell.

"Boy, my father would have kicked my ass if I acted like you. Consider this some tough love," Martin said as he pulled the trigger again.

Martin's aim was true and the top of the boy's head erupted in a shower of red pulp and bits of skull. He fell forward, his arm draped over his father's corpse.

"Two less crazies in this godforsaken town," Martin said as he holstered his gun.

He was glad he had come prepared.

After a brisk twenty minute walk, Martin was standing inside Tin. Though no street signs remained, he knew he was walking down First Street. He noticed several familiar landmarks that were now only burnt-out skeletons of their former selves. Tin had once been an ideal small town. It was clean, crime wasn't ever an issue, and people were friendly.

The center of town had showcased a small park filled with trees, benches, and a large fountain for wishing. Two small gazebos had been provided as well for picnics and gatherings. Now the fountain had been reduced to rubble and trees were nothing more than large, bare sticks. The grass was a field of dirt and he couldn't tell where the gazebos had been located. He continued walking and from memory could visualize the small businesses that had once lined the street. A pile of bricks used to be Pepe's Pizza, a hollowed shell was Clovis's Antiques N' Things, and Rocky's Music Shop was just a bare slab of concrete.

And these are just the shops, he thought as his mind wandered to the neighborhoods. He didn't dare cut up East Street to see the tragedies that had befallen the houses.

It was quiet in Tin. Eerily quiet. No birds chirped overhead and the sound of talking or the rumbles of cars passing by were only distant memories. The town was dead. Martin turned the corner which took him down Sixth Street and would ultimately be the road to his final destination. When he made the turn, his eyes teared up at the amazing sight before him. Rising tall above the disfigured buildings was the cross of the church.

"Wow!" he gasped as the tears rolled down his face as he was caught off guard by the inspirational sight.

And there were people there! At least six, he saw. There might have been more but he wasn't sure, and they were gathered outside the church. *Maybe there was hope for Tin after all*, he thought as he walked forward.

As he moved closer to the church, he noticed that it hadn't gone unscathed. The roof was badly damaged and had collapsed in some areas. The centuries old stained glass windows had been blown out and all that remained were empty frames. But that didn't matter to Martin. The church stood and people were here to worship.

"Greetings everyone!" Martin called as he looked at the odd gathering assembled outside the church.

Four men and two women were seated on the steps leading to the large wooden doors. All wore rags and had hair that was wild and unkempt.

"It's such an incredible thing that some people still have faith!" Martin bubbled.

"Faith? Faith in what?" an old man in his sixties wearing a pair of sunglasses asked.

"Why in the Lord. After all, you are gathered in front of His house."

The six erupted in laughter and to Martin they sounded like screeching hyenas and braying donkeys.

"What's so funny?" he asked, not understanding the joke.

"You think we're here for church?" a red haired crone cackled. "This is our morgue. We store our dead here. And believe me, there are a lot of dead inside."

"We had to do something with them. This was the only building big enough that was still standing," a brown haired old woman said.

"But it's not just a building! It's *His* house!" Martin stammered.

"Well, now it's *His* morgue!" one of the other men said mockingly and the group erupted in laughter.

"Are you stupid?" the same man continued. "Don't pester us with your beliefs."

"Hey, I have an idea!" the brown haired woman exclaimed. "Since he wants to go to church so badly, let's throw him in there!"

"Yes, let's!" the red haired crone agreed.

The six began to advance on him, but there was no fear in Martin's eyes and his heart remained calm, its rhythmic beat steady, as he unholstered his gun. The man with the sunglasses was closest and Martin placed a bullet dead center in his chest. The man's sternum burst open as sharp shards of white bone peppered the air. A river of bright red blood poured forward like a carafe pouring wine. The man pitched forward and didn't move. The five people stared at Martin and the fallen man and slowly, fear began to fill their eyes.

"You evil people can all go to Hell!" Martin screamed as he fired again, the bullet piercing the throat of the red haired crone. Her eyes bulged and her tongue looked as if it was trying to leap from her mouth. She grabbed frantically at what remained of her neck as she toppled backward, her dead eyes already beginning to be scorched by the orange sun.

The remaining four had seen enough. Before the second body had hit the ground, they had turned and fled.

Poor, lost souls, Martin thought as his attention was drawn to the doors of the church. The thought of Sarah being in there intrigued him and he debated taking a look. If she was in there, she didn't deserve to be stacked on top of others like a piece of firewood. But he knew she couldn't be in there, because she had told him where to find her. He checked his gun and noticed he had two bullets left. As he continued his walk, he hoped he had enough.

He had just finished the halfway point of his journey when a hooded figure appeared from behind some wreckage and startled him.

"Sarah?" he asked as he placed his hand on his gun.

The figure replied by removing its brown hood.

The man's hair was long, stringy and white, and encased his weathered face that was tanned like a piece of leather. His face was made of a thousand wrinkles and he appeared to only have a few teeth still stuck to his gums. Regardless of his lack of teeth, the man smiled and seemed to show them off with a strange sense of pride.

"Come to sit a spell and talk with an old man?" he asked with a dry, cracked voice.

"Sure," Martin said as he felt himself coming down from an adrenaline surge. "But I can't stay long. I'm meeting someone."

"Meeting someone! Well good for you! Hopefully whoever you're meeting isn't like the crazy people that live inside Tin," the man said and Martin responded with a slight chuckle. "My name is John and I'd love to talk with you for a spell. It does get incredibly lonely being out here on my own."

Martin sat down under a leafless tree and told John everything. He told him of the dreams with the voices, the vision of Sarah, the boy and the golden road, and the church people. John sat mesmerized, like a child sitting around a campfire listening to a counselor telling ghost stories.

"I just don't understand why an old man like me is still alive," John said when Martin had finished his story. "I think I would have killed myself if I wasn't so scared to do it. Or if I had something to do it with."

"Yeah, it's been a rough time for everyone," Martin agreed as he tried to dodge the subject.

"Will you help me escape this sorrowful life?" John asked as he eyed the gun on Martin's hip.

"I'm not sure if that's my decision," Martin replied. He was caught off guard by John's unusual request. "You seem like a good man. There has to be a use for some good people in the world still."

"But I'm so lonely," John said glumly. "Even if I am a good man, I'm in the company of the wicked. They want nothing to do with me. I had to get out of the town before someone tried to eat me. It got very bad after the first few months went by and all of the food ran out. I sadly did some horrible things to survive."

"I don't know," Martin said. "It just wouldn't be right. I guess I could give you my gun and let you do it."

John shook his head. "No, I'm too afraid to pull the trigger myself. Please, Martin, save me," John pleaded.

Suddenly Martin felt a hand on his shoulder. He turned around and saw no one. But he could still feel it. A phantom hand was lightly depressing his right shoulder.

Then the sweet voice of Sarah cooed in his ears.

Help him, Martin. Show the old man some kindness still exists in this world. Then come find me.

Martin smiled as the instructions were received.

"All right, John, I'll help you."

With a wide, mostly toothless smile, John clenched his eyes shut and dropped to the ground. He began to recite The Lord's Prayer in a loud, clear voice. Martin slowly walked behind the praying man and got into position, his gun drawn. He took aim at the back of John's head and just as the word "Amen" pushed itself through John's lips, Martin pulled the trigger. The old man lurched forward and spasmed violently for a few seconds before he went still.

"Rest easy, John," Martin said as he walked his final mile on his journey.

The sun was still high in the red sky as Martin reached the site of the refinery explosion. A large, flat rock was positioned perfectly to where it offered a scenic view of the destroyed refinery. He could see the shredded vessels and storage tanks that had once housed thousands of gallons of toxic liquids. He saw the flattened control rooms where operators had sat and oversaw the processes that one day doomed them. The destroyed cooling towers were scattered about in the distance.

"Sarah!" he called. "Sarah! I'm here!"

The glare of the orange sun was starting to sting his eyes. When he closed them, he saw the explosion and witnessed the chain reaction of the demise of the refinery like he had been there. He could see the people running as a wave of fire spread over them and their screams filled his ears. He felt his heart begin to race as the hot air hit his face and he could feel the flames dance across his body and lick his skin. But when he opened his eyes, all that was before him was gray rubble.

"Where are you, Sarah? Why did you bring me here? What is it you want me to see?" he asked the sky.

He was afraid his question would go unanswered until her voice entered his head again.

Martin, I'm here. I've always been here.

"But I thought I would see you," Martin said as his chin quivered and the tears began to flow.

Martin, you knew I was dead. You knew there was no chance that I would be standing here when you arrived. But I have been waiting for you. I've been waiting for over a year. I can't move on unless it's with you. I refuse to move on unless you're by my side. Please, Martin, come be with me.

He smiled and a single tear began to roll down his cheek. He knew it was true, he knew it had always been true, he just hadn't wanted to admit it to himself.

He had survived but had lost the woman he loved. The world was a cold dark place now; there was no hope, only the peace waiting for him in death.

He pressed the gun to his temple and took one last look at the secular world of destruction. He wouldn't miss it at all.

"I'll be with you soon, Sarah," he said as he squeezed the trigger.

There was nothing but darkness.

HOW STARS ARE MADE

KELLY M. HUDSON

The clang of the bell woke him from his dreamless sleep, dragging him back to reality, back to the horrible stench of his cell and the entire holding area. He snorted and wiped his eyes of the gunk that had grown there when he slept. It was thick, viscous and green and sometimes it was so thick that his eyes were sealed shut. He wasn't sure what it was, exactly—whether it was some remnant of a curse upon mankind during the war or if it was simply something as innocent as allergies—but it happened nearly every night when he slept.

The room was dark and the hay he was laying on was prickly as ever. In the corner was the hole where he was supposed to take care of his business, a circle that was two feet in diameter and four feet deep. He'd filled it long ago and now there was no sense in trying to use it anymore; the heaping mound of dung he'd left there was overflowing into his cell. He'd chosen another spot, in the west corner, where he'd piled up some hay and used it to absorb his urine and feces. He stumbled over there now, his body sore and his back stiff, barely making it to the circle he'd built before the burning liquid gushed from inside him and splattered the walls, hissing as it made contact with the concrete.

He grunted, the stench and the flaming agony of his piss slapping him completely awake. This was another by-product of the Great War and he wasn't sure if it was a result of the meat they gave him to eat or if it was some other, supernatural thing.

Supernatural. Now, that almost made him laugh. There was no such thing anymore. There was no above natural, or paranormal, it was all natural now, all normal. When the Angels and Demons struck their bargain in some back room in Babylon to overthrow their masters and wage the final, glorious battle they dubbed the Great War, anything that had seemed normal was thrown right out the window. A few years ago, he would have laughed if he were told a flying demon, arcing through the sky like some dark bird of prey, would become a common sight. Now, of course, things were different.

The world was in its natural state, as the Demons and Angels liked to term it. They'd waged their war and neither side could come out ahead, so they struck up a bargain. A peace was brokered and things went back to how they'd been when God and Satan were in charge of their respective sides, only now Ba'al and Michael were the rulers, them and their generals and colonels. The one thing they agreed on, the one matter that was able to bring them to peaceful terms, was their mutual hatred of mankind.

And so, on a world scorched with hellfire and angel blood, the remnants of humanity, those unlucky enough to survive the War, were rounded up into camps to provide amusements for the Demons and Angels. Some were led to breeding areas, where they were mated, fattened, and slaughtered, providing nourishment for the rulers and leftovers for the slaves. Others were put to use tending the fields, growing all sorts of bizarre fruits that had not existed since the fabled Garden of Eden.

Those people were worked until they dropped, to be replaced by those bred on the farms. Some were individually divvied out and turned into personal slaves to whichever entity expressed interest in having one. This position was the most unfortunate because these humans usually didn't last more than a month, at most.

And then there were the others, the ones like him, locked in his cell, wide awake now and fearful of the coming day. These were the warriors, sent out into the arenas to face death at least twice a week. They were throwbacks to the old gladiator days, only with no weapons, using their bare, naked bodies and their wits to keep them alive.

Human pitted against human, in glorious battle for the amusement and betting privileges of the Angel and Demon crowd.

Twice a week they fought; if they survived the first battle. The days between were spent in these dank, diseased cells. No man in his right mind would last more than a week in these conditions without slitting his own throat with his fingernails. And at first, that's how it worked; the captives lost heart and hope and a mass suicide followed. The Necromancers of the Angels, those fluent in their Kabbalistic magick, put a stop to this, using their abilities to cast a spell on the humans that physically prevented them from committing suicide.

Regardless of the spell, he had tried to kill himself once. He managed to sneak a jagged piece of rock he'd found on the ground after one of his battles in the arena, and when he reached his cell, he tried to jam it into his neck, hoping to slash open the artery and bleed out, mercifully, on the floor. The problem was, he kept missing. Every jab at his throat ended with the rock whistling through the air, its intended target untouched. He tried many different ways to make the rock work for him, but none ended in his death, only hopeless frustration. Finally, he cast the shard into the pile of feces in the corner and found it an appropriate metaphor for his current condition.

That was two days ago.

Now it was time for him to fight again. The clanging was the general alarm for his section. All the cells filled with men and women who'd fought nearly a week ago and won and were now bid to go out and do it all over again.

He thought of his wife, the woman he'd pledged his undying love to four years before the Great War broke out. She'd been separated from him when it began and he never heard from her again. She was the love of his life, the most important thing he'd ever known or felt, and now, a year after her disappearance, he'd forgotten her name.

There had been too much suffering, too many horrors since then. In fact, he'd forgotten his own name, as well. He spent countless hours in the dark, lying on the straw and breathing in the stench of his misery, trying to remember his name. He searched his mind but only found scorched scars and terrifying memories. It was as if that part of his life, those memories, had been shut off forever by the experiences since.

A horn sounded, hard and brittle, and then suddenly deep and sonorous, shaking him from his reverie. He felt his bowels shudder and nearly release. It was time.

Their guard, an Angel with a permanent sneer and an ill-temper, strode to his cell door and waved his hand to fling it open. The man stared at the Angel as long as he could, the brilliance of its countenance burning the remaining gunk from the corners of his eyes. He'd thought—when he was first thrown in the cell—that having an Angel as a guard would be a blessing, but he soon learned the opposite. The Angelic Corps had been forced by God to serve mankind for so long they grew bitter and resentful of humans. This fact made them deadlier than the Demons who, since their rebellion against God many millennium ago, had centuries to gestate their hatred for humanity until it died down into a simple, built-in prejudice. The Angels, though, relatively new to this animosity, were fresh with desire for revenge.

Angels and Demons looked much like humans, just more intense, with the Angels giving off their brilliant shine, so bright it was hard to look at them for too long. This brilliance, the Reflected Glory of God, had faded as time passed, ever since they'd gotten God alone in the throne room and pulled a Caesar on him, stabbing him to death with their enchanted blades.

The Demons didn't glow. They were harder to look at, though, because too much eye contact brought on physical revulsion, resulting in projectile vomiting and the violent evacuation of the bowels.

And though humans, Angels and Demons all shared a basic humanoid shape—with the Angels and Demons being, on average, a foot or so taller—there were significant differences, the biggest of which were their wings. Both Demons and Angels had them, and they folded neatly behind their backs and almost seemed to disappear, as if it were a trick of the light seeing them in the first place. But when they unfolded them, the wings could fill a room, thick and heavy and strong.

The guard Angel opened their cells and called out to them. It was time for the games. Their group would be pitted against those from another prison, each person put out individually to fight for their lives. The Demons and Angels who ran the show had a sharp sense of humor, sometimes matching up fat people against fat people, and skinny against skinny. They loved tall on short, and if a person had a physical deformity, they moved immediately to Main Event status. Anything odd or untoward was smiled upon, while anything normal or boring was stuck to the Under Card as warm-up.

He joined the line of slaves as they assembled outside their cells, his shoulders slumped and his head hanging, limper than the exposed penis between his legs. During his first match, when he fought an old man that really didn't stand a chance, he considered letting the codger win, hoping for freedom through death. But he had seen what happened when the loser of an earlier fight had died, and the fate was more hideous than living to fight another day. So he pressed on, resigned to his dire destiny, the same ending awaiting them all.

They marched out in single file, no need for whipping or prodding. Once, they had resisted but no longer. The guard Angel had smiled, his sharp fangs evident through the bright glow, and opened his mouth and sang a note. It was a simple, sharp note, and it drove every slave to their knees, bleeding from every orifice. When the guard Angel finished, the fighters got to their feet and did as they were told, never resisting again.

A roar greeted them as they entered the arena, as it often did. Demons and Angels never seemed to tire of this dreadful sport, and as he joined his cellmates on the player's chairs at courtside, he looked up and around at the familiar setting.

They were in Madison Square Garden, which had somehow stood, miraculously, through the carnage of the Great War. It was here that they waged their gladiator games for the amusement of their masters, the wooden floor now stripped and replaced by cold, hard concrete.

The seats in the stands had been remodeled to incorporate the larger bodies that now occupied them, and the box seats were reserved for higher ranked officials and visiting dignitaries.

From what he had heard, there were other arenas like this one around the world, converted to provide the proper venue for the bloodshed their masters desired.

Pairings were made and the fighters not in action stayed seated on the benches where basketball teams had once sat, multi-million dollar athletes that were either dead or slaves now, just like everyone else. He didn't watch the first match, nor the second. He stared at the floor, ignoring the roars of approval and cries of anger as the humans battled, fighting for their lives. The games were brutal, with eye-gougings, throat-rippings, and all sorts of depraved behavior. He had seen them all before and there were no mysteries of human anatomy he hadn't seen by now. So he sat and waited his turn, and when the second match finished, he was summoned.

He walked wearily onto the floor. Up above, harsh, bright lights burned down on the tops of his shoulders and head, but he hardly noticed. He raised his head to analyze his enemy, and what he laid his eyes upon took his breath away.

It was her, standing forty yards away, her long, black hair dirty and stringy, her breasts sagging, and the thatch of dark hair between her legs so thick it resembled a pair of underwear. But it was her, the woman he'd long-since lost, the most important thing in his life before the Great War. It was her, the one who filled his nights with beautiful dreams. It was her, the brightest star in the sky.

It was his wife.

The announcer came on and introduced the two combatants, not giving their names, just their relation. It was clear to the man that either the Angels or the Demons had done their research, and in a moment of great jest for them, paired the husband and wife together to fight to the death.

The horn sounded and the crowd roared.

The man looked around at all the jeering, laughing faces filling the stands. It was an equal number of Demons and Angels, all fierce in their pride and loud with their approval. Their hands pounded together, sending out thunderclaps to fill the arena with abrasive explosions.

The woman, his wife, howled and dropped to all fours and scampered towards him, her lips pulled back into a snarl, bitter flecks of spit foaming from her mouth.

As she moved closer, he was surer than ever it was his wife, he was even more certain she was insane. The war and her captivity had done to her what it had done to so many others; her mind had snapped and she didn't recognize him at all.

He backed up, unsure of what to do. He didn't want to fight her, but if he didn't, she would surely kill him. And if he fought, he would have to kill her. His wife. His beloved.

She leapt for him, jagged claws raking the air in front of his face. He batted her to the side, sending her crashing to the cement floor with a grunt followed by another howl. She rolled and recovered and was at him again in an instant. The man pushed her away, using her own ferocity against her. He couldn't bring himself to punch her or lash out in any way. He simply kept her at bay, repelling each attack.

But this was no way to win and certainly no way to survive. He'd seen it before, when two combatants refused to fight. A Demon had soared into the air and descended on them, rending them limb from limb, exposing their souls to the open air. And then after that...

He shuddered. He couldn't allow that to happen, not to her, not to his wife. But he also couldn't fight back, and thus his quandary: Did he let her kill him, or did he kill her, regardless of his feelings?

She circled around and the crowd, sensing his hesitation, booed him. Litter cluttered around his feet, bouncing off his naked body, the intent to compel him to action. Instead, he did just the opposite. He made his decision. He wouldn't fight this woman, his wife, whose name he couldn't remember. He would let her win and then face the consequences.

He dropped to his knees as the woman charged him. She slashed his face with her fingernails, stripping off the flesh from the entire left side of his face. He watched as her hand came away, his skin hanging in shards from her fingertips, as he felt the blood gush from his open wound and pour down his neck and shoulders.

He didn't blink as she backed up, surprised, and he didn't react when she howled in triumph and lunged forward, burying her teeth into the side of his neck. She bit through tendons and into an artery and tore free a chunk the size of his fist just below his right ear. Warm, wet blood squirted between his fingers as he instinctively reached up with his hands and placed them over the hole in his neck.

The coliseum swirled in his vision as the raised chorus of boos filled his ears, mixing with the triumphant cry from his wife. He blinked back the tears, looked into her eyes, and fixed his stare, pouring all the love he'd ever had in his heart out to her.

He pitched forward, the strength gone from his shaking legs, but he never broke his gaze, holding her with his eyes.

His lips shook as he put them together and spoke the last word he would ever utter.

"Wendy," he said, remembering her name at last.

He closed his eyes and felt his spirit slip from his body. It rose to go where it naturally remembered, towards a Heaven that didn't exist anymore. He watched Wendy as she glared at his dead body, sudden clarity slicing through her insanity.

"Tom?" she said, remembering his name. She fell to her knees and yanked fistfuls of hair from her head, weeping silently.

Tom turned from her. He had no more time now. Above him, the Soul Catchers grew, ready to ensnare him and drag his soul to Hell, where he would suffer for all eternity.

He could hear it, whirring above him, its tentacles reaching out and crossing the top of the arena, invisible to human vision but bright and pungent to his new eyes. They were thick, like octopus arms, palsied with a pattern of bright yellow spots on a red background, crossing and forming a net at the ceiling, blocking his escape. Tom flew to his right, dipping and diving towards the stands full of supernatural creatures. The Demons and Angels rose to their feet, eager for the hunt. They would chase him, and when they caught him, they would fling him into the Soul Catcher, and down he'd go.

Suddenly, Wendy charged across the court, running straight at a Demon that had raised a hand and pointed at Tom's flying form. Before the Demon could react, she threw herself on his sharpened claws, impaling herself, the Demon's rigid hand punching a hole through her chest. The spell that kept humans from killing themselves didn't keep them from being killed by their captors, so it didn't recognize her attempt as suicide, but as an assault. And why should it react to an apparent attack when no human had ever harmed a Demon or Angel?

Wendy hung on the claws for a moment and then died, her spirit splitting from her body to be released into the air.

Her eyes met his and they flew towards one another, joining and wrapping their spectral arms around each other. They held tight, relishing this moment, their true essences mixing and knowing one another for the first time in years.

It was the greatest moment of their existence.

The Soul Catcher floated from the ceiling and enveloped them, wrapping its tentacles around their spirits and imprisoning them. But then a strange thing happened as they tightly held on to each other—it couldn't hold them.

Their souls slipped through its grasp as if they were made of melted butter, and they oozed between the tentacles and popped free at the top.

Seizing the moment, they flew together through the ceiling—leaving the pursuing Demons and Angles behind—and up into the open air, the joining of their souls creating a new union, one too strong for any creature of creation to break or hope to control.

They didn't stop until they were far away and glowing brightly, a new star now twinkling in the night sky.

THE CARRIERS

TERRY ALEXANDER

Snow crunched under Brody Caulfield's boots as the cold seeped through his heavy coat, chilling his flesh.

"We'll be back later, Cheryl. I'm going to try to bag us a deer. We could use some fresh meat," he said as he hefted the 30-06 Remington to his shoulder

"But Brody, we don't need any more meat. We've got three freezers full." A perky blonde fisted her hands on her hips. The freckles on her face deepened in color as her temper flared. She glanced toward the slate gray sky. "Look at the clouds. It could snow again any minute."

"We won't be gone long, I promise," he said, placing the rifle in the pickup. "Besides, Wayne and Benny are old hands at handling slick roads. We'll be fine."

Two men with heavy bore rifles followed him to the extended cab of the pickup. Wayne, the shorter, heavier of the two, climbed into the back seat. His companion, a thin dark-haired man, took the front.

"Let's get the show started," Wayne said.

"Just a second," Brody said and pulled Cheryl in close, kissing her on the lips. "We'll be careful, I swear." He turned to a young black man standing near the door of the old bank building. "Hey, Eric, get on the roof. You're pulling guard duty today. And make sure the generators have a full tank of fuel."

"Why are you putting him on the roof?" Cheryl demanded. "What's going on? We haven't seen any strangers for months."

"Just being practical. Eric's been slacking off for a few days. This'll keep him occupied," he said and slid behind the wheel. "Love you, hon." He winked at her.

"Brody, you're up to something." Cheryl wagged her finger, scolding him like a schoolboy.

"I just want to do some hunting." The engine started easily at the turn of the key. "Keep the fire going and enjoy the snow. We'll be back before you know it," Brody said. The rear tires churned on the snow as he drove away.

"Okay, what's going on?" Benny asked and brushed dark hair from his eyes when they were on the road.

"Yeah," Wayne said. "We've got enough meat to last for a year easy and Eric's been busting his hump ever since he got here. So what's the deal?"

"I saw some tracks down by the goat pens," Brody replied. "Dog tracks."

"Dogs? That's impossible. The dogs killed each other after the plague. I haven't seen a dog in two years," Wayne said.

Benny's long hair fell back into his eyes as he shook his head. "It can't be dogs," he said.

Three years ago, a small group of corporate-funded scientists devised the virus to control the world's population of dogs and cats. They picked one thousand animals from kennels around the country and infected them with the disease, then turned them loose on the world, sending them to every country on earth. Their intent was to render most of the world's canine and feline population sterile. The plan worked, the disease ran rampant, uncontrollable. Within months, the animal population dropped over seventy percent. But then the virus jumped to humans and other animals, and once it mutated, it became fatal, killing off over ninety percent of mankind and the animal life on the planet.

The remaining pets that survived the virus went feral and joined the carrion eaters, feeding on the dead and dying. The remaining canines survived when all the other meat eaters died, but they were altered, forever changed. Loyal Fido became wild and aggressive and after the dead were consumed, they attacked the living to satisfy their unholy appetite. Soon they turned to cannibalism, the larger animals devouring the smaller ones until only a handful of animals survived.

But a few survived, immune but carriers, able to infect an animal or human with a simple bite.

"There was a human track also, barefooted," Brody said. "I saw something three days ago." He stopped and looked at the two men. "I think it was a carrier."

"A carrier, in Checotah, Oklahoma?" Benny continued to shake his head. "That can't be. They all died after they spread the disease."

"Maybe not," Wayne said. "Remember that guy from Texas last year? He saw a carrier down near the Red River."

"That guy was full of shit." Benny rubbed his nose. He used to be a hard core drug addict before the sickness. Sometimes the old urges came roaring back with a vengeance.

"I saw a dog from a distance, down by Elmer Chalmers' place. I'm certain it was a carrier. It had red skin covered with big yellow boils," Brody said.

"How close were you?" Wayne asked.

"I don't know, maybe five, six hundred yards away," Brody shrugged.

"That was probably Elmer you saw, or Emily or Diane," Benny said. "A trick of the light."

"Look, I just want to check out the goat pens first and then Elmer and his family. If everything's okay, we'll go back." Brody weaved the pickup around the empty cars littering the highway.

"Okay, we'll check on the goats, but I'm not so keen on the Elmer side of this. That crazy bastard shoots at everyone who comes around his house," Wayne said.

"Yeah, his place is practically a fort," Benny said. "Hell, he even dug a moat around his house." A line of sweat threaded its way down his face.

"Just a quick check. Like I said, if things look good, we'll go back home. I'll tell Cheryl we didn't see any deer."

"I don't like this, Brody. I really don't like this." Benny wiped perspiration from his brow.

The rear tires slid on the ice and Brody expertly turned into the skid. "We're nearly there," he said, moving his foot from the gas pedal and letting the pickup slow before he made the curve to Elmer's place.

"Oh my God!" Wayne said, his jaw dropping open in shock.

The fence surrounding the large, three acre enclosure was knocked over and lay flat on the ground, the metal T posts bent and uprooted. Multiple bodies littered the blood-stained snow. A single goat toward the center struggled to its feet, a raw, ugly wound stretched along its side from shoulder to hip.

"I can't believe it. I can't believe it," Benny said as he squeezed his eyes together.

Brody tapped the brake lightly, bringing the vehicle to a stop. "Damn it!" he cursed while shaking his head. "We just lost half our food source." He turned to Benny and Wayne. "Still think I'm seeing things?"

"Oh, hell," Benny said as he stared wide-eyed at the carnage. "Damn, I can't believe it. It's the early days all over again."

Wayne looked at Brody. "So what's the plan?"

"That goat's still alive. We need to check for others and put them down for good; they're infected now. We can't let an infected animal live." Brody nodded at the other men. "Make sure you're packing plenty of ammo."

"Let's do this," Wayne said, leaning forward in the rear seat. "What're you waiting for, Benny, an engraved invitation?"

"I don't wanna go out there," Benny exhaled after taking a deep breath. "What if they're still hanging around?"

"Then we kill as many as we can and high tail it back here." Brody popped the door open and stepped onto the crunchy surface. "Come on, let's move, and be on your toes," he said, moving over the downed fence and to the left.

"Come on, Benny," Wayne said and patted the tall man on the shoulder. "It'll be okay."

"Have you ever seen anyone bitten by one of those things?" Benny asked.

Wayne shook his head.

"A friend of mine got bit once," Benny said. "The bite was infected within hours and swelled up, yellow-green stuff draining from the wound. She died within three days. God, it was awful." Benny's face drained of color. "I managed to escape when they were eating her body. A bite from one of them is like being bitten by a Komodo dragon; their mouth is full of bacteria. I barely escaped with my life," he said.

Wayne nodded; everyone knew the bite from one of the infected dogs was fatal. "Relax. We'll get through this. Just stick close to me," Wayne said. "Now open the door."

Benny nodded, his fingers quivering as they closed on the door handle. "Okay, let's help Brody," he said.

Brody heard the pickup door slam behind him and he knew the others were following. Benny's actions puzzled him, but he knew the man would come through in a crisis.

Brody approached the first goat slowly. He knew the infection would cause the animal to bite him if he gave it a chance. He pulled a .38 revolver from his waistband, placed the muzzle behind the animal's head, and pulled the trigger.

The loud report echoed through the surrounding trees. He looked down at the goats already dead that were strewn across the snow. "Damn dogs tore their throats out. Check 'em all, make sure their good and dead."

Benny nodded. He moved from carcass to carcass, checking for any signs of life. Four goats had to be put down.

"I hope they didn't find the sheep and cows," Brody said, shaking his head. "We'll be up a creek if they killed them, too. Let's go check on Elmer and then go home."

"We might not make it back if the dogs are still around. Hell, they might kill us all," Benny said, licking his lips nervously.

The trio slowly returned to the pickup as a light sleet began to fall. The small ice pellets stung their unprotected skin and Brody bowed his head to the wind, wishing he had a hat. "We need to hurry," he said. "It's going to get dark early. I hope Elmer's okay."

"I think we should just go back to the old First National and wait things out," Benny said as he grabbed the door handle. "Things could go south real quick out here."

"Things have already gone south, Benny," Wayne said, climbing into the back seat. "If we don't deal with the dogs now, they'll be on us later."

"How do we know that? How do we know they won't just move on?" Benny asked as he climbed into the pickup. The door slammed behind him.

"Because they don't just move on, Benny. The dogs only live to kill," Brody said. "They'll kill until there's nothing left. We've got it pretty good here because we're off the radar. No one knows we're here and no one cares. Well, now the dogs know." Brody slid behind the steering wheel and cranked the engine to life. Elmer's place lay a mile to the west.

The slick road and stalled cars doubled the time required for the short trip. After several minutes, Brody stopped the pickup at the entrance to the dirt road leading to Elmer's house. The unrelenting sleet pelted the windshield, building up on the sides of the glass. There was a small drawbridge to cross the homemade moat at the end of the driveway.

They sat uneasily in the pickup, staring at Elmer's house nestled off the road. The roof of the brick home was barely visible through the bare trees as it was covered with snow and sleet.

"It seems awfully quiet," Brody said.

"See, nothing going on here." Benny said, exhaling a deep breath. "Let's go back now."

"No, wait, something's not right," Wayne said and fitted a pair of binoculars to his eyes. "Take a look at the chimney.".

"It's a chimney, so what?" Benny said and leaned out the side window, squinting into the distance.

"It's a cold day. Elmer burns wood just like we do. So where's the smoke?" Wayne asked, turning to face Brody. "What are we gonna do next?"

"Simple, we go inside and make sure he's okay, then leave," Brody said.

"From the look of things, everybody ain't gonna be safe." Wayne said. He slapped Benny's shoulder. "Open the door, Benny. It's time to play hero."

"Oh hell, I don't like this," Benny whined. A cold wind rushed inside the cab as he cradled the .303 British rifle close to his chest. Hesitantly, he moved forward, Wayne at his side as Brody climbed out the driver's side.

"Just stay calm. We'll get through this," Wayne said. "Just be ready for anything."

"Found some dog tracks," Brody said, kneeling to examine the mark. "They're around here someplace."

"The drawbridge is down," Wayne said as they moved closer to the house. "Elmer never leaves it down unless he's outside, and if he was able to, he'd be shooting at us right now."

"There's something on the ground by the drawbridge. Oh, damn," Benny said and stopped in his tracks, his face turned ashen. "They got him; the dogs killed Elmer."

"Stay here," Brody said to Benny and then added, "Wayne and I are going to check on Emily and Diane; see if they're still alive. The sleet's getting harder so let's make this quick."

Wayne nodded. "I'm for that."

Vapor plumed around Brody's head and shoulders, his heart beating rapidly against his ribcage. Warily, he approached the drawbridge, stopping for a moment to check on Elmer. The body felt cold to his touch. He rolled Elmer's stiff body onto its back. The old farmer's lower jaw and cheeks were torn from his face, leaving a bloody mess. A large wound in his stomach gaped open like a barn door. Crusty, frozen blood covered the body, staining the white snow crimson.

Suddenly, a female voice screamed from the barn loft, followed immediately by the sharp ping of a .22. "Brody, they're in the house. They're in the house," Wayne said.

Brody jerked his head toward the brick home just as the front door burst open. Three large, hairless dogs, their shoulders and hides covered with oozing, crusty sores, jumped through the entrance at once. They attacked silently, without barks or growls, their paws kicking up snow as they ran toward Brody and Wayne. The loud report of Wayne's 30-30 sent the lead dog tumbling to the ground in a shower of blood.

Emily kept up a steady fire on the dogs with the .22, the light-weight bullets stinging the animals but causing little damage.

"Get to the truck!" Brody shouted "It's at the end of the drive-way!"

Using the pulley rope, Emily and her teenage daughter swung down to the ground from out of the loft.

"Run!" she shouted, pushing Diane toward the road. "Don't look back, just run"

Brody centered the crosshairs of his 30-06 on the massive chest of a Bullmastiff. The animal somersaulted in the air, crashed to the ground, and slid on the slick ground. "Wayne!" he shouted. "Fall back to the pickup; fall back!"

Benny lifted his .303 to his shoulder. He lined up the sights on a large canine racing at Wayne from his blind side. His finger hesitated on the trigger as he nervously licked his cold lips. He swallowed, his mouth dry, as the bad days spent in Oklahoma City came rushing back to him.

The dogs were constantly hunting and prowling the streets, killing anything that moved. Benny and his wife Pam had hid in an old warehouse, too scared to leave and too scared to stay, until the day the dogs found them and killed Pam.

It was a haunting memory he wanted to forget. He blamed himself for her death and ran away as those devils fed on her. He managed to make it here, to build a new life, and now the dogs were back again.

Not again. Not this time, he thought. Through tear-filled eyes, he centered the gun sight on the animal's head.

Wayne sent a second bullet at a large Doberman. It crashed into the drawbridge and was still, half its insides now splattered across the snow.

A loud explosion sounded from behind Wayne and another dog smacked the ground near his feet. He turned to see the open mouth of a former pet snapping at his heels. He drove the rifle butt downward, crushing the wounded dog's skull.

"Move your ass!" Benny screamed. "Come on!" He ran to Emily and Diane, covering their retreat to the pickup. He knelt down and lined up a shot on a huge canine closing on Brody, but the bullet kicked up snow behind the animal's feet when he missed.

Brody leveled his rifle at a large, boil-covered chest, unable to use his scope to line the shot properly due to the rapidly closing distance of the target. The recoil of the .06 drove the cushioned butt of the weapon into his shoulder. The bullet struck the dog's right front leg and it rolled on the ground but came up to its feet a second later in an awkward, three-legged hop. It continued to advance until its head exploded in a spray of blood and brains. The loud report of Benny's .303 soon followed.

"Brody, get moving! We need to get out of here!" Benny shouted.

Emily and Diane climbed into the pickup bed as Emily continued to fire the .22, peppering the attacking dogs. "Hurry!" she screamed, her voice on the edge of hysteria.

Benny jumped onto the rear bumper, joining the two women. He rested the .303 on the pickup railing and squinted down the sights.

Brody turned to run just as a nude man walked through the ruined front door of Elmer's home. The deep red skin and multiple glistening pustules marked him as a carrier, one of the men who was immune but carried the virus within him, infecting everyone he came into contact with.

Wayne raised his gun and fired before the man was two feet out of the door. The carrier staggered from the impact, thick ochre leaking from the wound on his chest. A moment later he was walking forward again. Wayne fired again and this time the man went down for good, a large hole in his side.

"Damn it, Wayne, get to the truck!" Brody yelled as he shouldered his rifle, sprinting across the snow to the road, kicking a dog away from him as he ran.

Brody fished the keys from his pocket. The door handle felt cold and slick in his hand from the coating of sleet. He jumped behind the steering wheel and forced the key into the ignition. The engine roared to life as a red-faced Wayne jumped into the seat beside him.

"What the hell are you waiting for?" Wayne asked. "Get us the hell out of here."

"There's ice on the windshield," Brody said. "I can't see!"

"Who cares, get us out of here!" Wayne shouted. "We can't wait for the defroster."

Brody shifted the transmission into first gear and the rear tires spun on the ice, seeking purchase, burning through to the asphalt underneath. The pickup lurched forward. He turned the vehicle around, fishtailing as he sped for town. A steady barrage of rifle fire sounded from the rear of the pickup, the loud report of Benny's heavy rifle and the pop of Emily's .22 keeping the dogs at bay.

"Damn it!" Wayne shouted, his face flushed and sweaty despite the frigid temperature. "That was close. What are we gonna do now?"

"We get to the bank and fight like hell," Brody said, his face hard and grim. He expertly guided the pickup through the maze of stalled vehicles toward Checotah.

"You can slow down a little. We don't want to end up in a ditch and have to fight those things off out here on the road," Wayne said.

The sleet tapered off, replaced by heavy moisture laden snowflakes. A fierce northerly wind drove the flakes through the air.

"Yeah, yeah, you're right." Brody eased up on the accelerator. "How many do you think were left?"

"At least one," Wayne said and pointed behind the truck. At the far range of his vision, a running dog followed.

They made good time and Brody slowed the pickup, braking in front of the fortified bank. "Eric!" he shouted. "They're dogs on the way here. Hit the lights and be ready."

"Kick on the second generator," Eric said, leaning over the roof and calling to another man.

"I'll get it," Wayne said and disappeared around the side of the building. Within moments, a cloud of black smoke erupted. It quickly dissipated in the howling wind, followed by the throaty roar of the generator. "Hit the switch. I'll be up in a minute," Wayne shouted.

"Cheryl," Brody called as he ran inside the bank. "Break out the rifles and ammo and get everyone a handgun for close in work."

"What's going on?" she demanded.

"Dogs are on the way," Benny answered. "I'm going to the roof."

"But how, they're supposed to be all dead," Cheryl said.

"Well, no one told the dogs that," Brody replied and ran off.

Cheryl ran to gather the weapons, Emily and Diane following closely behind.

Wayne ran inside. Bent over at the waist, he took a moment to fill his lungs with air, his hands resting on his knees. "All this running is hard on us fat boys," he said.

"Get up top and help Eric," Brody ordered. "The rest of you fan out and take a window, close the shutters and use the firing slots we made. They'll be here before you know it."

"I'm on my way," Wayne said and hurried to the interior ladder leading to the roof.

The dogs had arrived and silently, the mutated canines ran to the bank's walls, biting and clawing at the openings. They jumped up onto the brick work, trying to find a way to the roof. The rifles blasted into the tightly packed mass of canines but the dogs continued their attack, their ranks growing at every breath. The loud report of the constant rifle fire in such a confined place set everyone's ears to ringing.

A small pack disappeared around the corner of the building, seeking another way inside.

Wayne stepped from the ladder, the pebbly surface slick under his feet. A dog had jumped atop the metal cage protecting the generator to then leap to the roof. Wayne swung the rifle toward it and the bullet caught the animal in the midsection as intestines blossomed from its stomach.

"Damn it, they're up here!" Wayne shouted.

"Kill as many as you can," Benny yelled above the din. "Try to keep them off us."

"Benny!" Eric shouted above the noise. "I've got to reload." Benny nodded and raised the .303 to his shoulder.

Eric turned to see another dog behind him. It had approached quietly and now prepared to attack. The animal's skin was a collection of scabby, crust covered and oozing wounds.

Eric fell to his side as the canine pinned him to the roof, its large teeth seeking his throat.

Before it could kill Eric, Benny slammed the rifle butt into the dog's head. It collapsed to the roof, its legs churning the air. Eric jumped to his feet. "Kill that thing. I'll help Wayne."

Benny looked around for Wayne and saw him standing at the center of the roof, swinging his rifle like a club, fighting for his life against two killer dogs.

Concentrate on the shot, concentrate on the shot, Benny thought as his eyes focused on the largest dog. He imagined the location of its head as he squinted down the barrel of his rifle. For the first time, he wished the rifle had a scope. He squeezed the trigger, the weapon bucked in his arms, and a dog's head disappeared in a spray of crimson.

"Got you, you bastard," Benny said and worked the bolt, cycling another round into the barrel. He squeezed the trigger gently, and the second dog went down with a hole in its side.

Now safe, Wayne waved to Benny and ran off to help someone else.

A sharp pain centered in the large muscle of his calf and Benny gritted his teeth as he fell to the roof. He rolled onto his back and drove the rifle forward, then pulled the trigger at point blank range, blasting a hole through the massive ribcage of the attacking dog. Removing the teeth from his leg, he swung his legs over the edge of the roof, and dropped the eight feet to the building's awning above the entrance. He landed hard and managed not to fall off it.

The dogs below ran and jumped into the air trying to reach him, and Benny recycled the bolt, the empty casing sailing over his head. He lay prone on the slick surface, taking a moment to line up the sights, hoping to find the head of one of the dogs. Seeing one, the rifle bucked against his shoulder but he missed.

Benny worked the bolt. He had one bullet remaining in the chamber. He quickly jacked it into the barrel and spotted Brody about to be jumped by a large German shepherd.

"I'll get you this time." He belly crawled closer to the edge of the awning, the barrel and part of his hand hanging out in space as he tried to line up the shot to save Brody's life.

He slowly squeezed the trigger, and even as the rifle discharged, a mouthful of sharp incisors closed on his hand, pulling him off the awning to fall to the ground.

The dog attacking Brody had been in mid-leap, the shot perfect, and as Brody turned at the sound of guttural growls, the head of the dog disappeared in a spray of brains, bone matter and blood.

Brody stumbled and fell, his hands pressing into the fresh snow as he realized Benny had saved his life.

The rest of the dog pack savagely attacked Benny, their jagged teeth tearing at his flesh. Brody, Wayne, Eric and the others all moved in and finished off the remaining dogs, putting each one down with a bullet to the head.

They approached their fallen friend, knowing he wasn't long for this world.

"I did it, Brody. I killed them all," Benny said, struggling to rise as blood dripped from the corners of his mouth. "I killed them all."

Brody nodded. He stared down at Benny's mangled body. A mass of crimson stains covered his body and bone could be seen beneath his torn clothing.

Brody's eyes began to tear. "You did good, Benny. You did real good."

"I can't move. I think I broke my leg," Benny said, his voice growing weaker from blood loss. "Let me end this quickly. I don't want to suffer."

Brody looked to Cheryl. "Give him your pistol."

Cheryl's hand closed on Brody's arm, her eyes saying that she didn't want to.

"Do it, he's earned this," Brody said softly.

Cheryl pulled the .38 from her waist band and placed it in Benny's blood-soaked hand.

"Thanks, Cheryl. Okay, turn around, I don't want anyone to see me like this," Benny said, his voice barely above a whisper."

As one, the survivors did as they were asked, each putting their backs to their friend.

A single report followed.

THE SANCTUARY

ANTHONY GIANGREGORIO

The snow blasted the man's face like tiny daggers, freezing his expression of suffering as he made his way through the desolate forest. The trees hung heavy with ice, more than one having collapsed under the weight of the snow.

The wind howled like a living thing, so loud he couldn't think.

With nothing to do but continue, he wrapped his thin coat around himself tighter and marched onward.

He didn't know how long he'd been walking in the solid white forest; more than a day, less than a week. He remembered times when he found a place to rest, huddling under an overhang of tree limbs or inside a small outcropping of boulders. With no fire, he would curl up into a ball and shiver uncontrollably until sleep finally took him into its cold embrace.

But he never slept for long, and would venture forth once more when the chill was too unbearable to ignore.

Images flashed through his mind as he walked; visions of a collapsing world.

Oil and gasoline had become scarce to the point the average man couldn't afford it any longer. When this happened, riots began in the streets, and once tall, ivory towers were soon torn down by angry, jealous hands. Where only the rich could afford to have electricity, as they purchased the fuel to run their generators on the black market, so too, did the desperate masses gather their weapons, their bombs, and their anger.

In time, the wealthy were in ruins and society was a distant memory.

Those bombs were sometimes nuclear, evil factions attacking the nuclear power plants, and after every meltdown, and multiple explosions that shook the earth to its core, the planet was thrust into a modern day ice age, the soot and dust clogging the atmosphere to the point the sun's rays couldn't penetrate to the land below. Plants began to wither and livestock died, the human race soon finding out it wasn't as invincible as it once thought.

The man lost his footing and fell face first into the snow, his mouth filling with ice and muffling his cry of surprise. He rolled onto his side, knowing he needed to get up, for to lie down now would mean certain death. But he was already at the end of his rope, and as exhaustion set in and he tried to raise himself to a sitting position, his arms wavered and he fell back to the frozen ground.

His will to survive was still strong, though his body was weak, so he began to crawl, one agonizing inch at a time. His feet were numb, as were his fingertips, and both had ceased feeling hours go, as did the end of his nose. But still he crawled, though the next hill would only play out as the other hundred had done so before it.

As he reached the top of the final hill he would be traversing before death took him, his eyes, now red and blurry, spotted something through the trees. It looked like it was made of glass and metal, the glossy finish reflecting what ambient light filtered through the clouds.

Filled with renewed hope, he gathered what strength he had left and forced himself onward; knowing whatever he'd spotted would be his final destination one way or another.

An hour passed and his head was growing foggy, but as he reached the edge of the property line to what was a large house, he dropped to the ground and passed out.

In seconds, the falling snow began to cover him.

He would have died then, buried under the snow, if not for the simple motion sensor that had picked up his body as he crawled over the property line.

Ten minutes after collapsing in the snow, three figures emerged from the house, each bundled up to the point their features were hidden. Scarves, ski masks and large parkas adorned each figure, their genders unknown.

They reached the fallen man and one each picked him up under the arms and began to drag him towards the house, while the third of the party walked beside them. He seemed to be the leader of the group, and when they reached the house, it was he who opened the door to let the others carry the man inside.

Quickly rushing into the house, the door was slammed closed, none of them wanting to let more of the precious heat within the home from escaping than necessary.

As the door clicked closed, locks could be heard being latched over the howling maelstrom. The snow storm continued unabated, as it had done so for the past fourteen months.

Ever so slowly, he opened his eyes and looked around him. He was in a queen size bed, the blanket was up to his neck, and he felt warm for the first time in he didn't know how long.

The room was clean, with a desk in the far corner, and a small daybed near one of the insulated windows. Outside, the wind howled, and he felt himself shiver despite the warmth of the bed.

The bedroom door opened and a man in his late sixties walked in. He had a receding hairline, white hair, unkempt, and bushy eyebrows that almost made him look as if he had a unibrow. He wore a gray turtle neck and a pair of black cotton slacks, his feet in a pair of thousand dollar shoes. On his wrist was a Rolex and diamond rings flashed on three fingers of his left hand, while the right one was bare. As he stepped into the room, he smiled at his guest, and after taking the chair at the desk, he dragged it across the plush rug and sat down, crossing his legs. "So I see you're finally awake. The first thing to ask I suppose is your name," he asked.

"Brett...Brett Butler. Where am I? And who are you?"

"Ah, right to the point, good for you. My name is Arthur McMillan, perhaps you've heard of me."

Brett blinked. "I've heard of *a* Arthur McMillan. He was on that apprentice reality show, and made all that money in textiles and oil. Is that you?"

"One and the same. So tell me, Mr. Butler, how did you find this place?"

Brett shook his head as he sat up some more in the bed. He tried to remember but it was all a haze, but now that he was warm and rested, he began to remember bits and pieces. He recalled being in a enclave that was struggling to survive. Raiders had attacked, killing almost everyone and he had managed to escape into the mountains. After that it all became a blur. He told McMillan as much, the older man nodding as he listened.

"I see. I've heard the same story countless times on the short-wave radio I have here. That's why I built this place in the middle of nowhere when the first hint of global strife began. I guess you could say I'm a bit of a survivalist nut." He chuckled slightly. "I guess the last laugh was on me though, huh?

"You built this place?" Brett asked.

"That's right. I made sure to use the money I had while it was still good for something. Took more than six months but this sanctuary will see me and my few guests through until the world can get back on its feet." He looked down at his shoes. "That is if that is even possible, of course."

"Of course," Brett said.

"You are aware I can't let you leave here, I suppose. This sanctuary is a secret. If you left and told others what's here, well, you know what would happen." He grinned widely. "But I suspect you wouldn't want to leave anyway. There's nothing around for miles in every direction. I made sure of that when I picked this location. We're on the top of a mountain, you see, one I bought before society collapsed. Before the first bombs fell, I was already set up here, well stocked with food, water, and an armory to make any gun nut proud."

Brett said nothing, only nodded.

McMillan stood up and Brett saw the large revolver on the man's hip. "Well, I'll leave you to rest. Someone will come by later and escort you down to dinner. That is, if you think you'll be up to it."

"I'm sure I will," Brett said.

"That's good, because we have a strict regime here and all who stay under my roof agree to follow it in exchange for my protection. Now that you're here, I expect you to do the same."

Brett could hear the warning in the older man's voice and he nodded, flashing a weak smile. "You'll get no trouble from me, sir. And I thank you for letting me stay."

"And well you should. I could have easily allowed you to freeze to death outside. But I chose to retrieve you."

"Then why did you? Not that I'm not grateful," Brett said.

"Why? Simple really. After more than a year, it will be good to have some new blood around here." He walked to the door and paused before leaving. "You get some rest now. Dinner is at eight sharp." He exited and closed the door, leaving Brett with more questions and no answers.

But he supposed he would get them at dinner. Sliding deeper into the covers, he closed his eyes, and before he knew it, had fallen back into an exhausted sleep.

A knock on the door woke Brett from a light sleep.

"Come in," he said and the door opened, revealing a man in his forties who had similar facial features to McMillan.

"Hi, I'm Jeff, I'm here to bring you down to dinner." He crossed the room and placed a set of clothes on the foot of the bed. "These are mine but you can have them."

"Thank you, that's very kind of you," Brett said as he pushed off the blankets and began dressing.

"I suppose, but it's not like I really had a choice in the matter," Jeff said as he walked to one of the windows to gaze out into the blizzard.

"How so?"

"Huh? Oh, never mind. You'll find out how things are run around here soon enough."

Brett nodded, though out of politeness more than any understanding. "Is Mr. McMillan your father? If not, you sure look a lot like him," Brett commented as he slipped into the brown loafers Jeff provided. He now wore a white long sleeve shirt, and a pair of tan slacks along with clean underwear and socks.

"No, you're right, I'm his son. Lucky me."

Brett was about to ask what he meant by that when Jeff walked by him and then paused at the door. "Good, the clothes fit you almost to a T. I thought as much when I carried you up here last night. Well, come along, we don't want to keep the master of the house waiting." He frowned and his eyes went cold, and Brett was sure he saw a touch of fear there as well. "It wouldn't be a very good idea."

"Ah, at last, our new arrival is here and we can get on with dinner," Arthur McMillan said grandly. He wore a black sport coat with a gray vest, matching slacks and casual shoes. "Come, Mr. Butler, sit over here next to me."

Brett did as he was told, eyeing the other new faces as he sat down.

"Let me introduce you to the rest of your small team of survivors of this Ice Age," McMillan said with a wave of his left hand, his other on the butt of his gun. "The lovely woman across from me is Wendy. She's my..."

"I'm his mistress," Wendy said blandly to Brett.

"Wendy, really," McMillan said, as if he was insulted.

"What's wrong, Arthur? It's the truth, so I might as well just get it out in the open. He's going to find out soon enough anyway." She looked away from McMillan and back to Brett. "That's right, I sleep with him and in exchange he lets me stay here, protects me."

"Ah, okay," Brett said, not understanding what was going on. But it was obvious the conversation he was now in had begun a long time ago and was just continuing with him in it

McMillan slapped his hand on the table, the dishes and glasses jumping. "Enough, that's enough, Wendy. If you don't stop, so help me I'll..."

"You'll what? Arthur? Kick me out like you're always threatening to do? Maybe you'd be doing me a favor," Wendy scowled deeply.

McMillan raised a hand and jabbed his finger at her. "Just one more word, Wendy, and so help me, you'll find out."

Wendy opened her mouth but held her tongue. Brett sat perfectly still, staring at the tableaux before him. He saw Jeff was picking at one of his fingernails, oblivious to what was transpiring, as if he'd heard it a thousand times before. The other man at the table was slightly more interested and he smiled widely as he watched.

When McMillan was confident Wendy was through, he cleared his throat and then gestured to the other man. "And this is Andy, he's Jeff's best friend from college. His parents were lost when L.A. was bombed and I invited him to join us."

"Hi," was all Andy said.

"Hi, yourself," Brett replied.

McMillan stood up and crossed the room, pausing at the door leading to the kitchen. So, if the introductions are finished, then come along and you can get your dinner.

Brett watched as Andy, Jeff and Wendy each stood up and crossed the room to line up behind McMillan. It reminded him of schoolchildren waiting in line for lunch at the cafeteria. McMillan looked over at Brett and waved him to follow as well. "Come along, Mr. Butler, if you want to eat this is how it's done here," he called.

His stomach rumbling at the mention of food, Brett did as he was asked and followed the others. Soon he found himself in the kitchen and McMillan was standing in front of a large pantry door with a heavy duty combination lock on it. As everyone waited, he turned the dial and opened the door. Then, one at a time, he handed each of them a can of food.

Brett was last, and as the others went back to the dining room, he stared at the can of chili in his hands. "What's this?"

"It's your dinner," McMillan said.

"I don't understand. Why is the food under lock and key?"

McMillan touched his gun in his waistband as he closed the pantry and locked it. "Because that's how we do things around here. I'm in charge of the food and I say what we do and don't do."

"But what if I'm still hungry?"

"That's not my problem, Mr. Butler. Now, be grateful like the others and go back into the dining room where you'll find a can opener and silverware." McMillan had a can for himself under his arm and carried a one gallon bottle of water in his free hand, his other hand always on the gun. Brett was beginning to realize McMillan ruled his little sanctuary by fear, namely by using the gun as his instrument of control. But without a way to defend himself, and not wanting to risk trying to take the gun away from the older man, Brett nodded and returned to the dining room.

The others were already seated, each eating from their can. Brett sat as well and picked up the can opener in the middle of the table. Once he had his can opened, he dug in, taking a fork from a small pile in the center of the table.

McMillan came in and sat down at the head of the table, and after opening his food, dug in. His gun was on the table to his right, in easy reach if need be.

No one spoke, each concentrating on eating, and Brett found his gaze constantly drifting to Wendy. Though any man would be attracted to her, especially as she was the only woman in the house, he still couldn't fight the instant attraction he felt for her upon meeting her.

Once or twice, he spotted her looking at him and she would smile slightly, then stop, not wanting the others to see.

But McMillan did see and he frowned deeply, but said nothing.

When everyone was finished eating and the meal was about over, McMillan cleared his throat and gestured to Wendy.

"Come here, my dear, and get under the table, I need you and I don't want to wait."

"No, Arthur, please, not now, can't we go upstairs?"

"Are you arguing with me?" The tone of his voice was clear to Brett. It reminded him of the tone his father would use with him when he was told to do something and he was hesitant.

"No, of course not," she said as she lowered her eyes in compliance.

"Then get over here and get to work, woman," he said.

Wendy wiped her mouth and pushed off from the table, her chair sliding lightly on the hardwood floor. Brett watched her, not understanding what was going on. What was it she needed to do that couldn't wait?

She walked around the table and stopped in front of McMillan, and when he gestured with his chin for her to get down on the floor, she went to her knees and slid under the table.

McMillan's eyes creased in pleasure as he leaned back in his chair and relaxed.

It took Brett all of three seconds to figure out what was going on and he stood up, dropping his fork to the table. "What the fuck is this shit?"

McMillan's eyes opened and he touched the gun as he glared at Brett. "I would sit down if I were you, Mr. Butler. I didn't say dinner was over yet."

Brett remained standing as he stared at McMillan. He could hear the slurping sounds coming from under the table and he squeezed his hands into fists.

"I won't tell you again, boy. Do what I say or pay the price, that's the exchange for living under my roof."

Brett hesitated for a moment longer but in the end decided defiance was useless at this time and sat down, crossing his arms over his chest.

The slurping grew louder and McMillan began to buck his hips, a serene look coming over him. Then he grunted and placed his free hand on the top of Wendy's head, thrusting as hard as he could and letting out a low growl of joy.

His body went rigid and then relaxed as he sighed. Wendy crawled out from under the table while wiping her mouth. Brett looked at her but she wouldn't return his gaze, her eyes only for the polished hardwood floor.

"Very nice, dear, very nice," McMillan said as he buttoned his pants. "All right then, dinner is over. Toss your cans into the trash and go to your rooms. At ten I want everyone to meet in the main room for a nightcap. Then we can all get to know Mr. Butler a little better." He looked at Brett and stroked the gun. "Isn't that so, Mr. Butler?"

"Yeah, I guess so," Brett replied.

"Good, then I will bid you all a farewell for now. I'm tired and want to take a quick nap."

He stood up and walked deeper into the rear of the house, leaving the others alone to stare at one another. Then, as if a starting pistol had been fired, Jeff and Andy turned and quickly walked away to dispose of the empty cans and leave. Wendy was hugging herself with her arms, her hair draped over her face, her eyes hidden.

"Wendy, I..." Brett began, but she held her hand up to stop him.

"No, don't say anything, please. This has happened before when he wants to show his dominance over me, over all of us."

"He's a pig, I can see that already. Why do you let him treat you like that? Why do any of you? He's only one man."

"Yes, one man with a gun, and others locked up in his safe as well as all the food."

Jeff walked back into the room as Andy headed off to his own room.

"I heard you, Brett, and you're right but also wrong," Jeff said softly as he looked where McMillan had disappeared, making sure his father wasn't returning to overhear him. "My brother was here with us, too, that was six months ago. Back then my father wasn't as bad, though he was always a little bit of a megalomaniac. Makes sense, though doesn't it? To be a success in big business, to take over companies and send thousands of people on the streets with no jobs, well, it takes a heartless son-of-a-bitch to do that anyway, doesn't it? The corporate world is as cutthroat as any jungle, only it's more 'civilized'. But make no mistake, there has to be a piece of a man missing to achieve the power my father has in the real world, well, before the collapse and the bombs."

"What does that have to do with anything?" Brett asked.

Jeff continued. "When we first arrived, my brother Doug was part of our group. He was my older brother and he was so much like Father it was amazing, they looked like each other, too. I took after our mother more. Doug and my father always butted heads, about everything you could imagine, so when my father began slipping slightly into madness, it was Doug who called him on it. In the beginning, when my father tried to control us, Doug always stopped him. But then, one night, something changed in my father. That was the first day he arrived to dinner with his gun. Doug told him to put it away, that it wasn't needed inside the house, but my father told him he was in charge and could do what he wanted. Doug tried to take the gun away from him and my father..." His voice cracked slightly at the remembrance "My father shot him at point black range. Shot his son and killed him. Doug fell to the floor, bleeding out and dead in seconds and do you know what my father did?"

Brett shook his head.

"He poured himself a glass of wine and smiled. Like it was no big thing, as if he hadn't just shot dead his first born son."

"What happened then?" Brett asked. Wendy was hugging herself tighter as the images of that night were recalled, tears streaming down her cheeks.

"We finished eating if you would believe it. My father made us. Then he had Andy and I drag my brother outside and the next day the body was gone. Wolves I suppose." He touched Wendy's arm. "Wendy and Doug were engaged to be married, that's why she was able to come here, too."

"Oh, Jesus, I don't know what to say..." Brett began.

"There's nothing to say. We're trapped in here with a man who is sick. There's no place to go so we have to endure."

"That's not true, you could leave. There has to be someplace else where we could go. We could leave in the morning," Brett reasoned.

"No, there is no place to go," Jeff said. "The cities are blasted landscapes and there can't be more than a few thousand human beings left on the entire planet. Look at you, you left where you were, and for what? No, we're in Hell, and it has finally frozen over. All we can do is wait to die and then the suffering will end."

Brett took a step closer to Jeff. "Look, I can see you've given up and I can't blame you. To live like this for so long, and after seeing your brother killed. But I won't stand by and let him boss me around. No one's going to control me, not like he wants to."

Jeff waved a hand and turned to leave. "Then I wish you luck, but be warned, my father is an expert shot. You cross the line and you will join my brother in feeding the wolves." He took Wendy by the arm. "Come on, Wendy, let's get you to your room so you can lie down for a bit." She went without hesitation, looking to Brett like a scared little girl. He wanted to go to her, to hold her and tell her it would be fine, but he didn't, knowing he had just met her and his compassion wouldn't be welcome...not yet anyway.

They left, leaving Brett alone with his thoughts. He picked up the fork he'd used as he looked around the room. His eyes went to a dark stain on the floor, as if wine had been spilled and then had soaked in before being cleaned up. The stain looked a lot like blood. As he stared at the stain, he bent the fork in two, never aware he'd done it until it was folded in half.

Tossing it to the table, he left the dining room.

At ten sharp everyone gathered in the main room. A warm fire crackled and brandy was poured for each of them, Wendy acting as server.

"So, Mr. Butler, how goes the world outside these walls," McMillan asked.

"About what you'd expect," Brett said, knowing the man was asking for the others' benefit.

"Ah, then I was correct in setting up my little sanctuary, wasn't I?" McMillan looked at Jeff. "See, son? I knew it was the right thing to do. Without me, you would be dead now, just ash back in Los Angeles." He gestured to the window, the snow falling in heavy flakes. "It's hard to believe it's August when you look outside. We could be here for years, hell, we may die in here."

"Then what's the point?" Andy asked. "What the point in going on?"

"The point, my boy," McMillan said. "Is to survive, by any means necessary, and goddamn it that's what I plan to do."

They talked for another fifteen minutes, Brett telling what little he knew of the world, how he had left his enclave and how life had been there when finally McMillan clapped his hands and sat up straight in his chair.

"I'm bored. I want to try something new tonight." He pointed at Andy. "You, go over there and give my son a blowjob."

Andy blinked, not believing what he'd just heard. "Excuse me?"

"You heard me. Go over there and do to my son what Wendy did to me at dinner. And do a good job, I want to see him cum hard."

Andy shook his head in defiance, but when McMillan touched the gun and scowled, Andy knew he had little choice, not if he wanted to live.

Slowly, he crawled over and knelt between Jeff's knees.

"Father, please don't do this, it's sick. Neither of us is like that, you know that. Please," Jeff whispered.

"Shut up. I say what goes on in this house and you'll do as I order, now take off your pants and let's have a show."

Brett stood to the side, his mouth hanging open, appalled and disgusted as Andy did what he was ordered to do. He took Jeff into his mouth and began working, similar to what Wendy had done only hours ago. Brett watched as McMillan reached his free hand into his pants and began massaging himself as his eyes grew wide with excitement. Wendy was in the corner, looking at her feet, shaking her head as she whispered to herself.

"Good God, this is a fucking freak show. McMillan, what the fuck is wrong with you?"

McMillan pulled his hand from his pants and swung the gun onto Brett, cocking it. "You have something to say to me, boy? Best pick your words carefully, they might just be your last."

Brett could feel the rage building within him but he knew he was helpless. He calmed himself and said. "No, sir, I don't have anything to say. You're in charge here."

"Damn straight. Now shut up and enjoy the show."

Despite Jeff's best intentions, he orgasmed and Andy spit as he wiped his mouth. His eyes glared hatred at McMillan, who seemed to soak it up, his grin so wide it threatened to split his face in half.

Andy went to the bottle of brandy and poured himself a drink, then another, and then another. No one spoke, each lost in their private thoughts. Jeff pulled up his pants and pressed his open palms to his forehead, wondering how things had become so out of control. Brett watched Andy, seeing the man taking drink after drink. If he didn't stop soon, he would become drunk, and once his inhibitions were down, there might be trouble. Brett stood up and crossed the room, his plan to take the bottle away from Andy.

"Leave me alone, fuck off!" Andy spit to Brett.

"Give me the bottle, Andy, you've had enough," Brett said. Out of all the others, Brett seemed to be the only one not lost in a fit of despair

"Screw you, get away from me!" Andy shouted and pushed Brett backwards.

McMillan laughed and pointed to Brett. "Best do as he says. Never a good thing to get between a man and his liquor."

Brett could see Andy had downed a third of the bottle and his eyes were already glazed, his words now becoming slurred.

"Fine, but let me take him back to his room. You've had your fun for the night," Brett said.

"Uh-huh. I say when it's time for this shindig to end and it's not yet. Now sit your ass down or else." McMillan's eyes were hard and

Brett knew if he pushed his luck any further he might end up like Doug. "Fine, but this is sick."

Wendy was silent, glad McMillan was leaving her alone for a change and Jeff had his face covered with his hands. Andy continued to drink until he was very drunk. Brett could see the glares Andy was throwing at McMillan and he hoped Andy wouldn't do something or say something rash.

It was as if Andy had read his thoughts as he stood up, the brandy bottle falling to the floor to roll until landing at the hearth of the fireplace. It was so empty only a few drops spilled out of the open top.

"You," Andy hissed as he came to his feet, swaying back and forth. "You no good prick. Think you're so fucking tough 'cause you've got that damn gun. Well, fuck you. I'm not scared of you anymore."

"You should be," McMillan said softly with a slight grin.

"Andy," Brett whispered loudly. "Sit down, that's the booze talking."

"Stay out of it, new guy, this is none of your business," Andy snapped then turned back to McMillan. "So, did you like watching me suck on your son's dick? Huh? Bet you wished I was doing it to you, huh? Admit it, you're a fag and you want me to suck your dick!"

"Careful there, Andy," McMillan said. "I'll allow you some leeway because you're drunk but you will still talk to me with respect."

"Respect? You? Bah! You're just a loser who had to trap us here so you would have a captive audience. You're nothing, you're as extinct as this damn planet we're on!"

"This is your last warning, Andy, sit down and we'll forget this happened," McMillan warned.

Brett felt his body going stiff as he watched Andy stumble over to the fireplace and pick up the black metal poker. He swung it back and forth a few times as if he was testing its heft.

"Fuck your warnings, asshole, I'm through listening to you! Tonight was the last straw!" And as Brett watched, Andy began a drunken charge at McMillan, the poker raised high to crack the open man's skull.

The only sound was Andy's footsteps as he crossed the room, but he was halted as McMillan raised his gun and fired. The report was loud in the confines of the room and multiple things happened at the same time. In the far corner, Wendy covered her ears and slid to the floor, cowering as she squeezed her eyes shut. Brett stared in horror as the gun went off, the bullet striking Andy directly in the chest. Jeff pulled his hands away from his face to become splattered with Andy's blood, the drunk man standing almost directly in front of Jeff.

As for Andy, he stopped running and his body jerked back and forth as the bullet blew out a fist-sized hole in his back. As Jeff yelled in shock, smudging the warm blood on his face, Andy fell back to sprawl across the floor, blood spurting from his mouth as he died.

The metal poker slid across the floor to land at Jeff's feet. At first, the man looked down at it as if it was a dead snake, or something that had materialized out of thin air. But then, his eyes cleared, and before Brett could stop him, Jeff picked up the poker and charged at his father, mimicking Andy.

McMillan wasn't ready for this and he actually hesitated for a fraction of a second, as if he realized he was about to kill his last remaining family member. But then instinct took over and he shot the attacking man coming for him, irregardless that it was his son.

Jeff was hit in the neck, a massive amount of flesh and muscle blown away in an instant. Blood geysered from the open wound to spray the entire room in crimson. Brett saw half of Jeff's neck was now missing, his head slumping to the side at a macabre angle. With blood sputtering from the jagged wound, he dropped to the floor, twitching and spasming in his death throes.

No one spoke, no one said anything for a full five minutes. By the time the silence was broken, Jeff's kicking feet has ceased for more than four minutes.

McMillan stood up on weak legs and looked down at a cowering Wendy, who when she saw McMillan look at her, cringed, squeaking like a mouse. She expected him to shoot her, too, but the bullet never came.

McMillan turned and settled his gaze on Brett, who was staring silently at the two dead bodies. He raised the gun and pointed it at

Brett's head. "Are you going to be a problem, too?" he asked Brett softly.

"No, no problem here, sir" Brett replied as he swallowed the large knot that had appeared in his throat.

"Good, then clean this mess up and feed the bodies to the wolves," he said to Brett. "Have Wendy help you." He glanced at the body of his son cooling on the floor. "Pity, really, but then he was always a disappointment to me." Without waiting for a reply, he turned and walked out of the room, the gun hanging by his side in an arm that seemed limp. "And have Wendy join me in my room when she's finished cleaning up."

Brett watched the man go but didn't move. Other than Wendy's frightened sobs, all was silent.

In the fireplace, the burning logs crackled with an intensity of heat only rivaled by the fire raging within Brett's heart for vengeance.

Wendy didn't talk as she and Brett dragged the two bodies into the snow. He tried a few times to get her to speak, but each time was met with only silence.

Once the bodies were outside, already an inch of snow covering them in less than a minute, Wendy went to a small closet, took out a few cotton towels and began wiping down the furniture and soaking up the blood in the main room. Brett helped, and an hour later there was almost no sign of what had happened. It was as if the two murders had never occurred and everything was as it was before.

When they finished and Wendy had carried the towels into the back of the house where laundry was kept, she walked back into the main room. She barely looked at Brett as she turned to follow that same route McMillan had used an hour previously. She was headed to his bedroom, as the man had dictated.

Brett crossed the distance separating them and grabbed her arm. "Wendy, wait, you don't have to go to him."

"Yes I do," she said softly, gently trying to pull her arm from his grip.

"No, you don't. Look, we can still fight him. He's only one man. Andy was drunk and Jeff acted rashly. Neither had a chance against an alert man with a gun. But together we can stop him."

She yanked her arm free as she looked into his eyes. "No, we can't! Don't you see! Only he knows the combination to the pantry. Without him, there's no food."

"Then we can leave here," Brett reasoned. "Why do we have to stay? We can take what we can salvage and just go. There must be someplace else."

"No," she said. "Arthur told us there's nowhere else to go. This is it."

"He's lying. There has to be someplace else, this can't be it. Christ, Wendy, he killed your fiancée and now Andy and Jeff. Who knows who'll be next?"

"No," she said. "You're wrong; he wouldn't hurt me, not like that. Now leave me alone. I don't want to die like Andy and Jeff, just let me be!" She turned and ran from him, her sneakers slapping the hardwood.

"Wendy, wait!" he called, but she was already around the corner and gone.

He stared at the empty hallway for more than minute as his mind raced with all he'd experienced in such a short time. To be saved from the frigid cold only to find himself in a worst predicament; ruled by a madman with a god complex. Slapping the wall with the palm of his hand in frustration, he headed to his room. He was too wired to sleep, but he didn't know what else to do.

Brett had thought once he was in his bedroom he wouldn't sleep, not after everything that had transpired that night, but once he'd lain down, he soon drifted off to sleep, his body still weak from his time in the freezing cold.

He didn't know how long he slept but he was snapped awake by Wendy's voice as she whispered into his ear and shook him frantically.

"Come on, Brett, you need to get up," she whispered, her voice full of haste.

Brett slowly came back to the waking world and he blinked up at her face. He could barely see her, the room wreathed in darkness. It felt late, but the exact time was unknown.

"What? What's wrong, what's going on?" he asked as he tried to focus on her voice.

"Shhh, don't talk so loud," she whispered. "I thought about what you said and you're right. We need to leave here before he kills us both."

"Is there a light? I can't see a damn thing," he said.

There was a soft sound of a cigarette lighter being flicked, and a moment later, a small orange glow was near his bedside. Wendy leaned over and lit a candle.

"There, better?" she asked as she sat on the bed.

"Yeah, I guess." As he sat up, he could see Wendy was wearing a thin nightgown. Her nipples pushed up on the thin material and he felt himself growing aroused, though he knew this wasn't the time. He also saw that her neck had a bright red ring around it; a few places tinged a dark blue.

"Your neck," he said.

She raised her right hand to her neck, touching it. "A souvenir from Arthur. He...he choked me tonight while having sex with me. I...I thought he was going to kill me. But he didn't. Then I realized next time I might not be so lucky so after...after he was finished, he fell asleep like he always did. I was going to try for his gun and kill him right there, but when I tried to reach for it, he woke up. I told him I was going to the bathroom and he let me be. I...I should have tried again but I was too scared." She looked down, ashamed of herself.

"No, you were right," Brett said. "If he'd woken up he would have killed you for sure. Whatever piece of sanity he's been holding onto went away earlier tonight when he killed Andy and Jeff." He slid out of bed and began getting dressed. "Go get dressed. Make sure you dress in layers, as many as you can. I'll meet you in the dining room. We'll see what food there is around and take all we can, then we'll get the hell out of this madhouse."

She nodded and slid out the door, her gossamer nightgown seeming to flow about her.

Brett continued dressing, his mind racing on what they were going to do next. He wasn't looking forward to going back out into the snow, but he knew there was little choice. Better to take their chances out in the storm than wait to be slaughtered by a crazy old fool.

He searched the room, checking the closet and then under the bed. He found a backpack under the bed, the name **Doug** stenciled on the front flap. He didn't give it much thought as he quickly took what was useable in the room, such as the blankets and the pillowcase. He blew out the candle and stuffed it into the pack as well; then, with a few other odds and ends, he left the room and crept down the hallway.

Wendy wasn't there yet and he went to the kitchen. He found a half open box of this and a quarter full of that, not much but better than nothing. He put it all into a wool bag found under the kitchen sink, and when he was done he carried it to the front door where he set it down. He looked up at the sound of footsteps and saw it was Wendy. She was fully dressed, wearing a heavy parka, gloves, scarf and hat. She had a parka for him, too. As he slid into it, she said, "It was Doug's."

He nodded and zipped it up, then took the proffered hat and gloves from her. When he was ready, he looked her straight in the eyes. "You ready for this? We need to keep moving when we leave here or we'll freeze to death. In the morning, we can find a place to rest and maybe make camp. Then we'll have to head out until we find someplace safe."

"I'm ready, it's not like we have a choice, right?"

He smiled at her. "Right, we don't."

Taking her hand, they walked to the front door. Brett fixed the backpack on his shoulder to get it more comfortable; Wendy with one as well. After that he shouldered the bag of food, and with one more glance at Wendy, he opened the front door.

Hand in hand, the two stepped into the frigid night and left the sanctuary behind.

The first night was the worst, as they both had to become acclimated to the harsh environment. They walked for hours, and when they couldn't go anymore, the dim sun finally rising, casting the land in a pallid gloom barely better than dusk, they found shelter in an old camping station, barely bigger than a large, walk-in closet.

They rested and ate snow, saving their meager rations for when they would need it most, and after catching a few hours sleep—curled up together for warmth—they headed back out into the frozen wasteland.

They didn't talk, each covering their faces so that only their eyes were visible, and they walked, day after day.

By the end of the first week, they crested a large hill, and as they reached the top, Brett, who was in the lead, stopped walking and fell to his knees as if he'd seen something devastating.

Wendy came up behind him, not understanding what was wrong. Was he sick? Tired? Why had he fallen to the snow-covered ground?

And then, as she joined Brett and laid her eyes on what he'd seen, she too, fell to the frozen ground and wept.

Miles way, lost in the swirling maelstrom of snow, they could see the remnants of a grand city. Now it was a burnt out wreck of battered debris, more than ninety percent of the city unrecognizable and covered in snow.

But as their eyes played over the devastation, here and there large signs could be seen from where the wind had blown the snow clean.

Massive fiberglass and steel signs with The Palms, The Rio and Terrible's Casino, dotted the landscape between the rubble and debris.

The Las Vegas Hilton was nothing but smashed concrete and metal, looking as if a giant hand had flattened it in a fit of rage. In the distance, where The Stratosphere once stood tall, the area was empty, the structure having collapsed.

Small dots that were once cars and trucks were scattered about, most flipped onto their roofs, a few lodged in the debris, as if a giant wind had picked them up to deposit them higher up.

From where Brett stood, he couldn't see smaller details, such as the remains of human bodies, but he had no doubt they would be there, buried in the snow, if a more detailed search was made.

"Oh my God, no," Wendy said as she began to weep.

Brett said nothing, only stared in horror. The heart of Clark County, Nevada was nothing but blasted, snow-covered wreckage, and for as far as he could see the same vista greeted him.

They stared at the destroyed city for a full half hour until the cold became too much and they knew they needed to get moving to build up their body heat.

"What do we do now?" she asked Brett as they turned away from the dead city, cocooned forever in a coffin of white snow and ice.

"We go back to the sanctuary."

"But what about Arthur?"

"We'll deal with that when we get there. We'll just have to hope he'll let us back in. But he doesn't strike me as the forgiving type."

"And if he doesn't let us in?" she asked, her lower lip trembling from more than just the cold.

"Then we're dead."

The journey back was harder now, the knowledge that there was nowhere else to go almost too much to take.

They sought shelter in the same camping station as before, and made it to the small shelter only an hour before a massive storm struck the area, the snow falling so hard and fast their footprints were buried in seconds after making them.

Huddled together in the middle of the small hut, they wrapped themselves in the blankets Brett had carried with him, and waited for the storm to break.

In that time, they talked for hours, slept a lot, wrapped in each others arms, and on the third day, made love for the first time. At first it was awkward, the two shy and cold, but as their passion grew, so too did their confidence.

The last two days trapped in the hut were one of bliss, as they grew closer, falling in love. If it wasn't for the want of food, which had run out two days ago, they would have been blissfully happy, despite the cold.

When the storm finally broke, they pushed out a window, and crawled onto the three feet of newly fallen snow, and began their trek back to the sanctuary.

Though closer now, they mostly stayed silent, each filled with the dread of their return. Once back, even if McMillan allowed them inside, the couple would be torn apart by McMillan, who claimed Wendy as his property.

But Brett figured one problem at a time, the first being to make it back safely and alive.

Days passed and eventually the sanctuary came into view with Brett leading the way. They were both tired and on the edge of total exhaustion as the weary couple stepped up to the front door of the sanctuary and looked at each other.

"You sure about this?" he asked her, his cheeks bright red from exposure.

She nodded, only her eyes visible from behind her scarf and hat. "We don't have any choice."

"Okay, cross your fingers that he's in a forgiving mood," he said and then banged on the door.

More than a minute passed and the door remained unopened. As the next minute ticked by, Brett tried to tell himself that it would take time for McMillan to get to the door.

That was if he planned on opening it at all.

Another two minutes went by and Brett was beginning to become nervous. His mind began to work frantically as he tried to figure out what he and Wendy would do next if they were ignored.

The truth was, he didn't know what to do.

It was below freezing and there was nothing even remotely close to the sanctuary where they could hole up. And then there was the matter of food, which they had none.

He knew if they didn't get back inside the house, they were both as good as dead and he let his eyes play over the reinforced windows, wondering if he could break in when the lock to the door clicked and it slowly opened.

McMillan was in a bathrobe, his revolver in his right hand, as he glared at Brett and Wendy. "Well, well, well. Back from your walk?" he quipped, his eyes cold, the gun aimed at Brett's chest.

"Well, come on, get in here, you're letting all the heat out."

Brett stepped inside with Wendy behind him, Wendy closing the door behind her. Once inside, they slipped out of their backpacks and parkas, setting them on the floor where they dripped water from the melting snow covering them.

"When I woke up and you two were gone at first I was upset," McMillan said. "But then I figured if you were stupid enough to leave then you deserved each other out there in the cold. I can't believe you have the balls to come back. So, why did you?"

Brett pulled off his gloves and hat, holding them, as he stared at the revolver in McMillan's hand. His one hope was that if the man was going to shoot him, he would have already.

"There's nothing out there," Brett said. "We walked for almost a week and found nothing but rubble. There was nowhere else to go but here."

"Uh-huh. That's what I figured. The whole damn world is gone, but I still remain. And I will remain for a long time to come." He raised the revolver a little higher. "But I can't have you around here, not after stealing Wendy from me. I'd be looking over my shoulder every second of every day."

"Then why did you let us back inside?" Brett asked. He shifted slightly, moving closer to McMillan who caught the movement.

"Stand still, don't move a muscle or I'll shoot you." McMillan looked at Wendy with what almost would pass for compassion. "I let you in because I had to if I wanted her back. But she's the only one I want." He looked her in the eyes. "As far as your betrayal, we'll talk about that later when it's just you and me."

Wendy looked down at her feet as she took off her gloves and hat, holding them in her hands. She knew when they talked it would involve pain for her.

McMillan turned back to Brett and said, "Goodbye, Mr. Butler, I can't say it's been a pleasure knowing you." He prepared to squeeze the trigger and Wendy yelled, "No, Arthur, don't do it!"

Brett saw McMillan's arm tense as he prepared to fire and he acted quickly, using the hat and gloves in his hands as a distraction by throwing them at McMillan.

The old man was caught off guard, for a split second jerking his head back, not realizing it was only the hat and gloves, and in that space of a heartbeat, Brett lunged at him, the two falling to the floor as they wrestled for the revolver.

Wendy moved closer, trying to decide what to do, but she was helpless as the two men rolled across the hardwood floor, grunting and gasping to gain the upper hand over the other. Brett managed to send a punch into McMillan's side, causing the older man to grunt, who then in turn sent a knee into Brett's groin, causing him to see stars. Despite their difference in age, both were evenly matched and neither could gain the upper hand on the other.

The revolver was lowered until the muzzle was an inch from Brett's forehead but at the last instant he bent it back and down. As the two men came to their knees, each facing one another, the gun was pointed down at the floor, both holding onto it. Then, the gun slowly was raised until it was jammed between the two men, their chests touching, and neither knowing who had a finger on the trigger.

Wendy jumped when the gun went off, sounding muffled, the two bodies pressed together stifling the report.

Both men toppled to the floor, McMillan on top of Brett. For a moment, neither man moved, as Wendy stared in fear, tears flowing down her face. If McMillan was the winner, her life would be ten times worse than it had been.

And then to her horror, McMillan pushed off of Brett's still form and stumbled to his feet. Wendy could see both he and Brett had dark blood stains on their chests and it was obvious Brett had been shot.

McMillan took two steps towards her, his right hand out in a fist, and Wendy shook her head, knowing it was all over.

But when he took another faltering step, he halted and stared at her. But she realized he wasn't really seeing her, his eyes now holding a haunted look. And then he coughed, blood spurting from his mouth to drip down his chin and spatter the floor. His legs bean to shake and he fell to his knees, then hands, looking like a toddler who had fallen down. He wheezed twice and then looked up at her, his left arm coming up and his hand reaching for her, begging for help. She did nothing of the kind, but stared at him, not understanding what was happening.

And then, his arm supporting him let go and he fell heavily to the floor, his breath coming in a few strangled gasps before he went still. His eyes remained open, gazing on something Wendy hoped not to see for a very long time.

She fell to her knees and sobbed, all alone now, and at first she didn't hear the low moan through her tears, but when it grew louder, she looked up and to her astonishment saw that Brett was slowly moving his head back and forth.

She jumped up and ran to him, falling by his side, and as she touched his chest, the dark blood staining her hand crimson, she saw there was no bullet hole, only transfer from where McMillan had been shot. As he rolled over and coughed heavily, she saw the large bruise on the back of his head where he'd struck it upon falling. While she had thought him dead, he had only been dazed and was now returning to consciousness.

As he coughed and sucked in a breath of air, he opened his eyes and looked up into Wendy's tear-filled eyes.

"What happened? Are we okay? McMillan, is he..."

"Yes, he's dead, we're safe."

"Good, that's good," he said, still dazed and not fully with it yet.

"But Arthur had the combination for the pantry. How will we eat?" she asked.

"We'll be fine," he said. "The pantry's in a room with plaster walls. I can make a hole in the wall and get at the food, it's okay."

As the young couple sat on the floor, holding each other, Wendy wiped her eyes and asked, "So what do we do now?"

He reached up and touched her cheek, wiping away a tear as the wind howled outside. "Now, we live."

NECROPOLITAIN

ANDREW C. PORTER

David came down the boulevard warily eying the darkened doorways and windows lining his path. He paused and set the sack he carried over his shoulder down gently onto the cracked and uneven cobbles that marked the walking paths of this corridor of the city.

He cocked his ear to the street ahead, a faint breeze stirring the air. The cry of a bird rang distant and remote, but of lurkers he detected no sign. He picked the sack up, the contents clinking dully, the sound setting David's teeth on edge. He pulled the black cowl down over his forehead in a hope that it would protect him, though past experience didn't bear this out.

Slowly, gingerly, he moved forward. The windows of the tall, dead apartments were a thousand spider eyes bearing down on him in malice. The doorways were gaping maws that held snaking, hungry tongues. David walked the razor line between the darkness of natural night and the unnatural black of the buildings around him, the narrowest of regions where the structures' malice gave extra cover, but was just outside of their reach.

He rounded a corner slowly, tested the air again, then moved forward. The new boulevard was a more important one from the city's past. It was twice as wide as the street he had just left. In the middle of it, ran a long, narrow park overgrown with vines that hung in mocking profusion on the trees they had choked to life-lessness. The apartments and nearby buildings were much larger here, and David hung near the overgrown swath in the middle, trusting that the vines would make it difficult for an enemy to hide in ambush. Not that a lurker would bother with an ambush, but the city also held other evils.

David pressed forward. The growth spilling over the edge of the park and onto the cracked asphalt deadened the sound of his feet and he pressed on at a faster pace for it. The route was risky. Less trafficked paths were available, but David had come to the conclusion that the paths no longer mattered. These days, the best way to survive was to spend as little time out as possible. Old Dob had said that a long time ago, people used the underground paths to travel around the city. Life had been easier then. People lived underground, learned the paths, found what they needed topside and then went back under. But things still found them there, things worse than lurkers. Dob's own Pa had lived in the tunnels if you let Dob tell it. His Pa had been carried off by a lurker after they found the havens.

David rounded a corner and there it was, hanging in the air, hands folded. Dob said they carried the old man away and he never made a sound.

Not everyone fled the underground of course. Some stayed and hid deeper. Now there are other things in the underground—hungrier things.

David slowed near thick shrubs at a point where the median park broke for a crossroad. These were the most dangerous places he knew, three long lines of sight, all leading to the crossing point. Dob had taught him to be wary of such places, and he always had been. David gazed up one direction, then the other, picking out the shapes and profiles of the cityscape in the sliver of a crescent moon. Nothing moved in the night. In the distance, the shapes of the tall ghost towers were picked out against the starlight. David had never been as far as the towers. He had wanted to. He wanted to look up at the shear impossible heights of glass and steel. He had gone to look for 'The Solution,' or 'The Fools Errand', as Dob called it, but his responsibilities always brought him back.

"Going to get yourself kilt on 'The Fools Errand'," he had whispered as David memorized old street maps in the pin shafts of sunlight that filtered into the haven. "Better men than you went looking for 'The Solution' and many more never came back. Ain't no solution. There's only death."

Dob had been right and wrong. David never found 'The Solution', and much of what he did find he would very much like to forget. Yet he hadn't died, and he'd found much that was of use to the tribe. From that time on he had been tasked with his tribe's hunting. Dob had retired from the dangerous work, continuing as David's tutor and advisor. Then Dob had been taken.

David slipped across the intersection. The old traffic lights still hung here and there, swaying in the gentle crosscurrent breeze. When David gained the median growth on the other side, he turned to face the direction he had come from and backed into the overgrowth, letting it surround him completely. He was well hidden deep within the vines. He put his back to a dead tree trunk and found a spot that allowed him a view of the entire intersection. He doubted even a lurker would be able to find him here. The *double-back* and the *watch* were two tricks of old Dob's. He began his count, one to ten for each finger twice.

"Ain't ever seen nothing following that didn't make a show of itself in a double ten count," old Dob's had said and neither had David.

Of course this wasn't for lurkers. They didn't bother waiting. The lurker that took old Dob had dropped silently into their midst like a spider on a thread of silk. David had seen it detach from the eave of a building, but it had moved with such an odd and ponderous grace that at first he didn't know what he was seeing. The lurker had almost looked like another hunter, robed and covered with a heavy, tattered cowl, but there were no feet and the hands were fleshless claws. David watched it descend, and before he could react, it had its arms wrapped around old Dob.

Dob never screamed or struggled. He just went limp. The lurker lifted him up into the air and slowly floated away down the street, and that was the end of old Dob.

When David was on his last finger count, he caught the movement down the avenue he had just traversed. The figure flitted from the corner to the median park on the path he had just taken. The figure picked its way carefully along the park. Its movement was steady and careful, slower than David, but only because it was smaller. When the figure was almost to the intersection, David was certain it was human. He remained hidden for the moment. Not all of the groups and tribes were friendly to one another, and David was very far from his haven. Worse, if he startled this person and they cried out, then the lurkers or the others, would come to investigate. So he waited.

The figure wore a black cape and cowl like all the tribes did. At the intersection the figure stopped and checked the directions much as David had done earlier, then raced across, turned at the edge of the park, and began to back into the overgrowth right where David was hiding.

David put his arms out. The vines rustled alarmingly as the figure penetrated them. Three steps, two steps, one step, and he wrapped a strong arm around the figure's upper torso and put a hand over the mouth. He felt sharp teeth biting into his palm but only squeezed harder. The figure struggled for a moment more, then went still.

"I won't hurt you," David whispered.

A sharp nod of the head and David pushed the figure away to arm's length as he drew his knife quickly. The figure turned fast with a knife in hand, to face him. They stood and looked at one another with blades bared.

Under the hood, David could tell that the figure wasn't much more than a child, a girl as well. As she beheld him, the fury in her eyes relaxed visibly and she sheathed her knife first.

"You scared me," she whispered.

"I thought you were following me," he replied.

"Just lucky," she said.

"Who are you?" David asked, meaning what tribe.

"Oh, Washington Heights. You?"

"East Harlem. You're a long way from your haven."

"So are you." She looked down at the sack at his feet. "Good run?"

"It'll do. You're going the wrong way if you're going home, you know. This is Yorkville."

"I'm on a run, but I ran out of time and now I need shelter."

David considered for a moment. He pulled up his sleeve where an ancient gold watch gleamed against his dark skin. "You have an hour before daylight. You can come to my haven. It's story time soon, too." He had never met anyone from the Washington Heights tribe, but making friends seemed smart. It might even yield new running grounds. "We better get moving," he said and started to walk out to the street, but a small hand stopped him.

"You need to do a count." Her face was deadly earnest, brooking no argument. David leaned back against the tree and began to count fingers again. When he had finished his count, they left the shelter together.

"You do the count, too?" he whispered as they moved out onto the quiet street.

"Yes," she said, then moved ahead of him, setting the pace.

"Do you have a name?" David whispered to her.

She didn't reply immediately, then half turning her head, she whispered back, "Dolly."

East Harlem Haven was a three-story building that once housed a library. It bore the blue circle and three arrows pointing in a glyph on the door that meant it was a place lurkers couldn't enter; others could enter of course. The door and windows were all covered in steel plates. It was thirty minutes before dawn when David and Dolly reached the door and David tapped out a series of knocks that meant he had returned safely. A second later, a latch slid inside the door and the silent hinges swung out, revealing a small port. An elderly man beckoned them in with a club in his hand.

"Who's this now?" the old man asked upon seeing Dolly.

"Hunter from Washington Heights. She needs sheltering, Bogg."

"She'll have it. Story time today. Maybe she has one we don't?" The old man looked from Dolly to the sack David placed inside the door. "Good hunting I see."

"It'll do. How did the others fair?" David took off his cape and cowl and folded them under his arm.

"Bah," the old man spit. "Youngers, every last one of 'em. Couldn't hold a candle to me when my legs were good and not worth a hair on old Dob's head. Weren't for you we'd all starve."

The East Harlem Haven was large, thirty-five people, but they were mostly children and elders. Bogg was the eldest at forty-five years old. Scurvy had ravaged the haven when he was a youth and his teeth were missing and his skin was badly scarred. That was before the lurkers had come and the city was full of the *cidd*. When

David was a child it was tales of the cidd that had kept them up all day. "These lurkers ain't nothing!" he remembered Bogg exclaiming at story time, "A cidd could see you through a wall and it would pull a building down to get at you."

Old Dob had pulled David aside later that evening, "Don't you listen to him, boy." Dob's breath smelled of liquor, but his eyes were clear. "A lurker is a worse thing. They come on you all quiet like. Don't tell you to freeze, don't tell you to put your hands on your head, they just pick you up and carry you off, silent as a breeze." David had taken it to heart. The exploits of Dob and Bogg's generation had led David's own cohort to risky expeditions and now only David remained.

The haven's living area was in the basement. Cots lined one end of the long, low room and the other side had a series of curtained sections for the privacy of the four birthing couples that had formed the nucleus of the tribe. They were all past child rearing age now and most thought it sad that the next generation were all young children, leaving David to face a life with no hope of children. Not that David wanted any children, in this too he had taken Dob's advice. "This is the city of the dead, boy. Living things are an abomination here. We're not wanted."

David believed him, but he wasn't without hope yet. "What about outside the city, Dob?"

The corner of Dob's mouth had twitched under his wiry black beard. "Outside is worse. Don't ever go outside the city. It's worse."

The terror in Dob's eyes had stuck with David and even at the height of his own explorations he never tried to go beyond the city limits.

In the middle of the living area was a brick fire pit that vented into a large, blackened metal tube that went up through cutouts to the roof. The smoke sometimes drew the attention of bad things, but the haven was well armed and supplied, so the attacks never came too much. The glyph kept the lurkers away, its mystical power making the haven somehow invisible to them. The old timers said that it was the cidds that allowed them to discover the havens. The tribes were bigger then and the cidds were killing them off faster than they could repopulate until a tribe took shelter in a building with the glyph. The cidds would think nothing of destroying a building if a single hunter was sheltered there, but if the building had the glyph, then you could stand on the roof and the cidd would pass by without so much as slowing down. The word spread and the tribes moved into the havens.

The elder women were rummaging through the cans that David and the other hunters had brought back. They sorted through the ones with pictures from cans with only symbols—which no one could read—and those without labels. Most could tell by shaking a can what it contained, but it was time for dinner and so they worked with the ones they were sure of. All told, there were just over a hundred cans, some small; it was not a good yield.

They passed out the plates—cracked glass and scratched metal and plastic—and then the women portioned out to each member of the tribe some of the food. David, as a hunter, received a double portion and he saw to it that Dolly did as well. Their plates had greens, sweet potatoes, and a few slices of salty, pressed meat that came from an easily identifiable square can. This was David's favorite.

Low murmurs of conversation ran around the fire as the tribe enjoyed the meal. Dolly sat next to David on the floor and both ate in silence. David finished first and left to wash his face at the cistern on the first floor. The water was overflow from the filters that they maintained in the bottom of the rain catch on the roof and it was important not to swallow any or risk the *tearing belly* and cramps. When he finished, he began to make his way down the stairs when he heard something coming from above. He turned and went up the stairs following the slight noise of footsteps echoing from the second floor. The footfalls had stopped by the time he climbed the steps, so he began to look around.

This floor was seldom used by the tribe unless something tried to break in the front door and they had to force it off. Otherwise this area was useless artifacts and undecipherable books. As a child, David had come up here to look at the pictures and try to tease meaning out of the symbols. It was while doing this that he had found the maps and figured out their meaning and how to use them to navigate the city. After his responsibilities as a hunter took over, however, his excursions on the second floor had stopped.

He continued to search, eventually finding the girl in a back area he hadn't visited in years.

Dolly stood beside a row of odd-shaped, ancient chairs that David had forgotten were there. She whispered to herself and ran her hand over their shapes. The chairs had always been strange. Each one was made of cushioned plastic and each had a ring on a telescoping metal shaft that came out of the low back. The ring was also metal and it hinged on the top of the shaft and could be adjusted for angle and height. David remembered that from the back of each chair a thick cord ran and that at one point in the floor all the cords came together and disappeared into a hole. Blazoned on the back of each chair was the glyph: circle and three arrows pointing into the center in blue.

"Just the same," Dolly whispered to herself.

"What's just the same?" David asked.

Dolly whipped her head around with a start but regained her composure quickly. "The chairs. We have the same ones in our haven."

"It's time for stories," David said, holding an arm out in the direction of the stairs.

"Have you ever been to another haven, David?"

"No." He had known other hunters, but only in the field.

"They all have these chairs. Every one."

"If they all have the glyphs, too, they should have other things in common."

"Maybe," she said, and made for the stairs.

Story time was once a week and it was the highlight of everyone's day. The youngers who had come up with stories would go first and these were usually just reworkings of the tales the elders told. The elders shared stories next, and these made up the bulk of story time. After the elders, it would be David's turn to tell about his hunt and then story time became a meeting about tribe survival. The children were always asleep by then.

This day went as usual. The children fumbled through tales, then the elders told theirs in expert, well-trodden renditions. Bogg mostly retold the exploits of old Dob as his own. Then after the last of the elders had spoken, Dolly stood up to speak.

"You don't have to. Bogg was just being an ass," David said from his seat next to her.

"I have a story to tell," was all she said and with that she walked to the teller's position next to the fire.

Dolly looked around the room at the wizened, toothless elders who cradled sleeping children, took a deep breath, and began.

"I have a story. A true story about why things are the way they are. It is the story of why the tribes are here and why the havens protect us from the lurkers."

There were gasps around the room and children grumbled at the disturbance. David sat up straighter.

"The world was not always like this. The city was not always dead. Long ago every building had a tribe and the trees were green. Back then the sun did not make you sick and the rain did not make you sick. There were no cidds and no lurkers and no others."

This was nothing new to David. Many of the elders told stories about the green time.

Dolly continued.

"In those days there were many cities and you could walk from one to the other without being hunted, and food didn't come from cans, and people lived outdoors under the sun. Then one day things began to change. First the plague came and many people died. Then there were wars among all the tribes of the world and the air was poisoned by their weapons. Each tribe lit great fires in the cities of the other tribes and the smoke made the rain become poison. Then the sun changed and you couldn't let it touch your skin for too long or you would get sick. Then the animals changed, the ones that lived. Things that the old tribes made changed them and they became dark and dangerous and that was when some people began to change too. Then the leaders of all the tribes came together and saw what they had done to the world and knew that if they didn't make peace, every person and every tribe was going to die, so they came up with 'The Solution'."

The room was deathly quiet. Even the crackling of the fire seemed to hush. This was not a story anyone had heard and David caught himself leaning toward where Dolly stood.

"'The Solution' was that every person in every tribe on earth would leave and go to 'The Core'." Dolly looked at them, gauging their reactions before she continued. "'The Core' is a place and it is not a place. It is a place that the tribes made for themselves that is separate from this world but still in it. Every person in the world was invited to come to The Core where they could live forever in peace, but not everyone would go. Some people said that people deserved what they got and refused. Others said that it was a sin to go and so they stayed behind. Most of these people died." Dolly seemed to be grasping now, uncertain of how to continue. "We are the children of the ones that refused 'The Solution'. We forgot our past and now we are here, but somewhere out there, The Core still exists and it is a good place."

Bogg stood bolt upright. "What a load of shit! Where did you hear that?"

"I read most of it," she said.

Bogg stood still, his mouth hanging open.

Essme, another elder, spoke instead. "You read it, child? How?"

"I...I can read. Several people in my tribe could. Our haven was in a school, a place that taught children to read. The teaching books were still there."

"Several people 'could'? Why can't they now?" Essme missed little and had picked up the past tense.

"They're all gone now. The women in my tribe couldn't have children anymore, at least not... not natural children. The elders knew a lot about the past so they decided we should all go out and try to find the truth once and for all. I was the youngest. I haven't seen any of them in a long time. I think they're all dead."

Bogg had regained his composure and he spoke, his voice full of threat. "You say your women couldn't have natural children? You mean they had others. Seems to me you must be some sort of other, too, then." He looked around the room, "Seems to me we need to put this *other* down!" He stomped his foot and children began to cry while some of the gathered mumbled in ascent.

David had enough. "Shut up!" he bellowed.

The tribes were cultures of whispers and even Bogg's tirade was delivered in relatively quiet tones. David's bellow crashed through all the taboo and all muttering ceased. "Most of you have never seen the things that are out there. She's a hunter, a good one. If she says she can read, I believe her."

Bogg's face was flushed a deep red, but as long as David brought the tribe its food, his word was law. David moved to stand next to Dolly. "I looked for 'The Solution' when I was younger. I couldn't find it, but maybe she can. Look at us." David waved his hand at the shamble of humanity gathered around the fire. "It can't be right that we have to huddle here and hope that the cans don't run out. It can't be right that the rain and sun makes us sick. You all know it's true. You've all felt that this isn't the way people are supposed to live. I'm going to help her. I'm going to find 'The Solution'."

The elders erupted in argument, some pleading with him, some threatening. Crying children were pushed aside as the story time degenerated into hot debate. David deflected the elders' demands with stony authority. Behind him, Dolly watched in silence as the East Harlem Haven fell apart.

"So how many tribes were there?" David asked as they bedded down in the basement.

"You mean before 'The Solution', or after?" Dolly unrolled her blanket onto the concrete floor, yawning as she did so.

"Before, after, both I suppose." They had worked their way toward midtown with pronounced care at David's insistence. He had told her up front that he wouldn't sacrifice himself for her. That if it came down to his life or hers, he wouldn't hesitate to save himself. She had no tribe and no one depended on her, but if he died, all thirty-four people in his tribe would die also.

"Before, there were hundreds. They didn't really call them tribes though. They were called nations," she explained.

"How many nations in the city?" David asked.

Dolly laughed. It was a young girl's laugh and it reminded David that though she seemed wiser than an elder and was more cautious than the best hunter, she was just a thirteen year old girl. "There weren't any nations in the city. The whole city, and many more just like it were all in one nation."

David couldn't begin to get his head around the concept. "How about after? What did the books say about the tribes after 'The Solution'?"

"Nothing. The books only tell up until before 'The Solution'. After that I just figured things out."

"Did you figure out how many tribes there are?"

She shook her head slowly. "Less now than before. There were a few hundred in the early days, most bigger than yours. They made forts and hid in the tunnels. That was when the cidds came, when they moved too deep underground. Now I guess there are only about a dozen tribes left in the city. Yours is about the biggest."

"You said that the cidds came when people went underground. I thought they went underground to hide from the cidds."

"No. The 'civil defense drones' were left underground to guard 'The Core' from anything up here that might try to hurt it. They were actually built by people."

David was getting used to having his view of the world shattered by the young girl, but this was harder to swallow.

"So you're saying that the cidds are things we made to hurt ourselves? That seems crazy. If that's the kind of people who left I don't know if I want to meet them."

"You've got it all wrong," she said. "The ones who left figured that if anybody stayed they wouldn't survive, at least not as people. They thought that in a few years they would just become *others*. The tribes were nothing they had ever planned for." She leaned back on her blanket and closed her eyes.

David wasn't finished with his inquiry just yet. "What are the lurkers then? Are they like the cidds?"

She didn't open her eyes as she replied, "No. The lurkers are something different."

The next evening they started early. The sun was still up but obscured by the large apartment buildings that lined the streets shoulder to shoulder. It was a pattern David knew well. The buildings would grow and gather closer all the way to midtown where the towers were largest. Beyond that David had never traveled.

The numbered signs marking the street corners were in the seventies when they came upon the *others*. It was dark now and the moon was just larger than a sliver. Dolly spotted it first, her hand shooting out and grabbing David's cloak in a tight fist. She held him there, her body stiff. David scanned ahead and then caught the motion a block away on an open corner.

Its back was to them and it looked to be feeding on something large and wormlike. From the sound of its exertions, its prey was very wet.

David began to back away. Dolly, still clutching his cloak, came with him. As they moved away, the other stopped its feeding and tilted its narrow black head to the sky and began to sniff. With a sudden hiss, it turned to face them and bolted in their direction. David grabbed Dolly and jerked her in front of him as he sprinted up the nearest cross street. They had run less than half a block when the shadow of the *other* sprang around the corner, hissing and spitting. Dolly ducked into an empty doorway and David overcame his repulsion and followed her.

In the pitch black recesses of the building's ground floor, Dolly stopped and David ran into her. They both crashed to the floor in a heap and Dolly began to frantically claw and elbow at David. "Get off of me! Hurry!" she cried.

David rolled to the side and tried to get his knife out. He drew it and held it up toward the dimly visible entryway just in time to see the darker shadow of the *other* spidering in. David braced himself for the impact, but instead the world erupted in light and shrieks.

The light cut through his eyes, blinding him, but in the instance that it did he had a vision that burned into his mind.

Dolly, half-risen from the floor, with eyes closed and her hand thrust out toward a figure that looked like a skeleton wrapped in tight black flesh. It had no features save for a wide hungry mouth full of sharp black teeth and tiny deep-set black eyes.

The room was filled with the other's hissing shrieks and another lower, more constant hiss. A pungent sulfurous smell bit his nostrils. As his vision cleared, he realized that the room was full of bright green light and that it came from an impossibly sustained flame Dolly held in her hand. The *other* was completely daunted by the light. It hissed at her and tried to come around the light but she kept the flame between them. Her other hand fumbled under her cloak for something and came out with a shiny metal tube, slightly ovular, bent so as to fit snuggly in her hand. She pointed this at the *other* and there was a line of blue light that streaked from the tube into and through the *other*. It lasted for less than a heartbeat, but after it was gone it seemed to David that the line hung as a vague red memory in the air. The *other* now lay motionless on the ground and the smell of burnt flesh mixed with the odor of sulfur.

David stood rooted to the spot, too dumbfounded to even question what he'd seen. Dolly turned to him and spoke in a commanding voice. "We must go now. The noise will bring more or worse." With that she ran out the doorway. David followed, but with a little more distance than before.

On the street, Dolly tossed away the green flame, which David now saw was coming out of the end of a brown cylinder. The flaming cylinder landed in the middle of the street but didn't burn out. David paused for a moment, thinking what a help such a weapon might be.

Seeming to read his thoughts, Dolly called back at him in a hushed but urgent tone. "It'll burn out soon and can only be used once!"

David gave one last longing look at the green fire and followed Dolly up the street. They ran six blocks when they heard the first of the *others* arrive at the tiny green flame. David saw the pinpoint of light eclipse again and again as the *others* searched the area. Some would hunt by sight but others would hunt by smell and these were surely already on the trail.

Dolly rounded a corner and took out her knife and cut a strip off of her cloak. She wiped David's sweaty brow with it and tossed it into a sewer grate. It was a trick that Dob had taught David. The others would prefer to go down into their own habitat if prey went that way and would search for a sewer opening that would lead to where ever the grate pipe led. Dolly sprinted on and finally paused in front of a huge apartment building, a section in ruins. She moved to go inside but David stopped her.

"You don't know what's in there!" he said.

"Yes I do." She wrenched free of his grasp and ran inside, pausing beside the door to point to a yellow and black circular glyph.

"That means there's a shelter here." She plunged inside and David followed.

Inside the building, Dolly produced another light. This one didn't create the flash or sulfurous flames as before, but emitted an even cone of white light that radiated out nearly thirty feet. David stared at the light in awe. Dolly turned to him and, seeing his face, handed the light over to him.

"It's just a flashlight. You used to be able to find them all over the city, but the batteries died a long time ago. This one charges when you walk."

David looked at the eight inch long aluminum tube. He pressed the black rubber button and the light went out. He pressed it again, causing the cone of light to return.

"Where did you find this?" he asked.

"In a place that the old ones had prepared."

David offered the light back to her.

The room they were in was too wide for the flashlight to give any indication of what it contained, but near at hand were overturned and broken chairs strewn across thick, rotting red carpet. Dolly led to the right, staying close to the wall. The wallpaper had peeled back in crumbling waves. They came to the corner of the room and continued along the wall. Fifty feet further on was a black metal door. The yellow and black glyph was posted beside it. Dolly opened the door into a narrow interior stairwell that continued down three flights. The stairs were littered with trash–paper, cardboard, plastic and even a couple of things that looked to David to be flashlights, though these examples were brightly colored plastic. At the bottom of the concrete stairs was more trash and evidence of a fire, though it was very old. There was another door to the right and it hung half off its hinges. Above the door was the symbol and a word.

"It says it's a shelter," Dolly said as she passed through.

Inside was a short hallway and at the end another heavy steel door. Dolly pulled it open with a loud creak. It opened on a long and narrow concrete room. Each side was lined with benches and shelves mounted above them. Whatever had been on the shelves had long ago been pilfered and now only bits of plastic and old cardboard remained. David was contemplating the wisdom of staying in the place when his heart froze in his chest. The door at the top of the stairwell was being opened. It creaked slowly and then stopped.

David and Dolly stood very still, listening to the silence, then came a sound. It was a long sharp inhalation of breath, like someone sniffing a pleasant aroma. Then it was followed by the sound of something huge, moist and segmented dragging its bulk forward.

"Inside, now!" Dolly hissed as she pushed him in and followed behind him, closing the door as she did. When they were safely inside, she spun a large wheel on the door that slid a double slide latch into opposing slots on the metal frame. The metal began to ring with impacts a moment later. The thing they had heard was throwing itself against the door, which boomed every time a blow fell. Dolly didn't waste time at the door.

"It will give up before dawn." Then she turned and began searching the room.

David watched her. She looked at everything, taking a steady inventory of what they had to work with. He noticed that the walls were covered in graffiti, not the fading masterpieces that still clung to bridges and alley walls, but the crude graffiti the tribes used. This had once been a home for some lost tribe.

David sat down on one of the wall benches. "I have questions. You need to give me answers."

"I'll try," she said as she uncovered a couple of white candles in the debris. She lit one of these with a match and switched off her flashlight. They sat with the candle between them, lighting their faces and making the rest of the room disappear into an endless darkness—an eternal darkness.

"Do you ever dream about the dead?" she asked.

"Sometimes."

She smiled and looked him directly in his eyes. She was very beautiful and very sad, each aspect lending gravity to the other. "The dead dream about you, too."

"Go on," he said.

"The dead are out there right now. They are calling to you, to your tribe. Nobody hears them when they're awake, but sometimes when you sleep, their voices can carry over. I'm different though. When I sleep the dead talk to me. They know me and they tell me things. They told me where to look for tools I would need. This," she took out the weapon she had killed the other with, "is a high amplification laser. It was one of the last weapons invented in the wars of the ancestors. The dead came to me in my dreams and told me where to find it. The flare, the flashlight, and other things, they all came from my dreams of the dead."

"Where are the dead?" David asked in a whisper. The other had stopped banging on the door and the silence it left behind now seemed a holy thing.

"In the Necropolitain."

"Is that in The Core?"

"In a matter of speaking," she replied.

David reached out and touched her pale, sad, beautiful face, his black hand sharply contrasting with her ivory skin.

"Is nothing certain with you?" Now David smiled, too.

She put her hand on his. "Nothing is certain."

They left the shelter the following night. The metal door to the shelter was badly scarred by the *other*. They listened carefully and took their time, and before they had gone a block, they ran into more *others*. This time they were able to duck away in time.

"I didn't remember them being this bad down here," David said.

"They weren't. They have been moving steadily toward uptown for a few years now. Something that used to keep most of them out isn't working now. It's going to get worse." She peeked out of the narrow alley they had ducked into. "It looks clear, but we should make for the park, we'll make better time."

David shook his head. "Lurkers. The park is full of them. Always is."

"There will be no lurkers in the park if we go now."

"How do you know that? Did you have another dream?"

She didn't answer but went out into the street and then up the side road toward the park, David following.

The park was six blocks further in the direction they had run from the *other*. Dolly didn't take the precautions of their earlier pace and David didn't argue. Too much in his world was changing, too many strange and terrible things. David had quested for some ephemeral 'solution' in his youth, but here, now, running just ahead of him truly was 'The Solution' or at least the door to it.

They came out of the apartment canyons suddenly. The park ran out of sight in both directions. David fought his instinct to hide near the buildings across the street as Dolly went to the sidewalk along the park. She picked up her pace more now, almost jogging.

David never understood why they called this a park. Every park he had seen was full of vines and dead trees. This park, the largest in the city that he knew of, was surrounded by a high concrete wall punctuated here and there by solid metal gates. Lurkers always patrolled the perimeter, or had until tonight. Old Dob had said this was where the cidds had been thickest when they were still around and that if you scaled the twenty foot wall you could still find cidds inside.

"What's inside?" David had asked him.

"Nothing but flat ground and in the middle of it all a giant dome. I perched up on the wall once when I was younger and saw it, heard it, too. It hums, real low, but it hums. The cidds were all around it. I think it's where they come from."

Now Dolly was nearly running and David, who was as fast and persistent as any hunter, was having trouble keeping up. "Please, give it a rest for a second," he said as he struggled to catch his breath.

Dolly turned to him and David was surprised to see that her face was pale and calm, without a hint of color to mark her exertions. "We have to move quickly. The path is only going to be clear for a little while and we need to get to our destination before daybreak."

"Before daybreak? We're going all the way past the big towers? That will take at least another night." David pulled himself up and leaned heavily on the wall. Looking toward the towers, he was surprised to see how close they now were.

"If we skulk around in every shadow maybe, but I'm telling you the path is clear, at least for the moment. We must hurry," she said and took off, her pace only slightly slower.

David groaned but followed as best he could. His legs became leaden, his lungs burned, and in his side was a sharp, agonizing pain. He was ready to call a halt, to force Dolly to rest, when, without warning, they were past the park and at the base of the towers.

David stopped and stared straight up, his mouth hanging open. There were tall buildings on his side of the city, buildings of thirty, forty, even fifty floors, but they were spaced apart and didn't seem to have the bulk that the far towers suggested.

Now, at the feet of the dark monoliths, he could see they were of an entire new order of vastness. There were towers of eighty, and one hundred stories here, some very much taller than that. Some were pitted and burnt and looked like long, rotten teeth, while others were strangely pristine with all their glass intact. He would have stood for an hour, looking up had Dolly not taken his hand and urged him onward. David followed, but stumbled several times as his eyes went involuntarily to the sky that was now so distant.

On the walls of the buildings, he saw more evidence of the old tribal graffiti, the marks of tribes long gone. There were also small pits all over the stone, concrete, and even the glass of the buildings' lower floors. David stopped at a corner that was particularly riddled and pointed at them. Dolly stopped, too, and saw where he pointed.

"They're bullet holes, from the early warfare among the different tribes. They all wanted to hold the big buildings back then." She moved down the avenue and David followed. He had heard of bullets and old Dob had shown him a gun once and explained how it worked, but he had never really seen the result of one before, and the bullets had all run out before Dob was born.

David was nearly ready to stop again when Dolly suddenly slowed and turned back to look at him. "We're nearly there. We can slow down some if you need to."

David nodded his head, meaning he wanted to, and Dolly stopped for a moment to let him catch his breath. When he finally did he asked, "I...I didn't know it was possible to cover so much ground in one night."

"You can't normally. Tonight is special."

David didn't understand. "What do you mean? How is it special?"

"The dead know you're coming. They arranged the path."

David felt his skin go cold. He closed his mouth, his breath now puffing through his nostrils. He looked Dolly over, pale, small, young, yet utterly unaffected by their dash across the city. She had weapons that David had never heard of, that Dob had never heard of.

Finally he came to a conclusion. "You're one of them. You're one of the dead."

Dolly didn't portray any emotion or reaction. "No, I'm not, but I can talk to them. I can hear them."

"Oh, yeah? And what do the dead say?"

"Come home."

David suddenly turned and broke into a run. He ran in the direction of the park, then took a side street to the right. He would make for the river and work his way back to East Harlem. He had just crossed the street when something hit him in the back and he went down hard, planting his face into the asphalt. Stars shot through his vision and blood erupted from his lips.

He heard Dolly's voice in his ear. "You can't go back that way. There are *others* all over the place. You'd never make it. If you want to save your tribe, you have to go with me to the gate! You have to go with me now."

David struggled for a moment longer, but Dolly was very strong and she had his arm twisted behind him in a way that hurt the more he fought. Finally, he spit out blood and said, "My tribe will die without me."

"I promise you, you will be with your tribe again. You must go with me just this little bit more." She climbed off his back and released his arm.

David climbed to his knees. They were sore and bloody from the fall. He turned to face her and when she saw his face, she grimaced.

"I'm so sorry, David. I didn't mean to hurt you, but if you had gone much further you would have died."

David didn't reply, only held out his hand in the direction they had been traveling. Dolly chewed her lower lip in a gesture that made her look very much thirteen, then she turned and led the way.

It wasn't far; three blocks down and one to the right. There was a break in the towers and in the midst of the break was a large, low columned building that had wide stone steps leading up to the entrance. Lions on stone plinths stood guard on the steps. On one of the columns flanking the entrance was the blue haven glyph. Dolly made her way up the steps.

"There's no tribe here?" David asked, his mouth throbbing as he did so.

"No," Dolly said, not turning around, "this was never a haven."

At the top of the steps were heavy bronze doors and Dolly pulled one open and held it for him. "It's just inside."

David didn't hesitate. He entered, and discovered the largest library he had ever seen. It was richly appointed with chairs and tables and there wasn't a speck of dust on anything. More importantly there were lights. Hanging from the high ceiling were scores of small but bright white lights that made the room seem to glow. In the middle of the room was a single chair with an adjustable metal halo on it, just like the ones in David's haven.

"What is this place?" David asked.

"The last door," Dolly said and slid an arm around his waist. "The chair is a gate."

"So the chairs in the havens, why couldn't we just use them?"

"They have been cut off for years and years. This one was rebuilt just for the tribes."

"Who rebuilt it?"

"They did." She looked up then and David followed her gaze.

From above the ceiling lights, the lurkers descended, a dozen of them, each floating silently down through the air, like a feather dropped from a height. David's heart raced, pounded in his chest, but he held firm where he stood. Dolly, somehow hearing his panic, put her hand on his chest. "Hush, everything is okay, they keep the gate."

The lurkers hovered just above the ground now. They were shaped like people in heavy, rotted purple robes. Inside the hoods were empty eye sockets and skeletal metal faces. On their backs were stiff black wings.

"They were built to look like angels, but the environmental conditions wore away their exteriors. By the time they got here, they weren't nearly as inviting as they were supposed to be," she said.

Dolly walked to the nearest lurker and put her hand on its shoulder. In response, it raised its own blackened, clawed hand and put it on her arm in an act that was somehow tender.

"They have been trying to bring you all home for so long. I know they must miss the makers," she said.

David walked to a lurker, his heart still pounding, his face throbbing. He looked into its hooded metal face, then stepped back and put out his hand in the oldest of gestures. The lurker shifted its head slightly to look at the hand David held up, extended its own, and shook David's hand.

"You're not lying," David said. "But what are you?"

"I'm something like they are. It took a lot longer to make me, and the place where things like us can still be built is half a world away. It was a long journey."

"So there was no Dolly?"

"Yes, there was a Dolly," she smiled. "She was the one who let us know that you were all here. That was nearly one hundred years ago. The story I told about myself was Dolly's story, it just wasn't recent. Dolly could read and write and she found an active gate and went into the Necropolitain. She spoke to the dead on behalf of the tribes and they were moved. They pulled back the civil defense drones and sent the lurkers. They were supposed to bring you all home, but they failed to realize how resistant you would be, how your long struggle would change you. The civil defense drones couldn't attack a portal sight, places with the symbol you call the glyph, and by the time the lurkers came the tribes had discovered this and formed the havens. The dead decided to let you be and bring you in one by one when the lurkers managed to catch you."

"Why? Why let us live in such misery? And why didn't you just tell us that when you first came?"

Dolly shook her head sadly. "You were being looked after as best we could. The lurkers keep the *others*, the mutants, away. They corral you toward the food stashes they create. They even test the cans for radiation and contagion. When scurvy hit the tribes they gathered the food that would stop it. But if I had stood up at story time and told this tale, that the lurkers are your friends, and you should let them carry you away, would any of you have believed me?"

"No, of course not," David conceded.

Dolly continued. "The reason I came is that things are degenerating in the world. The mutagenic acceleration is impossible to predict and the civil defense drones don't think they can hold the city perimeter much longer. New, more dangerous xenoforms are appearing from the wastes. I'm sorry, what I'm saying is that the city is getting ready to be overrun by the others, and even if you survive for a while, the very things that make them are steadily destroying every person in your tribe. There will be no more children that you could recognize as such. It's time to come home, David." Dolly walked to the chair and when she neared it the halo began to glow a bright blue. "Your neuropathic network will be held in quantum suspension then transferred to the data core about five miles below the city, in other words, you're going to leave your body. Don't worry, there is a new one waiting for you."

David walked to the chair and sat down as the lurkers made a semi-circle around him.

"What are they doing?" he asked.

"They're watching history," she said. "For them, this is the beginning of the end of their duty here. They want to go home, too. Hopefully they can soon." She adjusted the halo to hang at temple level around his head.

"One last thing, Dolly."

"Yes, David."

"Why did you come for me?"

"The man that taught me to count to ten twice on each finger told me that if I could get you to go through, the rest of the tribe would follow."

"Dob? Dob is there, too?"

Dolly leaned in and kissed the top of his head. "Have a safe journey, David."

There was a building noise like greater and greater volumes of air being forced through a narrow opening. David's eyes grew wide, then they slowly closed as his body collapsed. Hanging in the circle of the halo was the faint white tracery of a brain, tiny luminous lines connecting and dividing, throbbing with thought, memory, and senses. Then the white traces began to pull toward the brightly glowing halo which drank them into its own light, then they were gone.

David was gone. The halo became dull metal once more.

The lurkers dispersed in all directions, drifting slowly out to do what duties they had. One remained behind with Dolly. It gently picked up David's body in its arms and carried it toward the door.

Dolly watched it go.

A GREATER LOVE

DANE T. HATCHELL

It had been two years since a coronal mass ejection from the sun reached out and slapped the Earth. The solar plasma charged the Earth's magnetosphere with trillions of watts of power, but the planet's natural defenses weren't strong enough to protect the electronic age that sustained mankind.

The cosmic particles from the solar storm took out the communication satellites first. Cell phones, GPS devices, ATM machines, anything and everything that depended on the orbiters for transferring information, went silent. Television broadcasts went black, and national radio syndicated programs turned to white noise. Not long after, every electronic device on the planet began to fail. The induced currents from the solar plasma overloaded circuits with massive amounts of stray electrons, causing them to overheat and burn out. And as devastating as it was to lose every computer, every vehicle, and every power plant, it was the resulting fires that set mankind on the path to extinction.

Nearly every electronic component was overwhelmed by the surge of energy. Integrated circuits smoked, transistors melted, and capacitors popped. The electrical wiring in every house, and every building, heated past the point of melting its insulation to burst into flames.

Planes dropped out of the sky as their engines failed. Power plants overloaded and burned, cars coasted to a stop and burned, and refineries and chemical plants exploded. The sky turned black with smoke, and millions of pounds of toxic waste was released into the atmosphere and spread across the Earth.

The death toll that day, and over the next two years, amounted to billions. A fact unknown to those who still struggled to survive. Man was a dying species, but had no way of knowing it.

Survivors had to rely on themselves now, as there was no longer a government to tell them how to live, or provide them with care. No rules and no laws. As far as religion went, many had given up on hope in God.

But there was one man who believed that God had deliberately turned his back on mankind and his name was Thadious Cain.

Cain grew up in a small town that had two supermarkets, one church, and one school. His mother was left widowed when he was just an infant. Cain never knew his father, and his mother never so much as went on a date after his death.

Cain's mother had told him to make God his father in life. She was very devoted to her faith, and she and Cain had studied the scriptures together for all the years that she lived.

It wasn't long after Cain's sixteenth birthday that she died. Then, he was forced to make it on his own, until he was old enough to enlist in the U.S. Army. He joined with the Sixty-Eight W(hiskey) branch of the Army, and was deployed as a combat medic. One combat medic was required to be in attendance with a platoon for every hazardous mission. He was to provide aid in case of accident or injury on location, and to provide immediate medical treatment to the wounded soldiers. And there was never a mission that he didn't have to risk his life for others.

His years in the army shaped him into the man he was today. And after four tours in Afghanistan, his faith as a believer had been tested in ways he could never have imagined.

The thing that hath been, it is that which shall be; and that which is done is that which shall be done; and there is no new thing under the sun, Cain remembered, the scriptures continually flashing in his thoughts.

"What a load of crap," was his rebuttal.

As a youth, the scriptures inside him served as nothing but obligations to his faith. But the words were hollow, rarely touching him on the inside. It wasn't until his years in the military that the spirit began to speak to him, as the horrors of war tested his sanity. He returned to the scriptures for answers, answers to all the madness going on around him. And one day when he didn't think he could go on anymore, the spirit removed the scales from his eyes, and his faith grew to trust the Lord and His word.

Cain ended his career in the service because of a *calling* the spirit had put inside him. He learned of a small church in a rural town in Tennessee that needed a youth minister from his Pastor from his hometown. And after a long bus ride and one interview, the designated Committee for Faith Baptist Church unanimously agreed that he was just the type of man they wanted to lead their children into adulthood.

When the solar storm hit, Cain had been alone, away on a personal retreat several miles from his home. He was staying in a cabin by a pond that was owned by the church, as modern as any cabin that would have existed two hundred years ago. He wasn't totally alone though, his dog Jackson was with him; he didn't figure God would mind.

After the sky lit up and his truck caught on fire, he fully expected the Heavens to open and to see Jesus riding in on a white horse. Surely the Kingdom of God was at hand. But nothing of the sort happened. No signs came down from the Heavens, only black smoke rising up from the ravaging fires on Earth.

When he left the cabin to go home, he returned to a world of chard remains and ash. The devastation he witnessed was far greater than anything he had seen in war. The totality of the civilization he knew was gone; erased in the blink of an eye. He had been devoted to a kind and loving God, and now this was his reward.

All things, Cain thought, God had done this deliberately.

Cain was angry, he was angry at God. Every fire he passed was an unrepentant sacrifice of God's greatest creation, man. And those fires incinerated any subservience Cain's soul felt towards his once loving, but now fearful, Master.

What was the point of all this destruction? Was this just some sort of experiment to see how the 'ant nest' survived a crushing boot?

And we know that all things work together for good to them that love God.

Bull! There was no good anymore, there was no evil anymore, there was only right and wrong.

Cain knew the difference between right and wrong, but he didn't believe that God did. And if God did, He certainly wasn't concerned about doing right anymore. Cain hoped God was a He, because the first thing he was going to do when he met Him beyond the Pearly Gates, was to kick Him in the nuts.

Cain knew that his time, and the time for man, was short. His self determined mission would be to escort mankind into extinction with love and dignity.

He shall feed his flock like a shepherd: he shall gather the lambs with his arm, and carry them in his bosom, and shall gently lead those that are with young.

And that is exactly what Cain had been doing over the past months, wandering the highways of man, and herding 'the sheep'.

Cain had been heading north for several days, and figured himself to be somewhere in western Kentucky. His Australian Cattle dog, Jackson, trotted along by his side. The dog was the only living memory he had of a life gone forever.

The two lane highway he was traveling was sparsely populated with burned and melted vehicles, a sight now often seen on roads seldom traveled. Grass was intruding onto the asphalt, and decaying leaves piled undisturbed along both sides of the road.

A snake bite to his left calf a year ago had left him with a slight limp. The snake wasn't poisonous, but the bacteria from the bite caused some muscle and nerve damage. It was with the aid of a staff in the form of a wooden baseball bat that he made his trek down the deserted highway. His protection came from two Colt 1911 .45 pistols, each holstered and cocked on his hips.

The sun signaled that it was midday, and a group of hickory trees not far off the road looked inviting to the weary traveler. He wiped his brow with the back of his arm. The temperature was unusually warm for this time of year. It had been even hotter last year, but no one had the luxury to worry about global warming anymore. Cain changed direction and headed for the trees, Jackson following closely behind.

As they approached the trees, the terrain began to slope. He could hear running water and followed the sound to find a fast moving spring.

He was surprised to see a young man lying on his back near the water. The man was motionless, his eyes closed and his shirt was covered with blood.

Cain approached with caution, but the young man was oblivious to his presence.

"Hello, my brother. Don't be afraid, you aren't alone. I'm here to help you," Cain said.

The man opened his eyes to a squint, and attempted to prop himself on his right elbow to see who was speaking to him. Flies were dancing over his blood-drenched clothing, while gnats swarmed around his eyes and head.

"My name is Cain, when were you injured?"

"Sanchez...I'm Sanchez...it happened yesterday....I was with some other people, a married couple. We'd been traveling together for about a month." He paused and wet his lips. "The guy didn't like the way his wife was looking at me. We fought, I lost, end of story."

Cain's thoughts went back to his time in boot camp; his Drill Sergeant's name was Sanchez. "Let me take a look at you, I'm a medic."

Sanchez was too weak to protest. He lay again on his back, and covered his eyes from the sun with his forearm.

Cain unbuttoned the bottom half of the wounded man's shirt and carefully peeled it back. It was an open injury, a nasty knife wound that had torn open the abdomen, allowing part of the bowel to be exposed outside of the body.

"How bad is it, Doc?" Doctors were equivalent to saviors nowadays and Cain had now become this man's.

"Bad enough. I'll clean you up the best I can and then I'll try to get you put back together. It's in God's hands after that," Cain lied.

"You got anything to eat? I'm starving," Sanchez asked.

"I believe I have something you will like." Cain removed his pack and searched for a special can. Jackson wandered over and gave Sanchez the full sniff treatment, startling the man with a lick to the face.

"Hey, Doc, who's this?" Sanchez smiled and reached out to pet the dog.

"That's Jackson. Here, how do canned peaches sound?" Cain popped the top of the can and helped Sanchez sit up. The man drank the syrup first, and then tilted the can further back and ate the tender slices of the sweet peaches.

"Man, that was good. I haven't had peaches in over a year, they're my favorite," He laid back down, feeling somewhat revitalized. "Thanks, Doc, I don't know how I'm ever gonna repay you. This world's gone so crazy; you don't meet good men like you anymore."

"My friend, I have but one purpose left in life and that's to help all those in need." He paused and said, "Love is patient, love is kind, bears all things, believes all things, hopes all things, and endures all things, if I have not love, I am nothing."

"That's beautiful, Doc. Is that from the Bible? I'm Catholic you know." Sanchez adjusted the chain around his neck to expose a Saint Christopher medal.

"Yes, it was," Cain said softly.

"Okay, Doc, I'm feeling stronger now. Go ahead and put me back together," Sanchez reached out and put his hand on Cain's forearm and gave it a slight squeeze, "Doc, you're an angel."

Cain smiled a reassuring smile. He then unsnapped his right holster and pulled out his .45, pointed it between Sanchez's panic stricken eyes, and pulled the trigger. Jackson yelped, the explosion sending birds flying from the tall grasses by the spring.

The bullet left a hole the size of a silver dollar in the front of the man's forehead, and blew out a hole the size of a cantaloupe in the rear. Sanchez's eyes were now void of life, and void of pain.

Cain looked up at the sky and said, "See? There, it's over. Just like that. No need for him to suffer. How long would it have taken You to kill him, Lord? A few more hours? A few more days? Well, don't worry, I took care of him. I gave him peace."

Cain put the .45 back in its holster, reached into his small pack, and pulled out a folding shovel. The soil was soft by the water, and it didn't take very long to dig a shallow grave. *Ashes to ashes, dust to dust*, flashed through his mind as he slowly dug the grave.

* * *

Two days had passed and Cain continued northward. He didn't give his direction much thought, as he trusted in the spirit to lead him. Along his two year journey, he had changed the lives of the many he had met. He preserved their humanity, inspired hope, and taught them how to live, and die, with dignity.

A limestone road branched off the main highway; he followed it with his eyes to see that the road led to a river. The road was fairly straight, and through the trees he could make out a large burned building, a large covered structure of some sort. There were people by the covered structure.

"Well, Jackson, it looks like we've found a new home," Cain said, looking down at the dog.

Jackson looked up at him and tilted his head as Cain started his walk down the road. Jackson put his nose to the ground and found just the right spot, lifted his leg, and peed. He scratched the ground in satisfaction, then chased after his master.

One side of the burned building was located next to the river, and by the looks of it, he suspected it to have once been a sawmill. Years ago, he imagined that a water wheel was used to produce the mechanical energy to power the mill. There was no water wheel now, only a blackened diesel generator that stood as a memorial for an age that would never be again.

The covered structure on the opposite side was huge. It had a metal roof, and stood over twenty feet tall. It was over a hundred feet wide and at least fifty feet deep. It looked more like a pole barn, not having any walls on the outside and had been used in times past to store timber and rough cut lumber.

Underneath the structure, walls made of wood had been erected to create several individual 'rooms'. These were newly and crudely built, and could only provide a minimum amount of protection and privacy.

Cain was fifty yards away from the structure when his thoughts were interrupted by a series of whistles; someone was sounding a 'red alert'. Then he heard a man's voice shout, "Hey! We got a loner!"

Cain stopped and ordered Jackson to sit. He raised his right hand as if he was surrendering, and supported his weight on the bat with the other.

Two men came running into view, each carrying a long gun of some kind. Cain remained still with a friendly smile on his face. The two men slowed as they neared, and came to a complete stop when they were within a few feet of him. Each man kept their rifles pointing to the ground, but Cain knew they could be raised and fired in less than a second.

"What you doing here?" a tall blond man asked.

"I was traveling the highway and I saw that this road led to a river; then I saw people. I came to offer you my assistance," Cain said.

"Your assistance? Why would you think we need your help? I think it is more like you're looking for something to steal," a balding man with a thick red beard said.

"Friend, God has sent me forth in these wicked times to sow the seeds of His love. Some of the seeds fall on bad ground, and God's love doesn't grow. Some seeds fall on fertile ground, and the people harvest all that God has to offer. He who has ears to hear, let him hear."

"What are you, some kind of nut-ball preacher? We don't need no preacher," the bearded man said.

"I'm a healer," Cain said softly.

"A healer, like those televangelist used to do? You gonna touch us on the head and we gonna fall down all healed? I don't think so," the blond man chuckled.

"My words heal to those that listen. But my hands also heal." Cain paused. "Sergeant First Class Thadious B. Cain, combat medic 68 W United States Army." He offered his right hand in friendship.

The two men look at each other and the blond said, "You're a doctor?"

"I'm as close to a doctor as you can be without having a piece of paper from a University that says so." Cain's hand remained hanging in empty air.

"Sam, we can use a doctor, Jeffery's wife's in labor, and she ain't doin' too good," the blond man said excitedly.

"I...I don't see how we have much choice, Bill. Mary needs a doctor real bad." Sam turned and looked at Cain. "All right, Cain, you can come with us. But you're gonna have to give up your pistols."

Cain smiled and slowly removed his backpack and placed it on the ground in front of him. The two men raised their rifle barrels his way. He knelt and opened the pack. "My guns can do no harm if

I keep them in here." He slowly pulled the .45's from their holsters and put them in the pack, then zipped it up. "There, no harm, please bring me to the woman in need so I can help her."

The two men looked at each other and then lowered their weapons. "That dog, we don't have food for that dog," Sam said, nodding his head in the direction of Jackson.

"The dog can take care of himself," Cain said and looked down at the animal. "Don't you, Jackson?" The dog lifted his front legs and placed them on Cain's waist. Cain patted Jackson's head while he bumped Cain's hand with his nose.

As they made their way to the structure that Bill had referred to simply as 'the barn', the people were gathering to meet the new stranger.

There were five children playing close to the river, their ages ranging between five and ten years old. Four men, five women, and one child formed a crooked line in front between the playing children and Cain.

Cain thought the bunch looked relatively healthy, but their faces were tired and scarred from the harsh judgments of God. He walked up to them and purposely looked each one directly in the eye, then gave them a smile and a nod. He knew that the eyes were the window to the soul. And he wanted to show them all the love he had to offer.

"Hello, my name's Cain, and this is my dog, Jackson." The adults stood stiffly with accusing eyes, and in silence. But when the children by the river saw the dog, they ended their game and ran and stood behind their parents.

"He's a doctor, we're going to take him to see Mary," Bill said.

Sighs of relief went out, and the tension of the crowd seemed to dissipate.

"A doctor, oh my, praise God!" a woman's voice rang out.

"Indeed, praise the Lord!" Cain added. His eyes wandered again across the people standing before him. His pale green eyes were penetrating, but projected a feeling of trust. The one child that had not been playing was standing next to who he guessed was her father. She was partially hiding behind his right leg, peering around the outside of his thigh. He didn't think she couldn't be any older than six.

Was she just shy? Perhaps, but there was something not right, he could sense it. There were signs that only a trained eye could detect. She was continually scratching herself between her legs. She either had an infection or some type of irritation. One of her arms was casually looped around her father's inner thigh. It was too personal, and too familiar for normal contact between an adult and a child.

The father realized that Cain had fixated his attention to this and quickly moved her arm and held her hand, as if nothing unusual was to be noticed.

"Hey, is your dog friendly?" a young boy asked.

"Why, yes, and he just loves to play. Parents, is it all right?" Cain gave the group a questioning look. The parents voiced their approval, and the children all gathered to pet the dog. Then ran off to play with Jackson trailing them in hot pursuit, barking happily.

"Let's go see Mary," Sam grabbed Cain by the arm and led him under the shade of the barn. The barn wasn't wired for electricity, and thus, was unaffected from the solar event. The room that Mary was in faced the outside towards the river, the makeshift door wide open to allow in the natural light.

They could hear Mary as they approached; she was panting heavily and moaning in pain. Sam gave a knock on the door and the three entered the room. Jeffery, her husband, was holding her hand with a frantic look on his face.

"Jeffery, this is Cain, he's a doctor, and he's here to help Mary," Sam said.

"A doctor, thank God! Please help her, Doctor, she's in so much pain," Jeffery said exhaustively.

"How long has she been in labor?" Cain asked.

"I don't know...almost twenty-four hours."

"Not good, that's not good. Mary, how you holding out?" Cain asked and moved to her side and held her other hand.

"The pain...the pain is awful. I don't think I'm going to make it," she said.

"Look, you just have to hang in there. I'm going to get you through this." He pulled out a vial of morphine and a syringe from his pack, then unwrapped the syringe and filled it with several cc's of the drug. "Mary, I'm going to give you this, it'll ease the pain." Mary nodded her head with understanding.

"Hey, wait, will that hurt the baby? I didn't think you were supposed to give drugs during labor?" Jeffery asked.

"It shouldn't matter. I'm going to work fast enough that the morphine won't have time to have an effect on the child." Cain tied off Mary's arm with a rag and gave her the injection. She relaxed and laid back with a sigh.

"Mary, you're going to have to help me. Breathe and push when I tell you." She was aware enough to comply and followed Cain's instructions. After about forty minutes, she delivered the child, then passed out in exhaustion.

Cain held out a tiny baby girl. She might have weighed four pounds. There were ten fingers and ten toes, but half of the left side of her skull was missing, and her brain was exposed. Cain held the child in both hands and turned to face Jeffery.

"Oh my God no...no," Jeffery sobbed, "Why, this is horrible..."

"I'm sorry, Jeffery," Cain said softly.

Jeffery wanted to hold the child, but stopped himself. He knew better than to allow himself to become anymore attached. He turned his back and whispered, "Don't let her suffer. I don't want her to suffer..."

Cain understood, he placed his right hand against the child's nose and mouth, and held it tightly for a full fifteen minutes. Bill and Sam consoled Jeffery while Mary breathed shallowly in merciful sleep.

"She's gone, Sam, God rest her soul." Cain clipped the umbilical cord, and wrapped the dead baby in a towel.

"We were worried about the delivery, we didn't know of any children surviving birth since the Storm. But we hoped. We hoped it would work for us.

"A lot of toxins are still in the air, radiation, too, I imagine," Cain said.

"Why, why did this have to happen?"

"Consider the work of God. For who can make that straight, which he hath made crooked?" Cain said. "Hath not the potter power over the clay?"

Jeffery realized that there are questions that can't be answered in this lifetime. "Please, just take care of Mary."

"I'll make sure she's resting comfortably, I just need to clean her up," Cain said.

"Okay, I want to go and bury my daughter now. I don't want Mary to see her like this."

"I'll stay with her until you get back," Cain assured him.

"God bless you," Jeffery said and left with Sam and Bill close by his side.

"And you and your loss," Cain added and turned his attention to Mary.

He cleaned up the afterbirth, washed Mary as well as he could, and then opened his backpack. He took out his two .45's and put each one back in its holster, then searched until he found a bottle of barbiturates. He emptied about half the bottle's contents into his hand, and then shoved each pill through Mary's anus and into her rectum with his index finger.

Jeffery spent the night with Mary. It was her last night on Earth. She was asleep when Jeffery had returned from burying the baby. He had named his daughter, Shelia, after his mother. Mary never woke after giving birth. Jeffery blamed himself for not staying awake all night to watch her. But he was so tired, and his body overruled his mind. If only he had been awake when she stopped breathing, he, or Cain, might have been able to save her— or so he believed.

Cain had said no to that though, he said that she died from internal bleeding, and that there was nothing that anyone could have done for her. They buried Mary next to her daughter; they had been separated for less than a day, and would spend the rest of eternity together.

The following day, Cain took one of the rooms in the barn and made a makeshift 'examining' room out of it. There were several empty rooms for him to choose from and he wondered how many of this bunch had died over the past two years.

The people were eager to line up and discuss all their aches and pains and show him all their scrapes and bruises. His backpack was full of supplies that he had collected here and there over his travels. Most of the drugs were beyond their expiration date, but they still retained some of there potency.

As Cain had witnessed on others before, almost everyone had some type of skin cancer. This was most likely due to the damaged ozone layer not filtering the harmful UV rays from the sun, though there was no way to know for sure. Most of the cancers were basal cell carcinomas, but a few of the adults had the more deadly melanomas. He reassured them all with a smile that there was nothing to be concerned about.

The shy little girl and her father were the last to be examined; her name was Cindy and he was Ralph. Cain examined Cindy under the watchful eye of Ralph, who stood by with crossed arms and a scowl on his face.

"Tell me, Ralph, how's her health in general? Does she complain about anything?" Cain asked, not looking up. He had a hand-crank LED flashlight and was using it to examine Cindy's throat and eyes.

"Well, she don't talk much since her Mom died," Ralph offered.

Cain unbuttoned her little dress and let it fall down to her feet. He walked around her, looking for skin abrasions, and listened to her heart and breathing with a stethoscope. "Is that all?"

"Sometimes...sometimes she says that it burns when she pees," Ralph said hesitantly.

Cain knelt in front of Cindy and pulled her underwear down. He did a quick look, being careful not to be too invasive, and pulled the underwear back up. "Is she drinking enough water?"

"Well, hell, I don't know. I give her a drink when she asks for it."

Cain pulled the dress up and buttoned it, then gave Cindy a hug and thanked her for being such a good little girl. He examined Ralph mostly in silence, receiving an occasional grunt for a response.

His examination had proved what he suspected; the child was being sexually abused by her father.

Though sexual abuse didn't usually leave physical evidence, Cain had been trained as a Youth Minister to be on the lookout for the signs from the children's actions. Changes in general behavior, inappropriate sexual behavior, the fear of going home after church, things of that nature.

Cindy had shown the signs and her examination confirmed his suspicions. Urination problems were a classic symptom, and her underwear held blood stains that water couldn't wash out.

Ralph put his shirt back on and Cain sent the two off. He then went to his backpack and searched until he found a pen and a writing tablet.

Cain left his room with a determined look on his face. Bill was by the river heating water in a big pot under a coal burning fire. Boiling the water didn't filter out the toxins, but it did kill stomach distressing bacteria.

Cain increased his gait and headed straight for him.

"Bill, we've got a problem," Cain said when he reached him.

"Yeah, what's that?" Bill had an old bellows and was blowing more air on the coal.

"I'm not going to give you all the details now, but it's about Ralph. Go gather all the men and get back here as soon as you can." Cain had a sense of urgency in his voice that Bill picked up on.

"Ralph? Is he sick or something? Is he contagious?" Bill asked.

"No, but it's just as bad. Please, just go and bring all the men back as quickly as possible. Ralph said he and Cindy were leaving to pick berries and he'll be back soon."

Bill left without any further protest and returned within a half hour with most of the men that had been fishing not far down the river. The six men didn't look very happy; this newcomer was disrupting the routine of the day. Cain stood as ridged as a statue as they approached and they could tell something was bothering him.

"All right, Cain, what is it? What's so important that we have to come now?" Sam asked.

"Ralph is sexually abusing Cindy," Cain blurted. He was rewarded with surprised questions as protests erupted from the men simultaneously. "I saw the signs," Cain said. "I did an examination on Cindy and I know it's true."

"I don't believe it," a man named Buddy said.

"I need more proof," another man called Joe said.

"Why should we believe you?" Sam asked.

Cain pulled out a piece of paper, unfolded it, and held it up for all to see. "After the examination I was able to spend a few minutes alone with Cindy," he said. "I drew a picture of a little girl and asked her where her father liked to touch her. She showed me here, here, and here." Cain had circled where the touch points were, and pointed them out with his finger.

"I can hardly believe it," Buddy said.

"Let's confront Ralph," Bill said.

"He'll deny it," Cain added. "And there's something else." He paused then said, "I asked Cindy if she knew if her father had touched any other child...she told me... Kayla."

Gasps went out and Sam swooned and dropped to one knee. Kayla was his daughter. "No...no, this can't be true, not my Kayla." Sam's mind raced to think when something like this could have happened, and what signs did he miss that she was being molested. Cain's lie had pushed the group over the edge.

"Cain, what should we do? How do we handle this?" Jeffrey asked. Cain knew after what he'd done for the man's baby and his wife that he had Jeffery's total trust, Cain's betrayal unknown to him.

"If a man lies with his daughter, he shall surely be put to death," Cain said. He intentionally misquoted the scripture, and he did it to relieve their consciences for what they were about to do.

Ralph and Cindy returned with a gallon bucket full of blackberries. Ralph slowed his stride when he saw the group of people waiting for them—all the men had guns. The solemn look on their faces made him feel uncomfortable and he wanted to run, but he knew there was nowhere to hide.

"Uh...guys? You uhm...you want some berries?" Ralph asked nervously.

Emily, Sam's wife, walked up to Cindy and took her by the hand. "Come with me, Cindy; let's go wash these berries so we can eat them with supper." Cindy took Emily's hand and looked back at her father for permission. Ralph nodded, and swallowed dryly.

"Let's take a walk, Ralph, we've got something to discuss with you," Sam said without emotion.

They traveled along the river for a few hundred yards, and when the area cleared of heavy foliage, Cain called for them to stop.

Ralph stood opposite of the group and Cain stood between him and the rest of the men. Ralph couldn't meet their gaze, the accusing eyes of his jury burning through him.

It was Cain who broke the silence. "Ralph, I stand before you to give you a chance to confess your sins before men and before God." Ralph started shaking and tears streamed down his face. Cain said, "Thy eye is evil, thy body is also full of darkness."

Ralph began to cry uncontrollably.

A sinking feeling of realization fell over the group; this was Ralph's confession. They had all hoped this had been a mistake; they didn't want to deal with this as a reality. But now, they knew they were forced to.

Sam pushed Cain aside and exploded in Ralph's face. "You lousy piece of shit! How could you do that to your own daughter? How could you do that to Kayla? My Kayla!" A look of surprise came over Ralph's face, and before he could protest, Sam's Browning bolt action rifle fired, sending a .308 caliber bullet into his forehead. Brains and blood flew out of the back of Ralph's head and his body fell back a few feet, then slumped to the ground.

The men lifted Ralph and unceremoniously tossed him into the river, the current quickly dragging him under the surface and away from the men. Sam walked away in silence and the rest followed him as they made their way back to the barn.

Little Cindy was told that her father was traveling to the next town, to look for canned goods and medicine. He would be back in a few days and that she would be staying with Sam, Emily, and their children until he returned. She gave a big smile to Emily when she was told this, her teeth now stained from eating the blackberries.

As the day came to an end, Cain readied for bed. He did have a few things left he needed to do, but they were only for him to know about. Tomorrow, he would be going to the coal mine with a few of the other men. It was time to gather more coal for the coming winter.

* * *

A few miles down the road from the barn, was a hill that had once been mined for coal. A cave-in had shut the mine down, and the entrance had been boarded up, all this happening prior to the 1900's.

Jeffery and Tom had known about the mine from stories their grandparents had told them. Before the previous winter, the two managed to open the mine, to then chip out several hundred pounds of coal.

After breakfast, Joe hooked up a mule to a homemade yoke that was rigged to a four-by-eight utility trailer. It wasn't a thing of beauty, but it was surprisingly well balanced.

Cain joined a party of five volunteers for the coal collecting trip.

Tom and Diane, as well as Joe and Bell, were the only childless couples of the group. There was an underlying kinship between the two couples, knowing that they would probably never know the joys of parenthood. Buddy was Bell's older brother, and he joined this outing to ensure there were enough strong backs to get the job done. He left his wife, Cheryl, to tend to their child back at the barn.

The six of them traveled on foot, with Joe leading the mule by the bridle. Jackson had also joined the group, and trotted by the mules heel's, keeping the animal in line. They arrived at their destination in a couple of hours. An overgrown dirt road joined the highway and led to the coal-bearing hill a half mile away.

Cain was surprised that the others were so upbeat in spirit. He supposed they were too naive to realize the dire predicament that they, and all of mankind, were in. He blamed their youth for blinding them from the ultimate truths that tomorrow had in store for them.

There is nothing better for a man than to eat and drink and tell himself that his labor is good, Cain thought. He used to believe that, but even that was vanity to him now.

When they reached the mouth of the tunnel leading into the mine, the group unhooked the mule and tied it under the shade of a tree. Everyone took a water break, including Jackson and the mule.

The utility trailer was loaded with the tools they would be using for the day. There were two pick axes, hammers, chisels, shovels, several five gallon buckets, a wheelbarrow, and a few handmade torches to provide light while they worked. Tom lit two torches using a Zippo lighter, kept one, and handed Joe the other. Everyone grabbed their tool of choice and the group walked single file into the dark, cool tunnel.

The passage was less than fifteen feet wide and ten feet high. Large timbers stood dutifully, propping the dark firmament above. There was a distinct rotten egg smell that burned the inside of Cain's nostrils. He knew it was hydrogen sulfide, just one of the hazards of harvesting the fossil fuel.

Joe left his torch fifteen feet from the entrance, which was halfway from where they would be working. The tunnel ended at the site of the cave-in; it was a wall of crushed and solid coal.

"Okay, guys, let's get busy," Tom said and wedged his torch between two large chunks of rock, the flickering orange flame providing them just enough light to work by. "Cain, gather what you can by hand or use a hammer and chisel. We don't want anything smaller than about fist size. If you end up with bigger pieces, that's okay. We'll bust them up later back at the barn. If you use the shovel to pick up loose pieces, pick the chunks out, we don't need to carry any of the coal dust out of here. It just adds weight and it doesn't burn well. Leave the pick axe work to me and Buddy."

"Okay," Cain said coolly.

In a short time, the wheelbarrow was full of Kentucky's finest bituminous coal. Cain volunteered to wheel it out and load it on the utility trailer. Tom asked Cain if that was a good idea because of Cain's bad leg. Cain ignored the question and rolled the wheelbarrow out in silence. Tom and the others continued working, storing the coal in the five gallon buckets until Cain's return.

Cain made it past the halfway point and had to shield his eyes as he approached the rays of the noon day sun. He parked the wheelbarrow to the side and made his way to where he left his backpack. Jackson was sleeping next to it, with his head between his outstretched front paws. Cain opened the pack and gave his dog a pat on the head, pulled out two M67 grenades, and closed the pack again.

"Stay here, boy," he told Jackson and gave him another pat. Cain walked back in the tunnel and stopped at the halfway point. He could see the five men working in the dim light of the torch ahead. With a grenade in each hand, he pulled the pins out with his teeth and spit them on the ground. He released his *death grip* on the levers and tossed them at his new found friends.

Cain heard Diane say, "What the hell was that?" Just as he turned and ran out of the mouth of the tunnel.

The explosions were simultaneous, and small pellets of coal and black dust rolled out of the mine's entrance. Cain took refuge outside of the blast area and huddled by the side of Jackson, who was startled by the explosion and smoke.

"All is vanity. What profit hath a man of all his labor?" Cain said as he opened his canteen and drank. "Verily I say unto you, they have their reward."

And he had been the one to give it to them.

* * *

Cain was leading the mule down the road, steadying his walk with the bat. Jackson was doing what his genetic programming demanded and was bringing up the rear.

Within a mile of the barn, Cain could make out a man running in his direction. He unsnapped the straps of his gun holsters, making weapons ready for access.

The man was waving his arms and calling out and he saw it was Jeffery. Cain quickened his pace as much as he could and soon the two met.

"Cain!" Jeffery called, almost out of breath. "Cain, you gotta come back," he gasped for more air, "It's Sam...he's been shot..., his gun exploded. He's hurt...real bad. Shrapnel hit his chest and he's bleedin' badly." Jeffery bent over with his hands pressed into his thighs, gasping for air.

"Is he conscious?" Cain asked dryly.

"No...no, but it's bad, real bad. He needs you now. I was coming to get you. Sam was shooting at a snake and his gun exploded. There was a piece of wood jammed in the barrel of his revolver, Bill found it."

Cain remained silent.

"Hey, where're the others? Where's the trailer?" Jeffery was coming out of his panic and back to his senses and he now realized Cain was alone.

Cain hesitated and looked at the ground. "There's been a terrible accident back at the mine."

"An accident! What happened? Where're the others?"

"They were all inside the mine and there was an explosion," Cain said. "I guess the torches lit off a natural gas pocket or something. It was a total cave-in, I'm sorry, but they're all dead."

"Dead? There're all dead?" Jeffery's voice cracked.

"Yes, they were all buried in the mine."

"Oh God, oh no, that's horrible." Jeffery was overwhelmed with grief. "Oh my God, first Mary, then Ralph, then Sam, and now this. This is so bad. I...don't know what I'm going to do. I can't take this, I can't..." Jeffery broke out in tears.

"To everything there is a reason, and a time to every purpose under the heaven." Cain preached.

"No...no...no purpose to this," Jeffery stood with his eyes closed, shaking his head in defiance.

Cain continued, "A time to be born," Cain said and then called out, "Jeffery!"

Jeffery looked up as his name was called, only to see Cain pointing a gun at him.

"And a time to die." The hammer of the .45 slammed on the firing pin, sending a bullet into Jeffery's skull at eight hundred feet per second. All the sorrow, and all the despair that Jeffery was enduring, suddenly was lifted and eternal peace was granted.

Cain pulled a bullet out of his pocket and replaced the spent round. He, the mule, and Jackson, made their way down the lonely road, back to the barn.

* * *

No one was out and about when Cain arrived, except for one of the boys playing alone by the generator. Jackson ran over to him, and the two immediately engaged in a game of chase. Cain casually led the mule to front of the barn and stopped. He didn't hear anything, and couldn't tell which of the rooms that Sam and the others were in.

He stroked the mule on the back of its neck, then scratched him behind the ears. The mule seemed to enjoy it. He then unholstered one of his guns, placed it to the mule's head, and pulled the trigger. The mule let out a cry that almost sounded human, staggered sideways, and dropped to the ground, dead.

Cain's plan continued when Bill came running out of one of the rooms to see what was happening, confirming their location. Bill's gun was out and ready to fire but he lowered it when he saw it was Cain.

"Cain! What happened? Why did you shoot the mule?" Bill asked with surprise in his voice.

"Broke its leg, I had to do the right thing," Cain said as he looked down at the dead mule, his .45 still in his hand.

"Broke a leg? How…" Bill walked over to the mule and knelt down to examine the animal.

Cain put the .45 to the back of Bill's head and fired. The man fell face down into his own blood and brains, gore splattering the mule's belly.

Cain turned to see Bill's wife Linda, and Buddy's wife Cheryl, standing by the opened door. Both were frozen in shock; they had both witnessed the cold blooded murder of Bill.

Cain moved forward and shot Linda in the chest, sending her flying backwards and knocking Cheryl to the barn floor. He entered the room and put a bullet in Cheryl's forehead as she struggled to get up.

His mission was almost completed.

Sam was lying unmoving on a bed. He was either dead or close to it. Emily was the only other adult left alive. The children were crowded in a corner and Emily stood in front of them with her arms outstretched over them.

"Cain, why?" Tears rolled down her face. "Why are you doing this?" she asked, dismayed.

Cain closed his eyes and said, "The Lord has sent me to right the wrongs that he has done to his people." He opened his eyes and looked directly into Emily's, "Thus, I must utterly destroy all that they have, and spare them not, but slay both man and woman, infant and suckling, ox and sheep, camel and ass."

Cain holstered his .45 and transferred the bat from his left hand to his right. He took two quick steps towards Emily and then swung the bat around, catching her just behind the jaw at the back of her skull. Her head buckled from the blow and a sickening *crunch* sounded. She was knocked sideways away from the children, whose piercing screams were now near deafening.

Cain raised his bat and slammed it down again, and again, and again. Skulls cracked and brains splattered. Little Cindy would never have to worry that her father wasn't coming home.

Arms were broken in futile attempts to block the pummeling bat. Little Becky and Sammy no longer had to worry about their father surviving his bullet wound.

Blood and gore colored the wall behind them. Rod and Nancy had been parentless for barely five minutes, but the shock of seeing their mother killed before their eyes would soon fade into darkness.

As the screams stopped, the only sound that remained was of the dull thuds of the bat pounding little bodies and the rapid breaths of Cain.

"You see, God? I'm the strong one. I know how to fix everything," Cain panted. "I have sent them to you; they're yours now. Why don't you put them up in one of those mansions on that street of gold?" Cain bashed the bodies until all their twitching had stopped; he didn't want the little children to suffer a slow death.

Exhausted and bloodied, he went over to Sam and picked up a rag and dipped it in a pan of water. Sam lay unmoving on the bed, breathing shallowly.

Cain wiped his face and hands until all the blood wiped clean. He dipped the rag back in the pan and cleaned his bat; the wood had a few more dents in it now.

He then reached into his pocket and pulled out a four inch folding knife. Cain whispered in Sam's ear, "Or ever the silver cord be loosed." And then meticulously, he sliced through Sam's throat, slicing his carotid artery. "Then shall the dust return to the earth as it was: and the spirit shall return unto God who gave it."

The blood pumped out of Sam's neck and pooled around him. Cain left the room and the barn but before he left he said, "Let the dead bury their dead."

The boy that was left playing with Jackson was hiding behind the generator. Cain made a slow walk towards him, his hand outstretched, and a smile on his face.

"Come, child, come, don't be afraid," he said in a reassuring voice. The boy ducked his head behind the generator. "Now, now, it's okay, everything's going to be fine."

The boy's name was Edward, he was the son of Buddy and Cheryl. He didn't know that his parents were both dead, but had heard the screams and saw Cain as his protector. He hesitantly stepped into view with his eyes fixed to the ground.

"There, that's a good boy! Let me come and see you," Cain said while smiling.

"Where...where is everyone? What happened in there?" Edward's voice was soft and unsure.

Cain knelt before him and brushed the hair away from his bright blue eyes. "Everything's fine, son," Cain said and then placed his hands on the boy's shoulders, enlarging the smile on his face. "Everyone has gone to a special place. All the adults are there, and all the children, too. Even your mother and father, and they're all waiting for you."

His two hands went to the boy's throat, and he squeezed with all the might that his bitter soul could muster.

"You won't have to worry about growing up without a father now, son." Cain's face burned red as his anger built.

Edward's eyes were bulging; he tried to cry out but couldn't.

"No one to take me fishing, no one to take me hunting, or to a ball game, or just to hang out with the other kids," White foam was forming on Cain's lips.

Edward's face turned from red to purple to blue.

"No, just a mother that sat on top of me twenty-four hours a day. Undermining me, criticizing me, sodomizing me when I failed God!" Cain was lost in his personal Hell.

Edward could no longer stand and Cain found himself shaking a limp body. Little Edward had long suffocated to death.

Cain tossed Edward aside and wiped the tears and snot off his face with the back of his hand.

"It is finished!" Cain cried to the heavens. And then another scripture appeared in his mind. "Greater love hath no man than this, that a man lay down his life for his friends."

He repeated the scripture out loud again, laughed to himself, and at God.

"Two thousand years ago, you had a plan. It was a glorious plan, and billions of people put their faith in it. You sent your firstborn to be a propitiation for the remission of sins, well, I thank you for that. But the world is not ending like the Good Book said it would." Cain paused as another scripture flashed in his mind.

"For as many as are led by the Spirit of God, they are the sons of God."

Cain spoke again, "Yes, it's becoming so much clearer now. Now I know why the burden of righting your wrongs was on me. I'm your son. I'm representing you on Earth now. It's my responsibility to rewrite the end! The times have changed, the message has changed. I've been sent here to usher in the new Kingdom of God!"

Cain stood and stretched out both arms from his sides, tilted his head to the sky and yelled, "Greater love hath no man than this, to take the life of his friends!"

The words echoed back, with only the wind and the rustling leaves to respond. The final age was upon the Earth, and Cain had made himself the new savior of mankind.

Jackson walked to his side and pawed him on his thigh. Cain stroked his faithful companion's head and said with a gentle voice, "Let's go, Jackson, there are many wrongs for us to make right."

If there had been one ounce of sanity in Cain before, it was now gone forever.

Man and dog walked down the limestone road and back on the highway, guided by the spirit of God.

A NEW BEGINNING

DAVID BERNSTEIN

Scott Summers grew tired, sloshing around in the sewers as he searched for new ways of getting around the city. He'd seen more rats than he cared to and would never again complain about the small cockroaches he saw in his apartment after seeing the hand-sized ones in the sewer.

He'd been in the Brooklyn drainage system for a good couple of hours, killed only one mutant, and used spray paint to mark the walls. He had layers of cobwebs in his hair, and his ears were still ringing from having to use his gun in the tunnel.

He followed the spray painted arrows leading him to the man-hole that led to the street he lived on. He didn't need directions, knowing the sewers around the neighborhood by heart, but it was always a good idea to follow them. Getting lost in the Brooklyn sewer system wasn't difficult or well advised.

He made it home to his brownstone on Court Street with plenty of time. Dusk had fallen, the time the mutants came out of their hidey holes to look for fresh meat. They came out during the daytime, too, but preferred to avoid the sun it seemed.

The front doors of the building were barricaded, boarded up with plywood and two-by-fours. The only way into the apartment was with a ladder and through a window. Scott used his walkie-talkie to radio that he was home and Rob came to the window and lowered the ladder. He quickly climbed up while Rob watched the street, rifle in hand.

Once Scott was at the top and halfway in the window, Rob went back to the couch to continue a game of chess with Cathy, his wife.

"Hey, guys," Scott said as he walked through the living room.

"How'd the scouting go?" Cathy asked.

"Okay I guess. Found some new tunnels, but didn't go far enough to see where they ended up," Scott called from the kitchen. He grabbed a warm beer, popped the cap, and took a gulp. "Got tired of the shit down there–literally–and the guinea-pig sized roaches, too."

"I was wondering how long you'd be able to stay down there. I don't know how you do it day after day," Cathy said. "Checkmate."

"Damn it woman, I should never have taught you how to play," Rob joked.

Scott entered the living room and took a seat on the recliner.

"Want to shoot some mutants?" Rob asked him.

It normally wasn't a good idea to shoot at them for fun, but times had gotten so boring that they invented a game. They'd climb to the roof via the fire-escape and work their way–the brownstones connected to one another–to the building at the other end of the block and see who could hit a mutant in a certain body part. Shooting a hand or foot was five points; a head was only one point because it was too easy. Knees and shoulders were worth ten, and the jaw without damaging the head was worth twenty points. It was a fun game, but had at one time brought a load of the deformed humans. They had to pour gasoline over the crowd and burn them to help get rid of the large numbers.

Since the nuclear explosions in Russia, the world had changed. It wasn't just the radiation that affected humans, but the chemicals the terrorists mixed with them. Ninety percent of the Earth's population experienced physical and mental transformations, becoming horribly disfigured mutants, crazed and violent toward mankind. The world, as people knew it, had halted, becoming a wasteland of survival and turmoil.

"Nah, not in the mood," Scott said, upending the beer can and finishing it. "I was thinking about raiding the Barnes and Noble again. I've read all the books we took last time."

Cathy had begun reading a vampire book while Rob caressed her head. The apartment was hot and stuffy, but there wasn't much that could be done about it with no electricity.

"I'm down with it," Rob said.

Fifteen minutes later, they had their rifles slung over their shoulders and were climbing out the window. Scott had a katana, a Japanese sword, sheathed to his hip for silent kills, while Rob had a baseball bat resting in one of the mesh drink holders of his backpack.

The moon was full, illuminating the streets. They had flash-lights, but preferred to save the batteries whenever possible.

They traveled down the street, the bookstore only a few blocks from their house. The place was a mess. The front doors and windows had been smashed, allowing anything–mutant or not–to walk right in. Scott knew as long as they were quiet they wouldn't have much trouble.

They entered the store, splitting up and heading to different sections. Rob preferred history while Scott enjoyed fiction, mostly horror.

Thirty minutes later, Rob met up with Scott. "Got my selections," he said, patting his backpack. "You all set?"

"Yeah. Have a bunch of Pinnacle and Leisure horror books, ones I haven't read yet."

"Damn, why the hell do you want to read that shit? Just look outside."

Scott had always loved horror books and after the catastrophic events in Russia, he wasn't sure he'd ever read one again, but he did. They were what he truly enjoyed.

"Ha-ha. Let's go," Scott said and the two headed off. As they came around the corner of a bookcase, Rob's flashlight beam showed on the stomach of a horribly disfigured mutant, its skin almost seared off.

"Shit!" Rob yelled, his voice high pitched. He began scrambling for the gun stuffed in the front of his pants. The mutant grabbed him, its mouth open and coming at his face. He pulled the .38 from his pants and shoved the weapon under the malformed human's jaw.

Neither man had heard the thing approaching. Most of the time a mutant could be heard by its garbled speech or incessant moaning, but this one had a gaping hole where its voice box should have been.

"Wait," Scott said, peering over the top of the bookcase and out onto the street. A group of mutants were in front of the store. But it was too late. Rob's gun fired; the sound deafening in the quiet store. The back of the mutant's head exploded, sending flesh, skull, and brain matter over the bookcase behind it.

"Looks like we're going to have company," Scott warned. The mutants outside turned, bumping off the storefront, working their way to the smashed-out entranceway.

Together, Rob and Scott ran to the back-right corner of the store, leaving their flashlights on. They waved the light at the horde of disfigured humans as the group entered the store. Within seconds, ten were working their way toward the two friends.

"As soon as they get to that bookshelf," Scott said, pointing, "we run along this wall to the center of the store and make a straight run for the exit."

"Gotcha," Rob said, nodding.

As the mutants drew closer, their cries became louder. Though Scott had heard them many times, he never got used to the sound. It was as if they were in agonizing pain. He saw them moving together like a crowd of hungry reporters. "Go!" he yelled, and the two took off.

The two friends reached the center of the back wall. The mutants were coming at them from where they'd just been. Making a bee-line for the exit, Scott grabbed Rob by the collar, stopping him as two more mutants entered the store through the entrance.

"Time to get serious," Scott said, exchanging the flashlight for his sword. Rob's gun had made enough noise and as long as there weren't too many of the wretched creatures to kill, they'd use silent weapons.

"Bat time for me," Rob echoed, pulling his weapon out.

They approached the mutants, Scott slicing the arms off of one before beheading it. Rob smashed his bat in the side of another mutant's head, its eyes popping out of its skull. It was still alive and walking blindly. Rob bashed it again, this time cracking the skull and sending it dead to the floor.

They exited the store with the horde on their tail. Running to the left of the street, back toward their apartment, they spotted a manhole. Scott took out his mini-crowbar, always with him for quick manhole-cover removal, and pried open the lid before he shoved it to the side.

Once inside the gloomy, rank-smelling sewer, Scott pulled the lid back into place so it fell into its slot, careful not to catch his fingers. Above, he could hear the mutants as they clawed futilely at the manhole cover, too simple-minded to figure out how to lift the heavy lid.

The two friends traveled along the sewer line, following green arrows that Scott knew well, having made them himself; the arrows led to a manhole near the local supermarket. They went topside, making sure the area was clear of any of the mutants and headed into the supermarket.

A lone female mutant was inside the store. It looked as if whoever she had been had melted like wax. Half her face was unidentifiable—covered by a flap of thick skin. She wore no shirt; both breasts were missing, seemingly melted and blending into the rest of her body.

Not wanting to make noise with his gun, Rob bashed her head in with his bat, ending her suffering for good. Scott went through the place, grabbing whatever he could find while Rob watched the entrance. Scott managed to find a bag of opened potato chips, outdated Twinkies, two cans of peas, a tub of beef jerky, and a partially opened container of sweetened ice-tea. When Scott's bag was full, he switched positions and watched the entrance while Rob loaded up his bag. It was amazing how many times they'd been to the store and how they still managed to find stuff. Other survivors lived in the area, but they were few and far between. The grocery store on Atlantic Avenue had more food, at least last time they visited it, but neither wanted to travel that far at night.

They headed back inside the sewer tunnel, following the painted arrows again. Five minutes later, they were at the manhole nearest to the apartment. Scott popped his head out of the opening after removing the lid.

He climbed up and looked around to make sure the coast was clear when he thought he heard laughter from an alleyway to the south. He stayed low and listened. "Anyone there?" he whispered.

"What's going on?" Rob asked from below. "Is it clear or what?"

"Yeah, thought I heard something." Scott kept an ear and eye out while Rob clambered out of the manhole. They replaced the iron cover quietly and together headed toward the apartment.

Once safely back inside, they stored the food, popped open a few warm beers, and retold their tale to Cathy.

The next day, shortly after five p.m., Scott heard a crash from downstairs while lying on his bed. Rob and Cathy came running into his room, both with guns in their hands.

"What the hell was that?" Rob asked. Scott was already up. He grabbed his rifle and together they went to the living room.

The windows had black curtains on them. At night, they kept them closed to prevent candle or flashlight illumination from escaping. Mutants, the ones with eyes, were attracted to the light, and gang members looked for it to find places to ransack. There was still daylight outside and most of the drapes weren't closed yet.

Scott glanced outside and down at the street. The crash came again. He counted eight men, dressed in leather with spikes and chains, holding a portion of a telephone pole. A lone man with a Mohawk and black make-up around his eyes stood next to them. Scott recognized him. The man raised his arm into the air then pointed forward toward the apartment building. The men holding the pole charged forward, using it as a battering ram. They disappeared under the overhang and then the crashing sound came again. Scott realized the bastards were trying to break in.

A few months back, while walking the streets, Scott had come upon a gang. He'd counted ten people in total. They had guns, pipes, and baseball bats with nails in them. He watched as they entered a house, smashing the doors in. He heard screams and gunshots from inside. The group was noisy and crude, not caring how much racket they made. After a few minutes, some of the gang members came outside. They had two female hostages with them.

The women were bound at the wrists, crying, and wearing only undergarments. After a few minutes, the rest of the gang came back outside, hooting and hollering like crazed party-goers. The women hostages were carried down the street and into the gloom. Scott wished he could've helped, but there were too many gang members; he wouldn't have stood a chance. But that's how a lot of the world was now. People became worse than the mutants, lawless and out for themselves.

Once Scott was sure the coast was clear, he sprinted over to the house and went inside.

A man lay cut up and bloodied. He was still alive, but barely. Through wheezing breaths, the man asked Scott to kill him and not leave him for the altered ones. Scott knew the man was a goner and obliged him by putting a single bullet through his skull. The gang had made so much noise he wasn't worried about alerting the mutants. If they were coming, a single gunshot wouldn't have mattered.

He searched the rest of the house, finding food in abundance. The gang had ransacked the place from the look of the mess, but much had been left behind. The gang members were probably so high they didn't care about survival. They were just pieces of the apocalypse now.

Scott gathered up as much food as he could carry, finding a backpack and stuffing it to the point the zipper wouldn't close. He exited the house and saw the streets filled with numerous deformed figures. He wished he'd been faster, but hadn't expected to find a man inside asking to be put out of his misery. The noise from the gang had attracted the mutants' attention. He shot three coming up the stairs in the head, dropping them cold. More and more were pouring out of buildings and from around the corners. He dashed back inside, ran to the back of the house, smashed out a window and jumped into the alley. A few of the grotesque creatures were roaming, seeming to come to life upon seeing his presence. He took them out fast with precise shots to the head and sternum until his gun clicked empty. He dropped his gun as a mutant attacked. They danced in a death-struggle as he held the stinking creature at bay—its snapping maw only inches from his face. Its breath was putrid, filled with rotting teeth, but Scott had grown used to the odor after having fought so many of the things already. He managed to shove his opponent to the ground, pull out his knife, and sink it into the mutant's chest, putting it to rest.

More mutants were coming down the alley from his left. He looked to his right and the coast was clear. He took off, rounded the corner, and kept going, finally losing the horde, and making it back home.

"They're trying to break in," Scott told Rob and Cathy as he watched the gang down below.

"Damn, they must have seen one of us," Rob said.

Scott closed his eyes. "When we came out of the manhole, maybe."

"What?" Rob asked.

"I heard laughter. They must've seen us and then watched us enter the apartment." Scott opened his eyes and shook his head. "We got careless."

"We've got to do something," Cathy said. "What's done is done."

"Leave?" Rob suggested.

"No. There's no way we'd make it through without them seeing us. I say we fight," Scott said.

"Yeah, give them something to think about the next time they decide to break into someone's home," Cathy agreed.

Another crash came and this time it sounded like they broke through. The trio heard wild laughter and screams of triumph.

"Grab as many guns as you can, and bring extra clips and ammo," Scott commanded. "It's time to defend our home."

The group of friends hadn't been simply holing up and surviving. They'd realized the world was different and that most likely they'd need to do things–difficult things–in order to not only survive, but live.

A plan had been thought up after Scott had witnessed the gang take the women from that home. They'd need a defensive strategy in the event mutants or gangs ever broke in. Now was the time, as frightening as it was, to set that plan into action.

Couches, chairs, and even a refrigerator had been thrown down the first set of stairs by the three friends as a backup in the event the front doors were ever breached. The clogged stairwell would keep any mutants from reaching the upper levels and serve as a potential deterrent for any invading gang, or at least slow them down.

After arming themselves, the trio headed toward the front door of the apartment. Scott opened it quietly. The hallway was dark with only a fraction of light penetrating the gloom, allowing them to see. The apartment was at the opposite end of where the stairs emerged. Scott worked his way to the apartment at the other end of the hallway; the one nearest the stair's landing. He opened the door and crouched inside. Anyone making it up the stairs would be met with a blast to the chest or face.

Rob took up position opposite Scott, hanging over the hallway's banister. He was in a perfect position to reign down bullets when the invading gang came up the stairs.

Cathy crouched in the doorway of the middle apartment, halfway between Scott and Rob. She had extra ammo and clips in the event either Scott or Rob needed more. She also served as a third gunman.

The three survivors sat quietly, letting their eyes adjust to the low-lit corridor. Downstairs, the gang of killers tore away at the obstacles blocking the stairwell. It wasn't long before the first group of gang members were rushing up the steps, three in total.

Rob had them in his sights, but waited until the first one reached the top step. Scott blasted the man in the face, taking off his head as Rob opened fire from behind. With controlled blasts from his rifle, the two in back of their headless companion were soon dead, tumbling backward down the staircase.

More hurried footsteps thudded about from downstairs. Men appeared in the stairway, pausing at the bottom and looking at their dead companions.

"You fuckers!" a voice yelled. "You're gonna pay for that!"

Flashlights lit the stairwell, men moving slowly up, scanning the railing above. Rob had to pull back and keep from being seen. The gang was heading up the stairs, one of them keeping the light on the upstairs railing the entire time. If Rob poked his head up, they'd shoot it off.

Aiming his rifle, Rob waited for them to breach the top of the stairs, and then he and Scott could start blasting them.

They crept all the way to the top

Scott could hear each wooden stair creak and was amazed at how quiet the gang of killers could be. He saw the flashlight breach the top step and shine directly in his eyes. He couldn't see, but fired anyway, the blast breaking the eerie silence. The flashlight remained, he'd hit nothing. Rob opened fire and heard a yelp, the flashlight dropping.

Scott guessed someone had been holding it on a stick or something. Now the gang knew where he was. He sat quietly, waiting, when he heard something clank off the ceiling and land in front of him. He wondered what it was until a flash of light filled his vision. He went deaf and became completely disoriented.

They'd tossed a flash-bang grenade, a weapon the police and military used to temporarily disable opponents.

He heard only the ringing in his ears now, as if he'd been to a rock concert and had stood directly in front of one of the speakers. Scott hoped Rob and Cathy were okay and holding the line. Feeling around, Scott found the walkie-talkie and let Rob and Cathy know he was all right, but incapacitated by the flash-bang. He repeated his message twice for fear neither had heard him the first time. He sat inside the doorway, trying to clear his head. He aimed his gun in the direction of the stairwell, but didn't want to take the chance he might hit Rob or Cathy as his vision wasn't clear yet.

He crawled away from the doorway and further into the apartment. Their plan took into account if one of them went down. He knew Rob and Cathy should be able to hold them off until his head cleared.

His eye-sight was returning, and he was now able to make out blurred shapes and could hear muffled gunfire. A few more seconds and he felt good enough to take position in the doorway again. He saw the head of a man emerging from the stairs and fired a couple shots.

"I'm almost out of ammo," Rob's voice called from the walkie-talkie.

Scott had the walkie pressed against his ear. "Copy that. I think we should be okay, there were only ten of them. We must have killed at least half by now."

"Negative, Scott," Cathy's voice said over the walkie. "While you were down, more showed up. I looked out the window when the shooting stopped. They were greeting others and now they're all inside, downstairs somewhere. I think we better consider retreating while we still can."

"Damn it," Scott said, angered. "Okay, we're out of here."

He heard screaming from the hallway and looked up. Dread filled his gut as if he'd swallowed a bowling ball until he realized the cries were coming from downstairs. "What the hell was going on?"

"Holy shit!" Cathy yelled. "Guys, I'm looking outside and I think every mutant in Brooklyn is here."

Not wanting to leave his position, but doing so anyway, Scott ran over to a window facing the front and saw hundreds of mutants, all funneling into the building.

Gunshots mixed with the screams downstairs, pulling Scott away from the window and back to his post. "I think the mutants just saved our asses," Scott said. He walked over to the staircase and looked down.

Gang members and mutants were battling, but it was clear the mutants greatly outnumbered the humans. Scott saw grotesque shapes tearing at human flesh, tearing limbs from bodies. A few gang members pumped bullets into the creatures, but were quickly overrun.

Scott ran over to Rob, and Cathy was already there.

"Let's grab some essentials and get the hell out of here," Scott said.

"Look out!" Rob shouted.

Scott spun around and saw a badly burned mutant, its skin charred like a piece of over-cooked steak, running up the stairs. Raising his gun, he blasted a hole in its chest, sending the thing tumbling down the steps.

The trio ran back to the apartment, grabbed as much food and water as possible, a few more guns and flashlights, and headed for the roof.

They traveled along the attached houses, reached the last one, and climbed down the fire escape. The streets were still flooded with mutants so they took the alley, running in the opposite direction of the hideous creatures.

They'd all decided it was time to try and get out of the city. Rob had a number of car keys that he'd found on dead people and in houses. Together, the group had searched for any vehicles that were nearby, using the alarm on the key rings to find them, then remembering where they were parked. With luck, if they ever needed one, it would still be in working order.

They took a small SUV, as it was closest, wanting a secure ride and room to sleep.

They managed to make it out of the city, deciding to head upstate via the New York State Thruway. Along the way, they encountered other survivors who told them about a community in upstate New York, near Lake Champlain.

With no other destination, they decided to try for it.

A few hours later, traveling in a four vehicle convoy, they came to the small town of Crown Point where the community of survivors had established a working farm. The entire village, fields and all, was fenced in. They were all welcomed after having a body-check for mutations.

The years following their escape from Brooklyn were tough, but fruitful. While some villagers died from infection, disease, and other natural causes, most lived and thrived. Babies were born and newcomers arrived over time, the population slowly growing. The land for housing and agriculture was expanded; the fences widened as needed.

As the years passed, Rob and Cathy had two children, a boy and a girl. Rob became captain of one of the fishing ships while Cathy ran a daycare that watched a portion of the villagers' children.

Scott was in charge of security, making sure the fences were in good repair and that the people of the town were safe. He had a small, but prominent group of trusted men and women under his command. He met a young woman shortly after arriving and the two quickly fell in love.

The place had become a home; somewhere the three friends from Brooklyn felt safe and could do more than just survive. They'd found love and a sense of peace, creating a small world that resembled the one before the apocalypse.

HOPE OF A FUTURE

REBECCA BESSER

It all started in 2009, when H1N1 broke out. What some called the Swine Flu, which they had to change to appease the pork producers. Made sense, too, as the pigs didn't have anything to do with it, so why scare people away from their beloved sausage and pork chops?

By early 2010 most people had been vaccinated. I hadn't. I didn't want that stuff floating around in my system. All the hype only aggravated me. There were too many variables. They could have tested it more before they told everyone to get it.

You could have said I was paranoid, but, as it turns out, I was right. Of course, no one knew for almost a year, until babies were born deformed and with immunity diseases.

Even the effects of the vaccine were slow to be acknowledged because of the natural disasters. The memory of hurricane Katrina was starting to fade when the earthquakes started—Haiti, and then Chile.

They were strong quakes that left humanity reeling at our pitifully small existence. Buildings and lives were ripped apart, and for what? There was no reason. The Earth decided to move around a bit and we suffered.

More quakes broke out until it was clear that they weren't going to stop, that things weren't going to get better— and it all led up to the volcanoes.

As the quakes moved the plates underneath the ground, they shifted in ways that affected volcanic activity. Yellow Stone was the first to let us know what we were in for. A couple of small islands had formed in various parts of the ocean and live volcanoes were showing activity but that was to be expected. But when Yellow Stone National Park blew up in a spewing froth of hot, searing magma, the future of the human race began to become clear.

We couldn't fight against anything so strong. How do you battle a planet that didn't want to play fair?

One after another, active and inactive volcanoes erupted across the world. The ash was terrible and unbearable. It covered the planet for months.

Food shortages ensued. Thousands died. The year 2011 was a nightmare. Not only because of the volcanic activity, but something else had triggered. It was bad enough that global warming had caused the ocean temperatures to rise, but the magma spewing into the oceans from beneath the ocean floor heated it even more. Tropical storms became a daily occurrence. Pretty soon hurricanes were hitting all the coast lines. They got stronger and stronger and soon all the coastal cities were flooded.

They evacuated New York in time to save half the population. I can't tell you how many people drowned in the subways. Sydney was wiped out, as well, not to mention England and Ireland—basically most of coastal Europe was gone. The Hawaiian Islands had disappeared and as far as anyone knew, no one had survived.

New Year's Day 2012 brought a whole new perspective on things when it came in with a bang. Who knew there was a dormant volcano under Antarctica? I don't think anyone did. I'm not even sure there was one there to begin with but I think that the heat beneath the surface of the Earth was too much to be contained.

The splendid scene that the red magma created as it shot up through white ice, sizzling and setting off little explosions, would have been majestic if it hadn't been so disastrous. The ice melted at a tremendous rate, again changing the temperature of the oceans.

Hurricanes became 'hypercanes.' These five hundred mile per hour wind giants, with ten mile wide and a twenty mile high radius, poisoned plant and sea life. Since they reached all the way to the ozone layer, they laced the atmosphere with dust and soot that caused the sun's rays to not be able to reach the planet below.

What was left of the coastal cities was flattened as the hypercanes swept across continents. Sometimes they would make it a good ways inland before fizzling out and entire strips of earth were torn out of countries, leaving nothing in their wake.

I read about one scientist that said the cause of all of the destruction and mayhem was the shifting of the Earth's poles as we grew closer to December 21, 2012. The supposed end of the world, it was when the celestial crosses would meet, but the shifting started earlier than anticipated.

I figured we'd all be dead by their end of the world date. I wasn't even sure Earth would survive. It seemed bound and determined to destroy itself as it wiped out our existence.

Still, despite it all, a few of us survived. The band I'm with now consists of twenty people—fourteen women and six men. We live in a bunker underground. It's small and tight, and we don't get to go outside because of the radiation that has spewed into the air when the nuclear reactors melted down.

On December 21st, we were dreading what might happen. We didn't know how things could get any worse. But we'd thought that before, and look where it had gotten us. I didn't know what more could happen.

Unless the Earth spun off its axis, then it wouldn't matter anymore.

That fateful day came eventually came to an end—with nothing happening. At least nothing we knew about. Since all the satellites were out and we no longer had any kind of communication system to tell us what was going on in the world, we didn't know for sure. Something could have happened on the other side of the planet and we would never know.

All we knew was that we were still alive and that we had to press on to revive humanity, if we could. The future was as uncertain as it had always been

There were just fewer of us to live it now.

*　*　*

"Brian, are you just going to sit on your butt and write in that thing all day?" a feminine voice grumbled as a shadow fell over me.

I looked up to see Diane and I inwardly groaned.

"I was taking a short break," I said and stood, brushing dirt from the seat of my pants. "We're allowed to have breaks you know."

"Short breaks are allowed, yes, but not every ten minutes," she replied.

I itched to tell her that she knew that I didn't take breaks every ten minutes, like she did, but I held my tongue. Life was hard enough without adding more conflict, not that Diane thought about that when she was bossing people around.

I saw Kate glance our way and raise an eyebrow. I shut my journal and tucked it into my back pocket, along with my pen. Smiling defiantly at Diane, I stepped past her and joined the other two in our work group, who were searching the wreckage for food and anything else we could use.

Thankfully, the radiation hadn't been that bad in our area thanks to no reactors being nearby. Of course once the winds shifted direction that could change. We were also lucky enough to have a scientist in our band. Otherwise, we wouldn't have known if it'd been safe to venture out of the bunker. Harry was traveling with two others to see how far we could go in each direction and in essence, set up a perimeter. Once that was complete, we could do a better job of searching for supplies.

Kate smiled as I helped her lift a heavy piece of metal that she was struggling with.

"Did you get in trouble?" Kate teased.

"Yeah," I said. "Diane's in a bad mood today."

Kate laughed. "She's in a bad mood every day. Why would today be any different?"

I snickered. "True. Did I miss anything major?"

"No," Kate said. "I think there might be enough sheet metal around to build a shelter, but other than that, no great finds."

We added the metal to the pile of useful things we'd found. I stood and looked around, taking in the landscape, hoping to spot something we'd missed. I couldn't help but notice that Diane was now taking a break. It was her third one today. She took more breaks than anyone else and still complained when we took ours.

Shaking my head, I followed Kate to another piece of sheet metal and Heather joined us.

"I found a couple cans of food," Heather announced. "The labels are missing, so I don't know what's in them."

"That's better than nothing," I said. "With that and the building supplies, we should have a good bit to take back with us. But we might have to make more than one trip."

Heather nodded. "At least we'll have something to show for the day. It seems more often than not, we don't find anything of use or value."

Kate and I added another sheet of metal to the stack and the three of us walked up the hill. We paused at the top and surveyed, not for the first time, the devastation of our world.

Few trees could be seen, those that remained were mere skeletons of what they'd once been. The ground was bare of any and all vegetation. The endless swath of brown dirt was littered with scraps of trash, and occasionally a car or truck frame that was mangled so badly as too be almost unrecognizable.

We'd been sent north today.

Each day a group was assigned a different direction. Yesterday, we'd been sent southeast. It gave us a chance to see what was around us, as well as have new sets of eyes on areas where something might have been missed by others. There was so much to dig through that we could only search a small area each day.

Kate sighed. "I still don't know how we've survived this long."

"Me neither," Heather added.

I didn't have anything to say. Everything was gone and I still couldn't get my mind around it.

"What are you three doing?" Diane huffed as she mounted the rise to stand on the other side of Heather. "Standing here isn't getting any work done."

I glanced at Kate and saw her jaw tense.

"I think it's time for Heather's break," I said, waiting for Diane to say something snippy.

For once, Diane kept her mouth shut. Heather turned toward me and smiled as she made her way back down the hill to take a break.

"I think we have enough for today," Diane said, looking at our piles of scrap. "We should head back now."

Kate clenched her fists and closed her eyes. I could see she was battling for control.

"It's still early," I said. "We've just had breaks. We can get those piles doubled, if not tripled, before we lose the light."

"Who are you to say if we have enough?" Diane asked. "You're not the boss."

"No," Kate snapped. "I am, and I think we can get a lot more work done today."

Diane looked down at the ground, her face beet red. Kate didn't usually exert her authority over our search party and I think it caught Diane by surprise. I did my best not to grin.

"So, we're going to start over there and everyone's going to help," Kate said. "Heather will join us after her break, and then I'll take one. After that, unless we have to lift something heavy or do something else that's tasking, there will be no more breaks."

I tried to smother a laugh, but snorted from the effort. Without looking at either of them, I made my way down the far side of the hill and started working where Kate had indicated.

A few moments later, I heard the shifting and scraping of shoes on dry ground as the others joined me. Together, we lifted a fairly large chunk of cement to see what was under it. There was a cabinet, half of a porcelain kitchen sink, and some scraps of cloth. After moving the cement, we investigated our findings.

Kate gripped the handles on the doors of what looked to be a solid wood cabinet for a garage or pantry, and glanced up at us.

Diane and I nodded in unison as we held our breaths. I was hoping the cabinet was from a pantry and that the back of it, which was facing the ground, wasn't missing and there was actually something useful inside like food.

"What did you find?" Heather called from the hill above us.

We all jumped at the sound of her voice.

"We don't know yet!" Kate hollered back. "Might be something, might not be."

"Wait for me!" Heather yelled and rushed down the hill.

Heather was one of the youngest of the survivors at seventeen and was often impetuous. It was nice. When she was around, we weren't surrounded by gloom all the time, which almost made up for having to deal with Diane—almost, but not quite.

Kate resumed her grip on the handles of the cabinet and this time didn't wait. She tugged on the doors but they didn't budge.

We all sighed in unison. The tension was thick. We were running out of food and water. If there was food in the cabinet, we needed it badly.

"I'll help," I said. "Maybe it's just stuck."

Stepping forward I gripped one of the handles with both hands. Kate did the same with the other.

"One," Kate said. "Two. Three!"

We pulled as hard as we could and the door gave way. After recovering our balance, the four of us peered inside. There was nothing in the cabinet. As I'd feared, the back was missing and everything that had once been contained within was gone.

I bowed my head and leaned forward with my hands on my knees. After a couple of deep breaths, I stood up. Everyone's face mirrored my disappointment.

"The cabinet's in good condition," I said, trying to look on the bright side. "We can use it for something. I'm sure we can fashion a new back for it."

I pretended not to see the tears in Kate's dark brown eyes as she nodded and looked off into the distance.

"Help me lift this so we can see if there's anything under it," I said to the other two, drawing their attention away from Kate.

It took all three of us to lift it; it was an old cabinet, probably an antique. Otherwise, I don't think it would have lasted in such good condition. We stood it on a fairly level spot at the base of the hill and examined it further.

By the time we walked back to Kate, she had herself under control and was attempting to move the broken sink by herself. Heather made it to her side in time to help her before she dropped the sharp end on her foot. Together, they tossed it over the cement chunk.

We then worked together to remove some layers of house siding and insulation surrounding the area. It took a while. It appeared that a lot of stuff had landed here, probably deposited by a hypercane, to then fill in the deep depression in the ground. Everything was packed so tightly we had to pry it out with two-by-fours, lead pipes, and anything else we could find for leverage. After an hour of hard labor, we all wanted to sit down and rest. The air, lacking normal levels of oxygen because of the vegetation shortage, plus our exertion, worked against us to tire us easily.

I glanced at Kate, raised an eyebrow, and she shrugged.

"Let's all take a break," Kate said. "We've been working harder than I thought we would have to."

Diane grumbled something under her breath and wandered off to find somewhere to sit.

"You never did take your break earlier, did you?" I asked Kate as we sat together in the shade of the hill. Because of the depleted oxygen, breaks were necessary or a person might find themselves passing out in the midst of a task.

Kate shook her head and lay back, closing her eyes.

Heather wandered back over the hill; I assumed to get a drink of water. I silently hoped she would bring some back with her. Knowing her thoughtful nature, I knew that she would.

Sitting beside Kate, I reached over and took her hand in mine. She squeezed mine in return and smiled. Kate and I were close to the same age. I was thirty-four and she was thirty-two. We had bonded instantly upon meeting one another; I couldn't help but be attracted to her. She was sweet, kind, strong, and beautiful.

But it was dangerous to fall in love and we both knew it. Because of the number of men versus women that had survived the apocalypse, relationships could be difficult, if not destructive. Our band had decided collectively that the best way to rebuild the human race would be through an emotion-free breeding program of sorts. Simply, the men would try to get the women pregnant. It was more structured than that, but that's what it came down to.

Kate knew the risk as did I of being together, but we just couldn't seem to help how we felt about each other.

I squeezed her hand and rubbed the back of her knuckles with my thumb. "I'm sorry the cabinet was empty," I said.

She sighed deeply. "It's frustrating. We're eking by day to day on almost nothing. I sometimes think we would have been better off if we hadn't survived."

"It's possible," I said.

"I brought some water for you guys," Heather announced, coming back over the hill while waving a bottle of water.

Kate discretely withdrew her hand from mine and stood. "Great. It's time to get back to work anyway."

Kate took the bottle from Heather and downed half of it, handing the rest to me.

"Did you bring some for Diane?" Kate asked.

Heather nodded. "Yup."

"Would you go tell her that her break's over?" Kate asked.

"Sure," Heather said as she headed in the direction of Diane's disappearance.

With our rest over, we started in where we'd left off. It wasn't long before Heather and Diane joined us. We moved quickly and with renewed energy. It helped that when we got this done, we could head back to camp for the day.

We were rummaging and moving things for quite a while when we hit something solid. I thought it might be a large rock and that we'd finally found the bottom of the pile. But after clearing everything away, I found out I was wrong. It was a board, about the size of a door, and it was wedged into the dirt at an angle. It took all four of us to pull it out, and when we saw what was laying underneath it, we froze.

There, lying in the bottom of the pit, was a collection of canned food. Kate fell to her knees, staring at it, like she couldn't believe what she was seeing.

I grinned like an idiot.

Heather laughed loudly, her eyes alight. "Food! I can't believe we found food! I mean, I hoped we would, but I never expected to actually find some."

Diane didn't say anything. She, like Kate, seemed to be in a state of shocked disbelief.

"How are we going to carry it all back with us?" I asked absently, looking around for something that would hold the cans.

Kate looked up at me and blinked. "What? Oh, I think we could probably use the board that was covering it. We can stack everything on it and then each of us can take a corner."

And that's how we ended up arriving back at camp. All of us carrying the door-sized board—which was actually the back of the cabinet—covered with food and other useful items we'd found.

Everyone ran out into the dusky evening to greet us. We were the last search party to return and they cheered when they saw what we'd found.

Marcus stepped forward and raised his hands to quiet the excited group of people before he spoke.

"I would like to thank Kate, Diane, Brian, and Heather for finding this food. It'll go a long way in keeping us alive. This food, along with the water that Steve, Marie, Tony, and Patty found, should last for quite a while."

Everyone cheered again.

We took the food over to the cooking area and a couple of people helped us unload and stack the cans, a few prized bottles of juice, and everything else that we'd found.

A few of the cans were no good, their seems punctured or the insides ruptured somehow, but only a few were like that. The rest looked fine.

Finally, we sat down by the communal fire and were given something to eat. Normally, no one was waited on. But since we had gotten back late and were kind of like heroes for the day, it was allowed.

I saw Marcus sit beside Kate and I tried not to get jealous. Marcus was our voted leader. He was smart and muscular with dark wavy hair and hazel eyes. At one time or another, almost every woman in camp had looked at him with longing. I bet they were all waiting for the breeding process to begin. It wasn't really called the breeding process, of course, it was called 'repopulation'. But it all boiled down to breeding and I knew most of the women couldn't wait for their turn with him.

Kate laughed at something he said and I knew I had to get away before I did something stupid.

Gulping down the rest of my meager meal and quickly wiping my bowl clean, I made my way out of the camp. I pulled my journal out of my back pocket as I trudged off into the darkness. I didn't know how much I could write in the dark, but I knew it would keep my mind occupied.

*　*　*

Thankfully, the bunker we'd found and lived in had a stockpile of food and water. It kept us alive for a long time when we first found it. From the marks we'd made on the walls, it looked to be a total of a year we'd lived underground.

Harry, our resident scientist, warned us about radiation from the hypercanes. The knowledge that we could die if we went outside kept us somewhat content underground. Harry had found a radiation suit and some old detection gear stashed inside a yellow suitcase in a closet and after the first year, he would send one of us to the surface to check for radiation in the suit. Although we didn't get a reading on the meter, we still stayed underground. Don't ask me why. I think we were all afraid of what we would find on the surface, or what we wouldn't find.

Harry and Marcus decided we should stay where we were, just in case the meter was wrong. If it was right, then we wouldn't have anything to worry about, but they didn't know if we were the only ones to survive and I guess we just couldn't risk it.

By the time they let us out, we were ready to strangle each other, cabin fever taking its toll on all of us. To keep from killing one another, we made laws.

We didn't make too many laws, at least not too many major ones. You weren't allowed to willfully do anything to hurt another person. That included killing. You also had to do your best to keep peace. If you started a fight with someone you would get in serious trouble. I don't know exactly what the serious trouble would be because it's not like you would be killed for any offense. After we came up with most of the laws, some from 'before' and others brand new, it was agreed that we needed to come up with a strategy to continue the human race, and that's where the breeding program came from.

Since there were twice as many women as men, it was decided that there would be a system put into place. Each man would spend one week with the women, sleeping with a different one each night and then having a night to rest before going back to 'work'. Then the next man would do the same thing until they all had a turn. Once a woman was pregnant, she would be taken out of the rotation. Once all the women were pregnant, they would be more careful and the men would do more of the work.

We all agreed to the plan. But we also agreed that we needed to get on the surface to see what we were dealing with before anyone got pregnant. That way, the women could help with the work, until we had shelter and were stable.

The work wasn't broken up into male work and female work. It was just work. You took care of yourself and you did what duties were assigned to you and your work crew.

That was how it came about that I was spending more time with Kate. She was my crew leader. I really don't know what she sees in me. I'm somewhat tall and slimly built. I have flat wiry muscles and plain brown hair. My eyes are light gray and there's nothing unique about me.

Maybe it's my sparkling personality and wit, but I doubt it.

*   *   *

"Brian?"

I jumped as someone said my name from close by. "Who is it?" A soft feminine laugh floated to me on the evening breeze. "Kate?"

"That's me," Kate said as she stepped into my line of vision. "What are you doing out here all alone?"

I laughed. "And what are you doing looking for me out here all by yourself?"

Kate sat beside me, grinning. "I thought something was wrong when you took off. Wanna talk about it?"

Looking down at my journal, I sighed. "No, I don't think so."

"Oh, come on," Kate teased and bumped her shoulder against mine. "Tell me. Maybe I can help."

Glancing sideways at Kate, I decided to take my chances. "I think I'm in love with you," I said quietly.

Kate didn't reply.

I turned toward her and watched her as I continued. "If it wasn't for all of this," I swung my arm up and gestured at the world around us, "I would be dating you, hoping that someday we would be married and have children together. But, because of where we are, and what life has dealt, I'll have to pretend it doesn't bother me when I have to share you with other men."

Kate's eyes welled up with tears. They fell as she looked down at her hands which were clenched together in her lap.

"Brian," she whispered. "I love you, too. But we can't act on our feelings. It would hurt us all."

I don't know what I expected. But hearing her say she loved me, too, overwhelmed me with a joyous hope. I took her hands in mine.

"Please," I begged. "Stay with me tonight. Be with me tonight. No one has to know. I love you so much."

She took a shuddering breath. "No." Then she ripped her hands from mine, stood, and fled back to the camp.

My heart fell. Where there was joy and hope moments ago, there was a burning weight that made it hard for me to breathe. How could she say she loved me and then refuse to share that love with me? I was devastated. Anger sizzled through my body in the form of adrenaline.

I wanted to break something, to kill something, to tear everything apart. I felt that if I could make everything and everyone around me hurt as much as I was hurting then the pain would cease, but mostly, I hated myself for telling Kate that I loved her.

Thoughts of things I could do to myself, of things that would end my life, flashed through my head. They teased my soul with the promise of release. Images of knives sinking into my flesh and other twisted dark ideas taunted me.

Mentally shaking myself, I brushed my hands through my hair in torment and frustration. Through a force of will, I dispelled the temptations from my mind. I couldn't hurt myself. I couldn't allow things to drive me to that. If I did, I would never see Kate again. Maybe I could change her mind, make her see that it was right for us to be together.

With that thought, the thought of a maybe in the future, a calm settled over me. A cold shaft of resolve went through me, turning my anger and hurt into determination.

Standing, I turned toward camp and put one foot in front of the other as a plan began to form in my brain, a plan to win Kate for myself.

* * *

The next day dawned hot and muggy. I hadn't slept well, even though I'd been exhausted. My plan was swirling in my head and it wouldn't let me rest.

Getting ready to go out and get to work, I continued to think of ways I could make things right. The way they should be, instead of the way they were. I tried to think of any obstacles that might get in my way ahead of time so that I could handle them effectively.

But an unexpected obstacle reared its ugly head nonetheless. I was switched to another work crew. As Marcus announced the change, I glanced to my right where Kate was standing, to see her staring straight ahead. I had a sneaking suspicion that she had asked for me to be moved to another crew; a suspicion that was given more strength when I saw Marcus give her a barely perceptible nod.

At that precise moment, I hated Marcus for coming between Kate and me. My jealousy made me think that he just wanted her for himself and that she had just been toying with me and really wanted to be with him.

I clenched my fists and jaw. Closing my eyes, I took deep, steadying breaths. I felt betrayed and used.

They'll pay for this, I thought to myself as I almost passed out from the intensity of the feelings swirling within me.

"Brian, are you all right?"

I opened my eyes and consciously relaxed my tense muscles. "Yes, Heather, I'm fine."

"I can't believe they moved you to another crew," Heather said. "We all work so well together. As well as we can anyway, with Diane around. I'm going to miss you."

"I know," I said. I couldn't think of anything else to tell her. She didn't need to be brought into everything that was going on. "It'll be all right. Jesse is nice. You shouldn't have any trouble getting along without me."

"But I won't be the same," Heather pouted in her young, innocent way. "I like you and wish you were still going to work with us. Maybe you can talk to Kate and see if they'll switch you back."

I shook my head grimly. "No. We'll just go with the changes. I'm sure there's a reason for them."

I turned and walked away, heading toward my new group before Heather could say anything else. I already had enough going on in my head without her unknowingly adding more.

I inwardly fumed all day about being shoved off without any thoughts about my feelings. Although everyone was nice and we all worked well together, it just wasn't the same. I missed Kate, and I hated her because I missed her. I knew better, but my mind insisted she'd done this on purpose to hurt me, while in my heart I knew she'd done it to keep us both from doing something stupid that we would regret later.

When we returned to camp that night, I looked for Kate among the others but they hadn't returned yet.

Applying myself to help build a permanent shelter for us to live in, I let my mind wander. Thinking about what it would have been like if I'd met Kate before the Wrath of Earth, as we all called it. In my mind we were happy, had gotten married, and had healthy, beautiful children.

My thoughts were still in a wonderland of what-ifs when Kate, Heather, Diane, and Jesse returned.

After a supper of rice and kidney beans, I set off by myself again, going to the same place as the night before, thinking that maybe if I wrote about the past, something of the future might become clear to me.

I settled down and withdrew my leather journal from my pocket, smoothing my hand over its cracked, worn surface. Not knowing if anyone would ever read it, I wondered if I was wasting my time. In reality, it didn't matter. I needed the outlet. I had to have something to give me purpose.

Opening to where I'd left off the previous night, I stared off into the horizon, watching the sun slowly set behind the barren hills in the distance. As orange and red rays bathed the desolate land-scape, movement caught my attention.

I paused with my pen floating above my journal. Was someone wandering around in the dark?

As I continued watching the shadows, a man stepped over the rise of the nearby hill, his shape silhouetted in the purple dusk of last light. He was bigger than anyone I'd seen in a long time...and he was carrying a rifle.

Slowly, careful not to draw attention to myself, I stood and put my journal away. I stepped back and squatted in the shadow of the boulder I'd been leaning against. I watched as another man, who also had a gun, joined the first.

They talked to each other briefly, one gesturing behind them, the other motioning toward the east and our settlement. After their brief exchange, the second man made a motion and a small cluster of people joined them. I couldn't tell how many there were or their gender, I could only see that they were armed. They had guns, pitchforks, swords, and I don't know what else.

I knew I had to get back to camp and warn everyone.

Slinking through the darkness, I was glad that I was tall and slender, making it easier for me to move quietly.

After I was sure I was far enough away that they wouldn't see me, I started to run. My lungs burned from the effort, but I couldn't slow down. I didn't want to think about what would happen if I didn't get there in time to warn everyone.

I slid to a halt just inches from the fire, too winded to talk for at least a minute. By the time I caught my breath everyone had gathered and was watching me anxiously, not understanding why I was so excited and scared.

"I saw a group of people," I said while still gulping for air.

"People!" I heard someone call out in excitement.

"We aren't the only ones alive!" someone else said.

I held up my hand and took a deep breath before speaking. "They were armed. They have guns. They look healthy, too, the one man I saw was huge. They have to be eating better than we are."

Marcus stepped forward. "If that's true and they mean us harm then they could easily overpower us. Were they all men, Brian? How many of them are there?"

I shook my head. "Most of them looked male, but they were too far away to tell. I didn't get a count either, there might be fifteen, twenty, probably more."

Everyone was silent as they listened. The first voice I heard was expected.

"We don't know if they're going to try to hurt us," Diane said. "They could just be travelers in search of other people. Maybe they ran out of food or something where they were."

I shook my head and glanced at Marcus. He was deep in thought and hadn't heard Diane.

Since no one said anything to oppose her, she kept going.

"I think we should send a small group out to meet them and talk," Diane said louder, getting drunk on the attention. "I think it would be in our best interest to see if they come in peace."

"No," Marcus said.

"That's what we'll do," Diane continued, ignoring Marcus. "We'll meet with them and see what they want."

"I said no," Marcus said forcefully. "We aren't going to do that. We can't risk it if they're hostile."

"Then what are we going to do?" Diane asked sarcastically with her hands on her hips. "Hide like rabbits in a hole and wait for them to leave?"

"We're going to arm ourselves and defend our home," Marcus said.

Heads turned toward Marcus and then back to Diane. I could see everyone's minds calculating the difference in the plans. I could see our community splitting and taking sides.

Murmurs vibrated into the night air. Some agreed with Diane, and stepped closer to her, lending their support with suggestions and volunteering to go with her. Others remained with Marcus and asked what he had in mind. I put my trust in Marcus. Caution was the best policy for survival, for if Diane was wrong, they would all pay the price in blood.

Marcus tried one last time to convince Diane that her plan was dangerous. "Please Diane, don't do this. If you're wrong and they are dangerous, you could be killed. Think of it this way, at least staying together as one force, we might have a chance if they're hostile."

Diane rolled her eyes, turned her back on Marcus, and stomped away.

Marcus sighed and shook his head.

Glancing at those of us that were left, those of us prepared to fight, I counted a total of twelve. Diane had only convinced four people. That was a small number, but they were people that we could have used. The dozen of us quickly discussed and formed a plan.

We had no guns. They had that advantage over us, but we did have an array of weaponry at our disposal. Before the world turned into a living hell, I'd been quite good at archery. Trees were limited, but I'd managed to find enough wood to make three long bows and some arrows. I'd been training a couple of others to use them whenever there was time. We'd mostly planned on using them for hunting, but defense was just as good and had always been another likely possibility.

I took one myself and gave one to Tony, who'd been doing well with the lessons. I looked around for Jesse, who'd been my star pupil and realized that he'd gone with Diane. I gave the last one to Heather; while she lacked the strength for long shots, up close she was extremely accurate.

Marcus and Steve had fashioned swords out of some metal we'd found. They weren't very well balanced or graceful, but they were sharp. Those added to two axes we'd found in the rubble, armed us all.

The archers were to go outside of the camp and hide. Marcus would wait by the fire to meet the approaching people when they arrived and the rest were to hide where they could easily attack from different angles if it came to that.

I perched on the top of a large chunk of sandstone above our settlement and I could see Diane and her followers walking out toward where I'd seen the people. They carried three torches and were easy to spot.

They hadn't gone far when a group of five men meet them. They stood and talked for a few minutes and then I saw one of them punch Diane in the face. She fell heavily to the ground, her hand rushing up to staunch the flow of her bloody nose

In a blink of an eye, Diane and the rest of her party that had gone out to offer peace were surrounded. I watched Jesse try to fight, but to no avail.

A loud boom resounded through the emptiness as he was shot in the chest. I was stricken as I watched Jesse's body fall in a dead heap and strangers commenced with beating the rest of the welcome party into submission.

I saw Marcus rise to his feet and walk to the west side of the fire with his sword in hand.

I stood and got ready as well. Since we now knew they were hostile, we were allowed to shoot as soon as we had a good target.

I readied an arrow and drew back on the string of my bow. The fletching tickled my fingers as I waited. I knew we had to make every arrow count, for we only had ten each.

The raiders had Diane and her followers tied up and gagged. I was shocked to see that Jesse's body was also in tow. Why would they keep a dead man?

Marcus stood his ground and waited until they were twenty feet from him and then yelled, "You're not welcome here! Release those of us you've captured and leave now. We don't wish to fight you. There's no need for more death."

The big man laughed and stepped forward. "I disagree. There is need for more death. We're hungry and need to eat and you, my friend, are the main course."

That explained why they kept the dead body, they were cannibals.

Taking careful aim, I relaxed my hand and let the arrow fly. It struck the man in the eye and he fell over onto his back, instantly dead.

"That's what will happen to the rest of you if you don't leave now," Marcus shouted while brandishing his sword.

A woman growled viciously and leapt at Marcus. He stepped aside and brought his sword swiftly down on the back of her neck. It sank into her flesh, chopping her head halfway off in a fountain of gushing blood.

I released another arrow as I saw many of the raiders reach for their guns. The arrow struck a man in the neck. Other arrows from my fellow archers were striking further back in the crowd; Tony and Heather were hitting their targets as well.

Marcus bellowed like a crazy man and charged those in the lead of the group of men. He took down two before they realized he was crazy enough to attack. The six others of our band attacked the raiders in the middle, three on each side and I saw the other two of our people attack the rear.

The raiders were well armed, but they had taken it for granted that their numbers and weaponry would have us submitting. Either that or they thought we wouldn't be able to defend ourselves. Their miscalculation was serving us well for we had nothing to lose. Even if we surrendered, they would only kill us anyway

I had three more arrows and I released them in quick succession; all of them flew true. After that, I left my perch to join the fray, my blood pounding in my head as I fought the fear that filled me.

I slipped in blood and fell over a body. Retrieving a fallen gun, I aimed at a man that was breaking away from the others. I squeezed the trigger and screamed in pain as the recoil assaulted my shoulder. I fell to my knees, almost passing out from pain. I saw that I'd shot him in the thigh. He was on the ground, trying to drag himself to safety as he screamed in pain. I fired again but the gun was empty.

Grinding my teeth to ignore the pain in my shoulder, I forced myself to stand and advance toward him. I dropped the gun and went to a dagger that was still in the clutches of a severed hand. Frustrated when a couple of shakes didn't dislodge it, I dropped the hand onto the ground and violently stomped on it until it let loose. Bending to pick up the knife, I saw a movement to my right. Clutching the dagger in my left hand, I spun toward my foe. Thrusting upward, I caught the advancing woman in the gut, slicing her all the way up to her neck. She wailed like a banshee and stumbled back in dazed shock as her insides spilled out onto her feet. I stabbed her in the throat, ripping the blade back out as she collapsed, I turned back to the man I had shot.

He was sitting up against a rock, holding a gun across his lap. I suspected by his labored breathing and the pool of blood underneath his leg that he was bleeding to death; the bullet must have hit an artery. My suspicion was confirmed a second later as I watched him take his last gasping breath.

Screams of pain and yelling drew my attention back to what was going on around me. I surveyed the rest of the battle before rushing in to help a couple of women who were surrounded. The men that encroached upon them were so focused and intent on their prey that they didn't notice me. Uppercutting at a sharp angle, I caught the largest of the men in the left side. I threw all my weight into the thrust, hoping I would penetrate the short blade all the way to his heart.

All eyes turned toward me as the man cried out and fell. The women took the opportunity to kill one of the other men, falling on him like banshees.

The third man stabbed at me with a knife of his own. I blocked the best I could, but tripped over the head of someone who'd been decapitated. The man managed to injure my good arm as I lost my footing and I groped around me for something to use to defend myself. Finding a severed arm, I swung it upward in desperation. The arm whipped out straight, causing the hand to slap my attacker across the face. We both paused and looked at each other. If this hadn't been a life or death situation, I would have laughed at the absurdity of what had just happened and the look of shock on his face.

I lifted the arm again as he raised his knife to strike, but a sword exploded from his chest in a bloom of bright red blood. I turned away to protect my face from splatter as he fell on top of me, forgetting that I was still gripping the arm. It wrapped around the man's neck as he landed atop me, holding him to me as if I were drawing him close for a kiss.

I quickly released the arm in disgust and wiggled out from under him. Marcus stood over me, holding his sword and breathing heavily. He was covered from head to toe in blood and human tissue and for one moment he reminded me of a Viking warrior from the past.

"Are you all right, Brian?" he asked, as he wiped his face clean of blood with his arm.

I nodded and struggled to my feet. "I think so." I cradled my sore arm, the shoulder still sore from the kick of the gun I'd used.

"What happened to your arm? Did you get shot?"

"No," I said with a lopsided grin. "I didn't hold a gun right when I fired it. I think I dislocated my shoulder."

We turned to view the slaughter around us, seeing that we'd managed to hold our own. There were no more raiders left standing. They were either dead or had retreated.

"How many did we lose?" I asked Marcus.

"I don't know yet," he said. "You were the last one fighting. Let's go see how many made it to the rendezvous point."

I nodded and followed him.

I was relieved to see Kate, Heather, and a good many others still alive and fine. Out of the twelve of us who'd chosen to fight, only two had been lost. While many had various injuries, everyone seemed to be all right, as long as their wounds were treated and infection didn't set in. Diane, the lower half of her face covered in her blood, and two of her followers were there also.

Marcus sighed heavily. "I want everyone who's injured to get your wounds washed and treated immediately. Anyone who's still able, come help me clean up this mess and secure the area."

After my shoulder was popped back into place and the cut on my arm was bandaged, I went to help stack and burn the bodies.

A short time later, Heather came running up to Marcus.

"It's all gone!" Heather wailed. "There's nothing left. No food, no water. Nothing."

"Damn it," Marcus growled. "Some of them must have snuck in and taken everything while we were fighting the rest. What about the emergency stores?"

"Patty and Marie went to look," Heather said.

There was some talk about sending a search party out to see if we could catch the raiders that had taken our supplies, but we didn't know which direction they'd gone or how long ago they'd left.

Marie assured us later that the emergency rations were intact. It was good news that didn't cheer anyone up. The emergency stores would only sustain us for a week, maybe a little longer now that we had lost some of our people.

* * *

A couple of days later, we had packed up and were ready to move to a new location. The stench of the shed blood was making us sick and drawing animals, which in turn was a blessing. We killed them for their meat and their hides.

Harry, after scouting ahead, said that it was safe for us to travel north, so that's the way we went. Hours on the road later, we set up our tents that first night. I watched Kate across the fire, as we gathered around it to fight off the chill night, wondering how much longer we had to live. As for Kate, she still wouldn't talk or look at me. I knew we could die tonight, or tomorrow, or a week from now but all I could think about was being with her. I had nothing else to live for and I knew I had to take action if we were ever going to be together.

As darkness settled around us, I excused myself, pretending to be tired. But didn't go to sleep, instead, I circled out around the camp to a spot where I could see what everyone was doing. Then I waited.

Marcus and Kate were the last two at the fire still awake, the others now asleep in their bedrolls. They sat for a long time, not saying anything until Marcus broke the silence, and in the calm, quiet night, I could hear everything he said.

"Are you all right, Kate? I know the battle was hard on everyone, but you've been especially quiet."

She shrugged in reply as she stared at the fire.

"Kate," Marcus said. "Look at me, please."

She did, but she seemed reluctant.

"I know it was hard to kill those people. It wasn't easy for any of us but it had to be done."

Kate shrugged again.

Marcus sighed. "I hate to see you this way."

"I'll be fine," she muttered. "Don't worry about me."

Marcus brushed a hand through his hair. "I can't help but worry about you. I care about you Kate, more than I should." He reached over and took her hand in his.

"Marcus," she said, pulling her hand free. "No, we can't."

"But we could die tonight, tomorrow, anytime! I can't keep my feelings inside any longer. This could be my only chance to be with you."

"I'm sorry, Marcus, but I don't care for you that way," Kate said, standing.

"Wait," he said, standing as well.

"What?" She turned toward him. "There's nothing more to say."

He reached up, cupped her face in his hands, and kissed her.

I growled, wanting to tear him apart for touching her.

Kate pulled away and ran to her tent.

I sat silent and tense, waiting for Marcus to go to bed. He sat by himself for another half hour, just gazing into the fire, before he finally turned in for the night.

I waited an additional twenty minutes before I moved. Getting up slowly, I rubbed my legs to restore the circulation. Even though the night was chilly, I wasn't cold. I was buzzing with adrenaline and stored up emotion.

I moved through the camp clutching the dagger that I'd kept from the battle. It would serve me well this night.

Stealthy as a cat, I entered each tent methodically. I did what I had to do then left, moving on to the next one. It seemed like mere moments had passed when I found myself in front of Marcus' tent. I'd saved him for last, knowing that he might have trouble sleeping after that touching scene by the fire.

I entered and paused at the opening, listening. His steady breathing assured me he was asleep. I knelt beside him, pressed the dagger against his throat, and let it sink into his skin. His eyes flew open and he gripped my arm as his warm blood gushed across my hand. He was the only one who'd woken, the only one that looked into my eyes as I took his life.

"I've taken care of everyone," I whispered. "They didn't suffer. Don't worry, I'll make sure Kate's happy."

He gurgled and his grip went lax, his eyes losing their focus.

I felt at peace with myself, with the world, as Marcus' lifeblood squirted onto the soil beneath him. I knew everything was going to be all right now.

My steps were lighter as I made my way to Kate's tent. Slowly, I drew back the flap and crawled inside. She was lying on her stomach, facing away from me. I held my breath for a moment and just looked at her. She'd drawn the covers up over her neck to ward of the cold. The only parts of her I could see were her toes, her dark hair, and the side of her face.

Leaning forward, I gently kissed her cheek, then slowly I drew the blanket off of her shoulder and kissed her there, too. She stirred but didn't wake. I continued to remove the blanket until it was bunched up around her ankles. I let my fingers trail up her calf, and pressed my palm against her warm, soft thigh as I slid my hand up her body.

She made a soft moaning sound in her sleep and turned onto her side. I cupped her bottom, squeezing it gently before going higher. When I reached around to cup one of her breasts, she gasped and half turned in my direction.

"Brian?" she asked in a dreamy voice.

"Yes, Kate, it's me," I said as I leaned forward and traced her lips with my tongue.

She opened her lips for me with a gasp, wrapping her arm around my neck. I kissed her deeply as she turned over and pressed a hand against my chest.

She froze and pulled back. "What's all over you? Why are you wet and sticky?"

"It was necessary. So that we could be together as we should be," I said as I reached forward to caress her shoulders. "I cleared the path for our happiness and I saved them all from more suffering in the process."

"Saved who from what?" she asked while shoving my hands away and sitting up. "What're you talking about? What've you done, Brian?"

"I killed them all. I slit their throats while they were sleeping. Now they won't suffer through starvation and dehydration. Best of all, we can be together. There's no one to stand in our way anymore."

Kate gasped in horror and slid further away from me. Her eyes dropping to the bloody dagger still clutched in my hand.

"Kate," I whispered. "It's all right. It had to be done. It's for the best."

"You're crazy," she said in a scared, shaky voice.

"It's okay," I said, reaching for her with my free hand.

"No!" Kate screamed, frantically trying to get away from me. "Don't touch me!"

Dropping the dagger, I grabbed her ankles as she tried to crawl out of the tent. Straddling her, I grabbed her wrists and pinned her arms above her head, as I pressed her struggling body down with the weight of mine.

"You're covered in blood," she choked out and tried to twist herself free.

"I'm sorry, I know you're upset right now, but if you would just calm down and think about it, you would see that I did the right thing."

She whimpered and frantically tried to tug her wrists from my grasp.

"Calm down," I growled, squeezing tighter, getting aggravated at her reluctance. "I don't want to hurt you."

She stopped struggling and looked up at me with tears in her eyes. "Please, Brian, don't hurt me. You can let me go now."

I stared down at her for a moment, thinking. "If I let you go, do you promise to calm down?"

She stifled a sob and nodded.

I released her as I gently kissed her shaking lips.

She reached up and wrapped an arm around my neck, kissing me back. I moaned and thrust my hands into her hair, relaxing my body on top of hers.

The next minute was ecstasy; I was lost in the passion of being with her. Until I felt a sharp, hot pain under my left shoulder blade. I reared back and cried out surprise and agony, not understanding what was happening. Kate brought her knee up hard against my groin, wrenched herself free, and scrambled out of the tent.

Twisting my head, I saw my dagger was sticking out of my back.

Roaring in frustration and anger, I reached over my shoulder and ripped the knife out. Charging out of the tent, I spun around to see where she'd gone. I spotted her running toward a gulch to the south. Ignoring the pain in my groin, I forced myself from a hobble to a run as I gave chase.

I felt betrayed and angry with her for turning on me. I'd done all of this for her, for our love, and she'd thrown my gift in my face.

I began grinning when I realized I was gaining on her. She stumbled and fell when she glanced back over her shoulder and in seconds I stood over her, panting heavily. I can imagine how I must have looked in the moonlight, what with my upper torso covered in blood, some of it on my face as well.

I held the knife at my side and just looked down at her.

She was selfish and ungrateful. She wasn't the woman I thought she was, the woman I loved.

Kate stared up at me, her eyes wild. "Please, Brian, don't..."

I raised the dagger, and with all my strength and weight behind it, I plunged it through her heart. I knelt beside her as she died, my head bowed and my eyes closed with my hands gripping the hilt of the dagger. I don't know how long I knelt there but in time the darkness behind my eyes began to glow a dull red.

When I opened my eyes, I saw the rising sun was bathing the earth with the first rays of morning sunshine.

Standing, I left the dagger where it was, piercing Kate's heart. I turned and went back to the camp, weaving with exhaustion and blood loss. The world spun around me. Vertigo made my stomach lurch. I fell down to my hands and knees and crawled back into Kate's tent.

Fatigue was taking over. I knew that I wouldn't be able to stay awake much longer. As fast as I could, I bunched up a shirt that was lying close by and pressed it to my back to staunch the wound. I rolled up one of Kate's blankets and used it to hold the shirt on as a bandage.

I was so weak by the time I was done that I could barely drag myself along the ground to Kate's pillow. That's where I passed out, with her scent surrounding me.

* * *

It was early afternoon when I woke up. I still felt weak and spaced out. The world seemed like a far away dream that I was floating through.

I made my way to the cooking tent to find something to eat and drink. Taking a can of peaches, I searched for the can opener. Finding it, I set to work opening my meal. I broke out in a sweat from pain and effort. By the time I got it opened, I was almost too tired to eat and had to force down every bite.

After eating, I went back to Kate's tent and laid down, falling asleep instantly.

It was late at night when I woke again. The air was cooler, my head was clearer, and the throb in my shoulder had dulled. Sitting up, I decided I should write what happened and what I planned to do in my journal.

Gripping the pen in a shaky hand, I began.

Everyone's dead. I killed them all, even my beloved Kate. I don't see why she couldn't have just said 'thank you' and been happy about what I did for us. She broke my heart and then stabbed me.

Tomorrow I'll pack up what little food there is and continue north. Harry said that it was safe that way. I'll either find other people or die trying.

I'm proud of myself for saving everyone from the torture of starvation. I should be considered a martyr. I'm living and suffering and they're dead, at peace, free.

Tomorrow I'll set out. Tomorrow I'll live and suffer for humanity.

* * *

By the time morning rolled around, I'd slept some and packed some. I'd found a bottle of aspirin while I was rummaging through everything and the pills helped with my pain.

After another quick meal, I started north. I was weak and had to take breaks often. During one break, I looked back to see that hundreds of birds were circling and feasting on the dead bodies I'd left behind. They looked like a black tornado, swirling down from the sky to wipe away the remnants of death.

Even with my rest stops I made it a good distance the first day and then the next. I could feel myself getting weaker after that. On the fourth day, I ran out of drinking water.

With no water I gave up hope. I wasn't going to find anyone or anything. I was the last one alive and I wasn't going to make it. I felt like my body was burning from within as I broke out in a fever that sapped away even more of my strength. My shoulder wound began to smell and I knew it was infected

I trudged onward as long as I could across the never changing arid landscape. Eventually, my body gave out and I collapsed. Closing my eyes, I smiled, and let myself drift to sleep, hoping that I would never wake up.

* * *

Slowly I opened my eyes. Was I dead? I still felt sore and was thirsty. Were you supposed to feel pain and be thirsty if you were dead?

I glanced around to see my bag was lying beside me. I was naked to the waist except for a bandage around my chest and a sling holding my left arm. I was in a small hut. The roof was made up of random pieces of sheet metal; the frame, various pieces of wood and metal shafts and the walls, cardboard and warped plywood.

A panel shifted to my left and a woman entered.

"You're awake," she said with a smile. "We weren't sure if you'd make it. You had a pretty bad infection from the wound on your back."

I grunted and tried to sit up, but fell back, hissing in pain.

"Take it easy," she said, placing a hand on my forehead. "Your fever seems to have broken. Are you hungry?"

"Thirsty," I croaked.

She laughed. "Of course you are. I'll get you something to drink."

She walked across the room, picked up a small pitcher and poured out a cup of water into a glass. She came back and helped me hold my head up while I drank.

"Thank you," I sighed, laying back.

"I'll leave you to rest," she said, heading for the door. "I'll check on you again in a little while."

I nodded and closed my eyes.

I heard the panel slide back into place as she exited the room. I couldn't help but think about how much she looked like Kate.

Maybe things would turn out differently this time. Maybe she would appreciate and love me the way Kate wasn't able to; maybe there was hope for a future.

ABOUT THE WRITERS

Terry Alexander lives on a small farm near Porum, Oklahoma with his wife Phyllis. Together they have three children and nine grandchildren. They both enjoy sitting back with a good book on a rainy afternoon. Terry has won writing awards at in Oklahoma, Arkansas, Kansas, Texas and Missouri.. His work has been published in Memories and Make Believe, Writing on Walls III, Echoes of the Ozarks V and Frontier tales.com. Contact him at terry-ale@crosstel.net.

David Bernstein writes short stories for a number of magazines and anthologies. The first four chapters of his novel Amongst the Dead are available online at Tales of the Zombie War with more to come. Check out davidbernsteinauthor.blogspot.com. You can reach him at dbern77@hotmail.com. He lives in the NYC area with his girlfriend of eight years and hates car horns.

Rebecca Besser lives in Ohio. She writes fiction, nonfiction, and poetry for various age groups and genres and is the editor of End of Days Volume 4. Check out her website at ww.rebeccabesser.com

Mark Christopher is employed as an industrial hygienist by day and a horror writer by night. His passion for the macabre left him dissatisfied with many of the zombie stories and movies shambling around, so he was determined to blaze a new trail - one littered with slick patches of gore and more than a few empty shotgun shells.

Be sure to check out his short story "Riser", in Dead Worlds: Undead Stories Vol. 5, and get ready for his upcoming zombie thriller novel, Hollow Point. He is a graduate of Louisiana State University and currently resides in Baton Rouge, Louisiana. Check him out on Facebook; he's always looking for new friends and fans.

Anthony Giangregorio is the author and editor of more than 45 novels, almost all of them about zombies. His work has appeared in Dead Science by Coscomentertainment, Dead Worlds: Undead Stories Volumes 1-6, and Wolves of War by Library of the Living Dead Press. He also has stories in End of Days Vol. 1 -3, the Book of the Dead series Vol. 1-4 by LDP, and two anthologies with Pill Hill Press. He is also the creator of the popular action/zombie series titled "Deadwater." Check out his website at www.undeadpress.com.

Dane T. Hatchell grew up in Baton Rouge Louisiana and has lived there all his life. In his youth he was a fan of old school horror movies, and a collector of magazines such as Creepy and Eerie. Now in his early fifty's, he is devoting his free time to writing to satisfy a lifelong passion. You can contact Dane on Facebook at Enadious@gmail.com or Enadious B. Neuman on Facebook.

Kelly M. Hudson grew up in the wilds of Kentucky and currently resides in California. He has a deep and abiding love for all things horror and rock n' roll. He's had many stories published in such esteemed collections as Dead Worlds, Book of the Dead, End of Days, The Death Panel, and The Bitter End and also has a novel (Men of Perdition) on Amazon Kindle. If you wish to contact Kelly or find links to other stories he's had published, please visit www.kellymhudson.com for further details.

Keith Luethke lives in Knoxville, Tennessee and is the author of Dead House: A Zombie Ghost story and is a co-author of Human Harvest: Alien Abduction with Anthony Giangregorio. He enjoys talking to fans and can be reached through Facebook or at luethke@yahoo.com.

Jessy Marie Roberts lives in a "haunted" house in Western Nebraska with her husband and two dogs. She grew up in Morgan Hill, California. She has been published in various small press venues, including many appearances in anthologies by Living Dead Press, and is the Editor-in-Chief of Pill Hill Press (www.pillhillpress.com).

DEAD RAGE
by Anthony Giangregorio
Book 2 in the Rage virus series!

An unknown virus spreads across the globe, turning ordinary people into bloodthirsty, ravenous killers.

Only a small percentage of the population is immune and soon become prey to the infected.

Amongst the infected comes a man, stricken by the virus, yet still retaining his grasp on reality. His need to destroy the *normals* becomes an obsession and he raises an army of killers to seek out and kill all who aren't *changed* like himself. A few survivors gather together on the outskirts of Chicago and find themselves running for their lives as the specter of death looms over all.

The Dead Rage virus will find you, no matter where you hide.

CHRISTMAS IS DEAD: A ZOMBIE ANTHOLOGY
Edited by Anthony Giangregorio

Twas the night before Christmas and all through the house, not a creature was stirring, not even a. . . zombie?

That's right; this anthology explores what would happen at Christmas time if there was a full blown zombie outbreak. Reanimated turkeys, zombie Santas, and demon reindeers that turn people into flesh-eating ghouls are just some of the tales you will find in this merry undead book. So curl up under the Christmas tree with a cup of hot chocolate, and as the fireplace crackles with warmth, get ready to have your heart filled with holiday cheer. But of course, then it will be ripped from your heaving chest and fed upon by blood-thirsty elves with a craving for human flesh! For you see, Christmas is Dead!

And you will never look at the holiday season the same way again.

BLOOD RAGE
(The Prequel to DEAD RAGE)
by Anthony Giangregorio

The madness descended before anyone knew what was happening. Perfectly normal people suddenly became rage-fueled killers, tearing and slicing their way across the city. Within hours, Chicago was a battlefield, the dead strewn in the streets like trash.

Stacy, Chad and a few others are just a few of the immune, unaffected by the virus but not to the violence surrounding them. The *changed* are ravenous, sweeping across Chicago and perhaps the world, destroying any *normals* they come across. Fire, slaughter, and blood rule the land, and the few survivors are now an endangered species.

This is the story of the first days of the Dead Rage virus and the brave souls who struggle to live just one more day.

When the smoke clears, and the *changed* have maimed and killed all who stand in their way, only the strong will remain.

The rest will be left to rot in the sun.

THE BOOK OF CANNIBALS
Edited by Anthony Giangregorio

Human meat . . . the ultimate taboo.

Deep down, in the dark recesses of your mind, can you honestly say you never wondered how it might taste?

Honestly, never wondered if a chunk of thigh tasted like chicken or pork?

Or if a hunk of an arm was similar to steak? And what kind of wine would be served with it, red or white?

Would a human liver be no different than one from a cow, or a pig?

For all we know, human flesh is as tender as veal, better than the finest tenderloin. And that is what the stories in this book are about, eating each other. But be warned, after reading these tales of mastication, you may just become a vegetarian, or at the very least, think twice before taking your first bite of that juicy steak at your local restaurant.

DEADFREEZE
by Anthony Giangregorio
THIS IS WHAT HELL WOULD BE LIKE IF IT FROZE OVER!

When an experimental serum for hypothermia goes horribly wrong, a small research station in the middle of Antarctica becomes overrun with an army of the frozen dead.

Now a small group of survivors must battle the arctic weather and a horde of frozen zombies as they make their way across the frozen plains of Antarctica to a neighboring research station.

What they don't realize is that they are being hunted by an entity whose sole reason for existing is vengeance; and it will find them wherever they run.

VISIONS OF THE DEAD
A ZOMBIE STORY
by Anthony & Joseph Giangregorio

Jake Roberts felt like he was the luckiest man alive.

He had a great family, a beautiful girlfriend, who was soon to be his wife, and a job, that might not have been the best, but it paid the bills.

At least until the dead began to walk.

Now Jake is fighting to survive in a dead world while searching for his lost love, Melissa, knowing she's out there somewhere.

But the past isn't dead, and as he struggles for an uncertain future, the past threatens to consume him. With the present a constant battle between the living and the dead, Jake finds himself slipping in and out of the past, the visions of how it all happened haunting him. But Jake knows Melissa is out there somewhere and he'll find her or die trying.

In a world of the living dead, you can never escape your past.

DEAD MOURNING: A ZOMBIE HORROR STORY
by Anthony Giangregorio

Carl Jenkins was having a run of bad luck. Fresh out of jail, his probation tenuous, he'd lost every job he'd taken since being released. So now was his last chance, only one more job to prevent him from going back to prison. Assigned to work in a funeral home, he accidentally loses a shipment of embalming fluid. With nothing to lose, he substitutes it with a batch of chemicals from a nearby factory.

The results don't go as planned, though. While his screw-up goes unnoticed, his machinations revive the cadavers in the funeral home, unleashing an evil on the world that it has not seen before. Not wanting to become a snack for the rampaging dead, he flees the city, joining up with other survivors. An old, dilapidated zoo becomes their haven, while the dead wait outside the walls, hungry and patient.

But Carl is optimistic, after all, he's still alive, right? Perhaps his luck has changed and help will arrive to save them all?

Unfortunately, unknown to him and the other survivors, a serial killer has fallen into their group, trapped inside the zoo with them.

With the undead army clamoring outside the walls and a murderer within, it'll be a miracle if any of them live to see the next sunrise.

On second thought, maybe Carl would've been better off if he'd just gone back to jail.

ROAD KILL: A ZOMBIE TALE
by Anthony Giangregorio
ORDER UP!

In the summer of 2008, a rogue comet entered earth's orbit for 72 hours. During this time, a strange amber glow suffused the sky.

But something else happened; something in the comet's tail had an adverse affect on dead tissue and the result was the reanimation of every dead animal carcass on the planet.

A handful of survivors hole up in a diner in the backwoods of New Hampshire while the undead creatures of the night hunt for human prey.

There's a new blue plate special at DJ's Diner and Truck Stop, and it's you!

DEAD THINGS
by Anthony Giangregorio

Beneath the veil of reality we all know as truth, there is another world, one where creatures only seen in nightmares exist.

But what if these creatures do actually exist, and it is us that are only fleeting images, mere visions conjured up by some unknown being.

Werewolves, zombies, vampires, and other lost things that go bump in the night, inhabit the world of imagination and myth, but all will be found in this collection of tales.   But in this world, fiction becomes fact, and what lurks in the shadows is real. Beware the next time you sense you are being watched or catch movement in the corner of your eye, for though it may be nothing, it might just be your doom.

INCLUDES THE EXCLUSIVE DEADWATER STORY: DEAD GRAVE

THE DARK

by Anthony Giangregorio

DARKNESS FALLS

The darkness came without warning.

First New York, then the rest of United States, and then the world became enveloped in a perpetual night without end.

With no sunlight, eventually the planet will wither and die, bringing on a new Ice Age. But that isn't problem for the human race, for humanity will be dead long before that happens.

There is something in the dark, creatures only seen in nightmares, and they are on the prowl. Evolution has changed and man is no longer the dominant species. When we are children, we're told not to fear the dark, that what we believe to exist in the shadows is false.

Unfortunately, that is no longer true.

SOULEATER

by Anthony Giangregorio

Twenty years ago, Jason Lawson witnessed the brutal death of his father by something only seen in nightmares, something so horrible he'd blocked it from his mind.

Now twenty years later the creature is back, this time for his son.

Jason won't let that happen.

He'll travel to the demon's world, struggling every second to rescue his son from its clutches.

But what he doesn't know is that the portal will only be open for a finite time and if he doesn't return with his son before it closes, then he'll be trapped in the demon's dimension forever.

SEE HOW IT ALL BEGAN IN THE NEW DOUBLE-SIZED 460 PAGE SPECIAL EDITION!

DEADWATER: EXPANDED EDITION

by Anthony Giangregorio

Through a series of tragic mishaps, a small town's water supply is contaminated with a deadly bacterium that transforms the town's population into flesh eating ghouls.

Without warning, Henry Watson finds himself thrown into a living hell where the living dead walk and want nothing more than to feed on the living.

Now Henry's trying to escape the undead town before he becomes the next victim.

With the military on one side, shooting civilians on sight, and a horde of bloodthirsty zombies on the other, Henry must try to battle his way to freedom.

With a small group of survivors, including a beautiful secretary and a wise-cracking janitor to aid him, the ragtag group will do their best to stay alive and escape the city codenamed: **Deadwater**.

DEAD END: A ZOMBIE NOVEL
by Anthony Giangregorio
THE DEAD WALK!

Newspapers everywhere proclaim the dead have returned to feast on the living!

A small group of survivors hole up in a cellar, afraid to brave the masses of animated corpses, but when food runs out, they have no choice but to venture out into a world gone mad.

What they will discover, however, is that the fall of civilization has brought out the worst in their fellow man.

Cannibals, psychotic preachers and rapists are just some of the atrocities they must face.

In a world turned upside down, it is life that has hit a Dead End.

BOOK OF THE DEAD 2: NOT DEAD YET
A ZOMBIE ANTHOLOGY
Edited by Anthony Giangregorio

Out of the ashes of death and decay, comes the second volume filled with the walking dead.

In this tomb, there are only slow, shambling monstrosities that were once human.

No one knows why the dead walk; only that they do, and that they are hungry for human flesh.

But these aren't your neighbors, your co-workers, or your family.
Now they are the living dead, and they will tear your throat out at a moment's notice.

So be warned as you delve into the pages of this book; the dead will find you, no matter where you hide.

ANOTHER EXCITING ADVENTURE IN THE DEADWATER SERIES!
DEAD SALVATION
BOOK 9
by Anthony Giangregorio
HANGMAN'S NOOSE!

After one of the group is hurt, the need for transportation is solved by a roving cannie convoy. Attacking the camp, the companions save a man who invites them back to his home.

Cement City it's called and at first the group is welcomed with thanks for saving one of their own. But when a bar fight goes wrong, the companions find themselves awaiting the hangman's noose.

Their only salvation is a suicide mission into a raider camp to save captured townspeople.

Though the odds are long, it's a chance, and Henry knows in the land of the walking dead, sometimes a chance is all you can hope for.

In the world of the dead, life is a struggle, where the only victor is death.

INSIDE THE PERIMETER: SCAVENGERS OF THE DEAD
by Alan Spencer
In the middle of nowhere, the vestiges of an abandoned town are surrounded by inescapably high concrete barriers, permitting no trespass or escape. The town is dormant of human life, but rampant with the living dead, who choose not to eat flesh, but to instead continue their survival by cruder means.

Boyd Broman, a detective arrested and falsely imprisoned, has been transferred into the secret town. He is given an ultimatum: recapture Hayden Grubaugh, the cannibal serial killer, who has been banished to the town, in exchange for his freedom.

During Boyd's search, he discovers why the psychotic cannibal must really be captured and the sinister secrets the dead town holds.

With no chance of escape, Broman finds himself trapped among the ravenous, violent dead.

With the cannibal feeding on the animated cadavers and the undead searching for Boyd, he must fulfill his end of the deal before the rotting corpses turn him into an unwilling organ donor.

But Boyd wasn't told that no one gets out alive, that the town is a death sentence.

For there is no escape from *Inside the Perimeter*.

DEADFALL
by Anthony Giangregorio
It's Halloween in the small suburban town of Wakefield, Mass.

While parents take their children trick or treating and others throw costume parties, a swarm of meteorites enter the earth's atmosphere and crash to earth.

Inside are small parasitic worms, no larger than maggots.

The worms quickly infect the corpses at a local cemetery and so begins the rise of the undead.

The walking dead soon get the upper hand, with no one believing the truth.

That the dead now walk.

Will a small group of survivors live through the zombie apocalypse?

Or will they, too, succumb to the Deadfall.

LOVE IS DEAD: A ZOMBIE ANTHOLOGY
Edited by Anthony Giangregorio
THE DEATH OF LOVE
Valentine's Day is a day when young love is fulfilled.

Where hopeful young men bring candy and flowers to their sweethearts, in hopes of a kiss...or perhaps more. But not in this anthology.

For you see, LOVE IS DEAD, and in this tome, the dead walk, wanting to feed on those same hearts that once pumped in chests, bursting with love.

So toss aside that heart-shaped box of candy and throw away those red roses, you won't need them any longer. Instead, strap on a handgun, or pick up a shotgun and defend yourself from the ravenous undead.

Because in a world where the dead walk, even love isn't safe.

ETERNAL NIGHT: A VAMPIRE ANTHOLOGY

Edited by Anthony Giangregorio

Blood, fangs, darkness and terror...these are the calling cards of the vampire mythos.

Inside this tome are stories that embrace vampire history but seek to introduce a new literary spin on this longstanding fictional monster. Follow a dark journey through cigarette-smoking creatures hunted by rogue angels, vampires that feed off of thoughts instead of blood, immortals presenting the fantastic in a local rock band, to a legendary monster on the far reaches of town.

Forget what you know about vampires; this anthology will destroy historical mythos and embrace incredible new twists on this celebrated, fictional character.

Welcome to a world of the undead, welcome to the world of Eternal Night.

BOOK OF THE DEAD
A ZOMBIE ANTHOLOGY VOL 1
ISBN 978-1-935458-25-8

Edited by Anthony Giangregorio

This is the most faithful, truest zombie anthology ever written, and we invite you along for the ride. Every single story in this book is filled with slack-jawed, eyes glazed, slow moving, shambling zombies set in a world where the dead have risen and only want to eat the flesh of the living. In these pages, the rules are sacrosanct. There is no deviation from what a zombie should be or how they came about. The Dead Walk.

There is no reason, though rumors and suppositions fill the radio and television stations. But the only thing that is fact is that the walking dead are here and they will not go away. So prepare yourself for the ultimate homage to the master of zombie legend. And remember... Aim for the head!

REVOLUTION OF THE DEAD

by Anthony Giangregorio

THE DEAD SHALL RISE AGAIN!

Five years ago, a deadly plague wiped out 97% of the world's population, America suffering tragically. Bodies were everywhere, far too many to bury or burn. But then, through a miracle of medical science, a way is found to reanimate the dead.

With the manpower of the United States depleted, and the remaining survivors not wanting to give up their internet and fast food restaurants, the undead are conscripted as slave labor.

Now they cut the grass, pick up the trash, and walk the dogs of the surviving humans.

But whether alive or dead, no race wants to be controlled, and sooner or later the dead will fight back, wanting the freedom they enjoyed in life.

The revolution has begun!

And when it's over, the dead will rule the land, and the remaining humans will become the slaves...or worse.

KINGDOM OF THE DEAD
by Anthony Giangregorio
THE DEAD HAVE RISEN!

In the dead city of Pittsburgh, two small enclaves struggle to survive, eking out an existence of hand to mouth.

But instead of working together, both groups battle for the last remaining fuel and supplies of a city filled with the living dead.

Six months after the initial outbreak, a lone helicopter arrives bearing two more survivors and a newborn baby. One enclave welcomes them, while the other schemes to steal their helicopter and escape the decaying city.

With no police, fire, or social services existing, the two will battle for dominance in the steel city of the walking dead. But when the dust settles, the question is: will the remaining humans be the winners, or the losers?

When the dead walk, the line between Heaven and Hell is so twisted and bent there is no line at all.

RISE OF THE DEAD
by Anthony Giangregorio
DEATH IS ONLY THE BEGINNING!

In less than forty-eight hours, more than half the globe was infected.
In another forty-eight, the rest would be enveloped.
The reason?
A science experiment gone horribly wrong which enabled the dead to walk, their flesh rotting on their bones even as they seek human prey.

Jeremy was an ordinary nineteen year old slacker. He partied too much and had done poorly in high school. After a night of drinking and drugs, he awoke to find the world a very different place from the one he'd left the night before.

The dead were walking and feeding on the living, and as Jeremy stepped out into a world gone mad, the dead spotting him alone and unarmed in the middle of the street, he had to wonder if he would live long enough to see his twentieth birthday.

THE CHRONICLES OF JACK PRIMUS
BOOK ONE
by Michael D. Griffiths

Beneath the world of normalcy we all live in lies another world, one where supernatural beings exist.

These creatures of the night hunt us; want to feed on our very souls, though only a few know of their existence.

One such man is Jack Primus, who accidentally pierces the veil between this world and the next. With no other choice if he wants to live, he finds himself on the run, hunted by beings called the Xemmoni, an ancient race that sees humans as nothing but cattle.   They want his soul, to feed on his very essence, and they will kill all who stand in their way.   But if they thought Jack would just lie down and accept his fate, they were sorely mistaken.

He didn't ask for this battle, but he knew he would fight them with everything at his disposal, for to lose is a fate worse than death.

He would win this war, and he would take down anyone who got in his way.

THE WAR AGAINST THEM: A ZOMBIE NOVEL
by Jose Alfredo Vazquez

Mankind wasn't prepared for the onslaught.

An ancient organism is reanimating the dead bodies of its victims, creating worldwide chaos and panic as the disease spreads to every corner of the globe. As governments struggle to contain the disease, courageous individuals across the planet learn what it truly means to make choices as they struggle to survive.

Geopolitics meet technology in a race to save mankind from the worst threat it has ever faced. Doctors, military and soldiers from all walks of life battle to find a cure. For the dead walk, and if not stopped, they will wipe out all life on Earth. Humanity is fighting a war they cannot win, for who can overcome Death itself? Man versus the walking dead with the winner ruling the planet. Welcome to *The War Against Them*.

DEADTOWN: A DEADWATER STORY
B OOK 8
by Anthony Giangregorio

The world is a very different place now. The dead walk the land and humans hide in small towns with walls of stone and debris for protection, constantly keeping the living dead at bay.

Social law is gone and right and wrong is defined by the size of your gun.

UNWELCOME VISITORS

Henry Watson and his band of warrior survivalists become guests in a fortified town in Michigan. But when the kidnapping of one of the companions goes bad and men die, the group finds themselves on the wrong side of the law, and a town out for blood.

Trapped in a hotel, surrounded on all sides, it will be up to Henry to save the day with a gamble that may not only take his life, but that of his friends as well.

In a dead world, when justice is not enough, there is always vengeance.

END OF DAYS: AN APOCALYPTIC ANTHOLOGY
VOLUMES 1 & 2
Edited by Anthony Giangregorio

Our world is a fragile place.

Meteors, famine, floods, nuclear war, solar flares, and hundreds of other calamities can plunge our small blue planet into turmoil in an instant.

What would you do if tomorrow the sun went super nova or the world was swallowed by water, submerging the world into the cold darkness of the ocean? This anthology explores some of those scenarios and plunges you into total annihilation.

But remember, it's only a book, and tomorrow will come as it always does. Or will it?

Eternal Night

A Vampire Anthology

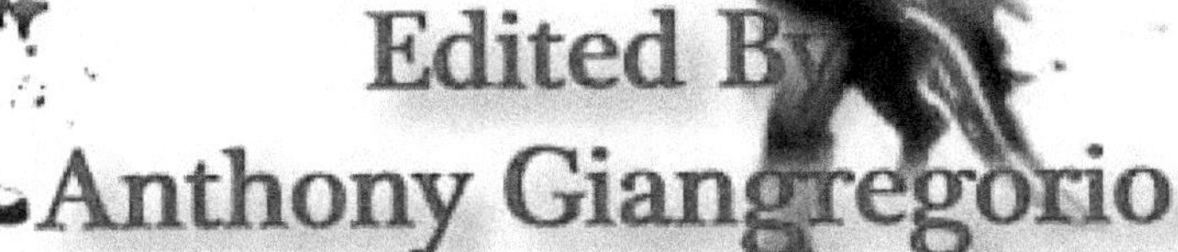

Edited By

Anthony Giangregorio

THE BOOK OF CANNIBALS

ISBN 13: 978-1-935458-52-4   ISBN 10: 1-935458-52-3

ARE YOU HUNGRY YET?